To Gabe:

The Case

of

Too Many Clues

All the Best!

Cindy Vincent

Also by Cindy Vincent

Bad Day for a Bombshell,
A Tracy Truworth, Apprentice P.I.
1940s Homefront Mystery

Swell Time for a Swing Dance,
A Tracy Truworth, Apprentice P.I.
1940s Homefront Mystery

Yes, Carol . . . It's Christmas!

The Case of the Cat Show Princess:
A Buckley and Bogey Cat Detective Caper

The Case of the Crafty Christmas Crooks:
A Buckley and Bogey Cat Detective Caper

The Case of the Jewel Covered Cat Statues:
A Buckley and Bogey Cat Detective Caper

The Case of the Clever Secret Code:
A Buckley and Bogey Cat Detective Caper

The Mystery of the Missing Ming:
A Daisy Diamond Detective Novel

The Case of the Rising Star Ruby:
A Daisy Diamond Detective Novel

Makeover For Murder:
A Kate Bundeen Mystery

Cats Are Part of His Kingdom, Too:
33 Daily Devotions to Show God's Love

The Case
of
Too Many Clues

A Buckley and Bogey
Cat Detective Caper

Cindy Vincent

Whodunit Press
Houston

The Case of Too Many Clues

A Buckley and Bogey Cat Detective Caper

Published by Whodunit Press

A Division of Mysteries by Vincent, LLC

For information, please contact:

Buckley.CatDetective@mysteriesbyvincent.com

BuckleyandBogey.com

ISBN: 978-1-932169-59-1

Printed in the United States of America

Dedication

To all the fantastic foster Moms who give helpless, homeless kittens and cats a fighting chance, including Cindy, Kellie, and Brenda, and most especially, Deb, who saved and fostered our own precious Miss Magnolia Belle.
You are love and kindness in action.

CHAPTER 1

Holy Mackerel!

For as long as I live, I don't think I'll ever forget that week in August. Hands down, or, um . . . I mean . . . *paws* down . . . it was one of the strangest weeks that I, Buckley Bergdorf, have ever been through. First of all, we were just wrapping up the last of a long string of big cases. And I don't mean the good kind of string, either, the kind a guy like me could chase around the house for hours. No, I'm talking about the kind of string that means a whole bunch of things that happen right in a row. For us, it had been one huge case after another after another after another. In fact, the BBCDA — or the Buckley and Bogey Cat Detective Agency — had been so busy that I couldn't even think straight anymore.

Then, our sweet, twelve-year-old human sister, Gracie, finally convinced our Mom and Dad to let her have a cell phone. She'd been asking them for weeks. She said all her friends had one and she should have one, too. So there it was, in a pretty purple case, and in her hand wherever she went. She even held it whenever she cuddled me.

And if all that wasn't enough, well, then the strangest thing of all happened — somebody left us a big, giant clue!

Right on our own front porch.

Okay, maybe the clue wasn't *actually* all that big or giant. The truth was, it was really kind of small. Even so, it was still *important.* Very important. And I've been a cat detective long enough to know that major clues almost *never* just showed up out of the blue like that. Especially ones that are placed all nice and neat inside a little glass jar with a shiny black lid. No, when it comes to finding clues, it usually takes us lots of time and lots of work.

But not this time. Instead, somebody saved us a whole bunch of trouble and set that clue right out where we would see it.

Of course, we didn't exactly *know* it was a clue at first. My big brother and best friend, Bogart — or "Bogey" as I call him — spotted it before I did. We'd just wrapped up a big confab on our last case when we wandered by the front window in our dining room. By that time, we both needed a change of scenery and a chance to stretch our legs.

Naturally, Bogey glanced out the window the second he walked into the room. Exactly like a good cat detective is supposed to do. And that's when he saw it, just outside the window on our porch. Pretty close to the front door. The clear glass jar was about as tall as two cans of cat food stacked on top of each other. It didn't have a smudge on it, and the black lid was almost as shiny as Bogey's black fur. But oddly enough, the only thing I could see inside that jar was a stack of four little wooden squares. They were the kind that came from a word game I'd seen our Mom and Dad play sometimes. So I already knew that each one of those little squares had a letter on it. I could see the letter *G* on the top square from where I sat.

And as I stared at that little jar, I couldn't help but wonder how someone had managed to sneak it onto our front porch. Without us even noticing. I guess we'd just been too wrapped up with wrapping up our last case!

Bogey raised an eyebrow and reached for a bag of cat treats that he kept stashed behind a potted plant. "This is new."

"The cat treats?" I asked as he passed one to me. They sure tasted like the same fish-flavored treats that he always kept hidden there.

Bogey shook his head. "Nope, kid. I mean that jar sitting pretty on our front porch."

I put my paw to my chin as I ate my treat. "Well, I guess it *is* kind of pretty."

Bogey grinned. "Just an expression, kid. It means it's in a good spot."

"Oh . . . okay," I nodded. "Anyway, I've never seen it before, either. And it looks like there's a piece of paper taped to the lid."

Bogey passed me another treat and took one for himself. "Probably a message."

I felt my eyes go wide. "Somebody sure went to a lot of trouble to fold it up so small. And to make it fit on that lid. I wonder what it says."

"Your guess is as good as mine, kid." Bogey gave us each another treat before he returned the bag to its hiding place. Then he moved from side to side in front of the window, trying to get a better look at the jar.

That's when I suddenly realized just how suspicious the whole setup seemed — no matter how we looked at it. And believe me, my brother was taking it in from every angle he could. Even though we run our agency together, he is still the pro and I am still the rookie. But I've come a long way since I was adopted into our forever home and Bogey took me under his paw. He taught me how to be a cat detective and, before long, we started the BBCDA on the Internet. Then we got our first case through an email from a cat who was in trouble. Big trouble. That case turned out to be a real doozie, and after we solved it, we got more and more cases. And more. Lately, with business booming, we sure could've used a few extra cat detectives on the payroll! We even convinced one of the other cats in our house, Lil Bits, to come out of retirement and lend us a paw.

Because, not only do we crack cases for cats in trouble, but we also solve plenty of mysteries for humans, too. Of course, we only converse with humans by email, so they have no idea that the BBCDA is actually run by a couple of cats! To be honest, they might not be too happy if they found out the truth. That's because most humans have no clue what cats are capable of. Bogey always says we can use that to our advantage, but I'm still not sure what he means by that.

And I wasn't sure about that jar on our front porch, either. Just looking at it, I wondered if we were about to end up with another case.

I turned to ask Bogey what he thought, but he answered my question before I even asked it. That's how good a cat detective the guy was.

"Yup, kid," he said. "Looks like we'll have another case on our plate before the day is done. Somebody left that jar out there for a reason. And my *gut* tells me we'd better find out why. That, or maybe I just need to cut back on the cat treats. Could go either way." He patted his tummy and grinned.

Well, to be honest, I thought Bogey *had* been overdoing it a little on the cat treats lately. Probably because we'd been so busy, and he'd been downing treats instead of taking time to eat our good, healthy cat food. The only problem was, I wasn't sure things were going to get any better any time soon. Not if we were going to take on another case, when we should probably be taking a break.

That is, *if* we took on another case.

"I wish we could get a better look at that jar," I told my brother. "It's only a few inches from us, but we can't even touch it."

Bogey scooted closer to the window until his nose was pressed against the glass. "You got that right, kid. We need to see that jar up close and personal. And give those squares the once over."

"But how?" I asked him.

After all, we were basically housecats. We couldn't exactly open the door, run outside, and inspect that jar. Sure, Bogey and I are pretty smart, but so far we haven't figured out a way to open the heavy front door of our old house. And when I say "old," I do mean old, since the place was well over a hundred years old. In fact, it was one of the oldest houses in all of St. Gertrude, the town where we live.

Yet being a housecat never stopped Bogey from figuring out a way to investigate *outside* our house. That's probably just one of the reasons why he's one of the best cat detectives in the business. I only hoped I could be just as good as he was one day.

To tell you the truth, sometimes I'm pretty amazed at how different Bogey and I are. Sure, we're both black cats with gold eyes. But that's as far as it goes. I'm huge and fuzzy with fur that sticks out a mile, since I'm a Maine Coon Cat. And in case you've never heard of Maine Coon Cats before, well, let me tell you, we're gigantic! Enormous, even. I'm only two years old and I'm already twice as big as Bogey. And he's a full-grown guy!

To top it off, my paws are so large they could double for snowshoes. It seems like they're always growing, and I barely get used to them before they grow some more. Then I have a really hard time making my paws go where I want them to go. When I want them to go there. Especially since I just had another *big* growth spurt over the last couple of weeks.

But Bogey never has that problem. He is sleek and lean, and he can run so fast that even some say he can fly. His paws always go where he wants them to go.

Now he stepped back from the front window and grinned. "Cover me, would ya, kid? I've got an idea."

Before I could answer, he turned and raced from the room. He was nothing but a black streak as he flew into the front hallway and past the front door. He didn't slow down until he reached our Mom's home office, right across the hall from the dining room.

Of course, I knew exactly what he wanted me to do. I was supposed to keep watch and warn him if any of our humans were headed our way. That's because the people in our family don't know that we use the computer. So far, we think it's probably best to keep them in the dark. Which has been pretty easy, considering we mostly use the computer when the house *is* dark, and our family is sound asleep. Or when they're out of the house during the day. But there are times when we have to make exceptions.

And I guess this was one of those times.

Thankfully, our Mom was in the kitchen, since it was her night to cook dinner. Gracie was in the family room, tapping away on her new cell phone. And our Dad hadn't come home from work yet.

That meant the office and the computer were free.

So Bogey made a beeline for the keyboard and started to type away. Seconds later, he jumped down off the desk. Then we heard Gracie holler to our Mom.

"Mom, how did you do that?" she asked with a giggle. "You

sent me an email and you're not even near your phone. Or your computer."

I glanced at my brother. "Did you . . .?"

"Yup, kid," he said with a grin. "I sent the email from our Mom's account."

I crinkled my brow. "And it sounds like Gracie got it already. She sure stares at her phone a lot."

Bogey tilted an ear toward the kitchen. "She's like a cat with a new toy, kid. You know how it is. You play and play with the thing until the catnip wears off. And then it just ends up under the couch. Collecting dust."

I nodded. Bogey had a good point. Though these days, we sure didn't have time to play with any of our toys.

Our Mom answered Gracie from the kitchen. "No, honey, I didn't send you an email."

"You didn't?" Gracie replied, and we could hear her feet padding along the hardwood floor from the family room to the kitchen. "But an email came in that says I should open the front door."

"That's strange," our Mom laughed. "Maybe we'd better go check it out."

And the next thing we knew, they were headed our way.

Bogey stood at attention. "Get ready, kid. We'll make our move the minute they open the door. I'll distract them and you push that jar inside."

I gulped. "But why do *I* have to push that jar into the house?"

After all, I wasn't too excited about going outside all by myself. And I definitely did not want to get locked out for the evening.

Bogey put his paw on my shoulder. "Let's face it, kid. You're bigger. And those paws of yours are perfect for the job."

Well, when he put it like that, how could I refuse? It was nice to know that my big paws came in handy sometimes.

"I'll do it," I told my brother.

Then without another word, Bogey and I crowded next to the front door. Our beautiful Mom walked into the entryway first, with her dark, curly hair in a long ponytail. Gracie, who had the same dark hair and eyes, followed behind. I noticed she was holding her cell phone in front of her. She kept looking at it as she followed our Mom to the door.

"Hello, boys," our Mom said as she reached down to pet Bogey and me. "Looks like you heard someone at the front door. Strange that no one knocked or rang the bell."

If only she knew just *how* strange!

She peeked through the peephole and glanced outside. "Well, no one's there. Maybe someone left a package for us."

She unlocked the door and glanced at Gracie. "Hang onto the boys, would you, honey? So they don't get out?"

"Sure thing, Mom." She put her cell phone in her pocket and wrapped her arms around both me and Bogey.

"We seem to have a problem, kid," Bogey meowed. "Think you can get out of Gracie's arms to get that jar?" Of course, he switched to cat language, just like us cats always do when humans are around.

"Uh-huh," I meowed back. "I know just what to do."

Of course, I usually liked it when Gracie wrapped her arms around me and gave me a nice, big hug. But when you're a cat detective, sometimes you've got to stay focused on the job.

So when our Mom opened the door, I reached up and gave Gracie a big kiss on the nose. She giggled, and I wriggled right out of her grasp.

Then Bogey let out a howl that practically echoed through the whole house, if not down the entire block. He held up his paw and dangled it, like it was limp. Possibly broken.

Our Mom's eyes went wide and she turned to him. "Oh no, Bogey! Did I step on your paw?"

"Bogey," I meowed. "Are you hurt?"

"Nope, kid," he meowed back, just under his breath. "It's my distraction, remember? Now get that jar inside."

"Oh, right," I said before I scrambled out the door.

Bogey followed up his first distraction by flopping over onto his side. He continued to howl and even panted really hard between his cries. Just for effect.

By now, Gracie was petting his head, trying to calm him down. "I'm sure no one stepped on Bogey's paw. I was just holding him." She started to check him over, to see where he was hurt. After all, she planned to become a veterinarian one day. And I had to say, she was going to make a very good one.

Our Mom leaned down to check on Bogey, too, while he

kept up his act. He was putting on such a show that I could see why he was once hired to be in cat food commercials. A long time ago.

In the meantime, I raced across the front porch and, right away, I wished I hadn't. Because I'd barely stepped outside when the wind suddenly picked up. It ruffled my fur and sent icy chills running down my spine. In the distance, I spotted big, angry black clouds blowing our way. As near as I could tell, we were in for a very nasty thunderstorm.

And I do mean nasty!

Holy Catnip!

Needless to say, I didn't exactly *like* thunderstorms. All that flashing lightning was scary enough, but those rotten storms also gave my fur plenty of static. In fact, our Dad always said I was a walking sparkplug during a storm. Yet the worst part for me was the really loud, booming thunder. Sure, I know I'm supposed to be a big, brave cat detective. But the truth is, thunderstorms almost always sent me racing for a nice safe spot. Usually right under our Mom and Dad's bed.

So, let me tell you, when I saw that storm coming, I was suddenly in a very big hurry to get back inside our house. I put one of my huge paws on the side of that jar and batted it with everything I had. Like I was batting a cat toy. Thankfully, it didn't matter that my paw didn't go right where I wanted it to go, since the jar was bigger than my paw. My aim was close enough, and that jar went sliding straight into our house. Once it was past the door, I scurried back inside and batted it into the dining room. With one last swipe, I slid it behind the same potted plant where Bogey stashed his cat treats.

Then I returned to Bogey.

"Got it, kid?" he meowed.

"Got it." I gave him a "paws up."

Bogey grinned. "Good job, kid." And just like that, he quit his howling. Then he rolled over and bounced to his feet.

Gracie and our Mom both gasped and looked at each other.

"What in the world . . .?" our Mom sort of muttered.

"I guess Bogey is fine." Gracie rubbed his back and he purred in return.

Our Mom shook her head. "I don't know . . . He certainly acted like he was in a lot of pain. I wonder if we should take him to the vet's office. Just to be sure he's all right."

With those words, Bogey made a giant leap into the air and then loped around in a big circle. Just to prove he was okay.

Anything to avoid a trip to the vet's office.

Gracie picked him up and cuddled him. "I guess he doesn't need to go to the doctor. But I'm going to keep an eye on him."

And that's when something caught *my* eye. Something outside. I turned my head and saw a yellow-haired woman racing right up our front walkway! In fact, it seemed like she practically flew in on the wind that was blowing in our direction. The gale ruffled the fur of the scrawny, calico kitten the woman carried before her with outstretched arms. That tiny kitten had huge, wide eyes and a look of confusion written all over her face.

"Yoo-hoo!" the woman hollered as she came closer. "Mrs. Abernathy, could I please speak to you?"

Our Mom picked me up, probably to make sure I stayed in the house. "Well, hello, Mrs. Bumble. I haven't seen much of you since you moved into the neighborhood. And please call me Abby. Everyone does."

"Then please call me Bea, my dear," the woman said as she came ever closer.

Now I could see the lady was wearing a blue, bee-print shirt. She also had on big, black glasses with sparkly bees attached to the corners.

"'Bea' it is," our Mom said. "So how is the honey business?"

"Buzzing," came the lady's reply.

By now the kitten looked even more dazed than she had before. In fact, I could see that she'd started to shake just a little bit.

Our Mom smiled. "And what shall we call this little one you're carrying around with you?"

Bea frowned. "Well, she doesn't actually have a name. And that brings me to the reason why I'm here today. You know I take in foster cats."

"Yes, I'd heard something about that," our Mom nodded as the lady stepped onto the porch.

"Excuse me, Mrs. Bumble," Gracie said. "But what does that mean? Foster?"

Bea held the little kitten up high and looked her over from head to foot. "It means that I take care of cats and give them a home for a short time. Until I can find forever homes for them, where they'll stay for the rest of their lives."

"Oh, I see," Gracie murmured. "So the poor homeless cats can have a place to stay. While they're waiting for someone to adopt them."

Bea nodded. "That's right, young lady."

Our Mom hugged me tighter. "It's wonderful that you take them in, Bea. Especially since I've heard the shelters are full right now and some poor animals have no place to go."

I thought of the cat shelter that our friend, Luke, the church cat, ran at our family's church. The shelter was named after Bogey and me. And last I'd heard, it was full, too.

Bea raised her dark eyebrows. "Very kind of you to say, Abby. And now I'm hoping you might help me out. I found this little calico chasing the bees in my backyard. I don't know where she came from, and none of my neighbors have ever seen her before. So, as near as I can tell, she's a stray kitten. But I'm afraid I just don't have room to take in any more foster cats at the moment. Then I remembered that you have cats and you take very good care of them. So I was wondering if you'd be a foster Mom to this little kitten for a few weeks. Just until I have room at my place. Or until I can find her a forever home."

"Well, we do have a houseful already . . ." our Mom started to say.

"Please, Mom," Gracie chimed in. "That little kitten looks really scared. And if we don't take her in, what will happen to her?"

Our Mom sighed and laughed. "Well, I guess we could take in one more. Until you can find a permanent home for her, Bea."

"Thank you so much," Bea gushed. "I'm sure she won't be much trouble. She's such a tiny little thing."

"But don't you think we should give her a name?" Gracie asked.

Bea shook her head. "I wouldn't bother. She'll get a whole new name when she gets adopted into a permanent home. And then she'll just have to learn her name all over again."

Gracie frowned. "Oh . . ."

Bea darted a glance at the sky. "Well, it looks like I'd better buzz on home before this storm hits!"

And without another word, she plopped the tiny kitten onto our hardwood floor. Then she turned on her heel and raced off into the wind, while thunder boomed in the distance.

I looked at those mean, black clouds in the sky, and I was really glad that our Mom was holding me nice and tight. Because it sure looked like we were in for a real doozie of a storm! And all of a sudden, I started to shake almost as much as that little kitten.

Holy Catnip!

CHAPTER 2

Holy Mackerel!

There we were, with a big, ugly thunderstorm headed our way, and a cute, little kitten who was already here to stay. For a while, anyway. A kitten with no name. What in the world were we supposed to call her?

And on top of it all, the clue that we'd found on our porch was still hidden behind the potted plant.

Our Mom shut the front door and set me gently on the floor. "I guess we've got a new addition to the family. Even if it's only temporary. Welcome to our home, little one." She reached over and petted the tiny cat's head.

"She's so adorable," Gracie said right before she kissed Bogey on the head and set him on the floor. Then she scooped that shivering kitten up off the floor and cuddled her in her hands.

"Don't be scared," she cooed to the cat.

The kitten's green eyes went even wider than before as she snuggled in to Gracie. "I'm not s-c-a-r-e-d," she meowed down to Bogey and me in a shaky voice.

Well, I had to say, that really surprised me. Because she sure looked scared to me. And she sure sounded scared. And I just happen to know a thing or two about being scared. In fact, you might even say I'm sort of an expert on the subject. So let me tell you, if I've ever seen a cat who was scared before, well, she was it.

Yet the more I watched her, the more I realized how different she looked from any other cat I've ever seen. That was the thing about calico cats, cats with coats of many colors. No two looked a thing alike. The colors in their fur came out in every pattern and design that anyone could ever imagine. And then some.

This little kitten had one orange arm and one black arm, and black around both her eyes, like she was wearing a mask. She had white ears and a little black mustache beneath her pink nose. Above her nose, she had an orange-striped patch that reached all the way up to her forehead. But her neck, paws, and belly were all white. She looked like someone had tried to color her with crayons, but couldn't decide which color to use.

Though I didn't care about any of that when thunder suddenly boomed outside. And I nearly jumped to the ceiling when a big lightning bolt flashed just outside our window. Talk about being scared!

Without thinking, I scampered around and hid behind Gracie's legs. Not that a big guy like me could possibly hide behind her thin legs. Still, I did my best.

Gracie giggled. "Oh, Buckley, there's nothing to worry about. It's only a storm. You're safe inside our house."

Our Mom smiled at Gracie. "Honey, would you mind taking care of these kitties for a little bit? While I finish cooking dinner?"

"Sure thing, Mom," Gracie said as she kneeled down closer to me and Bogey. All the while, she kept the kitten snuggled up at her shoulder.

But our Mom had barely gone back to the kitchen when Gracie's cell phone made a *ding-ding* noise from her pocket. It sounded like she'd gotten a message.

She immediately put the kitten on the floor. "You just wait here for a second, little one. I'll be back with you in a minute." Then she grabbed her phone from her pocket and tapped on it a few times. "Oh look, it's from Olivia!" With a big smile, Gracie wandered over to the staircase and plopped down on the bottom step.

Seconds later, she started to tap away on the phone with

her thumbs. Really fast. As she did, she kept her eyes absolutely glued to that little screen. She didn't look up, down, right, left, or anywhere else. She just kept on staring at her phone.

As near as I could tell, it must have been a pretty important message, for her to just walk away like that. Especially after our Mom had asked her to watch over the little foster kitten. And us. Gracie was usually a very responsible girl, and she always took very good care of all the cats in our house. To tell you the truth, we loved her like she was our real sister.

So I decided to lend a paw and step in where Gracie had left off. "Welcome to our house," I told the little calico. "My name is Buckley and this is my brother, Bogart. Or Bogey, for short."

I was about to ask her name, too. Just to be polite. But then I remembered she didn't *have* a name. Somehow, that seemed really wrong to me. After all, I had a name! One that I liked a lot. And Bogey had a name. And the other three cats who lived in our house all had names. Some of the cats even had two. For instance, one of the cats who lived here was named Princess Alexandra, but the humans called her Lexie. And we mostly just called her Princess. Then there was a really, *really* old cat who we called the Wise One. But her real name was Miss Mokie. And finally, there was Lil Bits, and we usually called her Lil.

All the cats in our house had great names. I couldn't imagine what it would be like not to have one. If you don't have a name, how do you know who you are? And what do you call yourself? No matter how I looked at it, it didn't seem fair to me that this tiny kitten didn't have a name, too.

Another round of thunder rumbled outside and the little cat jumped. Well, to be honest, she wasn't the only one. I may have gone airborne myself a little bit.

But the kitten quickly put on a brave face and looked up at me. "Buckley and Bogey . . .? Wait a minute . . ." She paused and her mouth fell open wide. "I've heard of you guys! You're cat detectives, aren't you?"

I smiled at the tiny creature. "Uh-huh, we are. We run the BBCDA."

She gasped. "I've heard of that, too! Wow, I can't believe

it! Here I am, staying at the house where Buckley and Bogey live!"

Then all of a sudden, she leaped into the air, practically bursting with excitement. She danced across the room and back, before she started to race around in tight, little circles. Around and around and around she went. As near as I could tell, she had a lot of energy inside of her and it seemed to be coming out all at once. And she didn't show any signs of stopping any time soon.

It made me dizzy just watching her. *Really* dizzy.

I turned to my brother. "Um, Bogey . . . what do we do about this?"

Bogey let out a little chuckle. "Don't sweat it, kid. I've seen this kind of thing before. I've got it covered."

And the next thing I knew, Bogey had grabbed a hidden bag of cat treats from under the stairs and was waving a treat in the air. A fish-flavored treat. Known in our house as one of the tastiest of all treat flavors. And like someone had turned off a switch, the kitten suddenly stopped moving. She sniffed the air and made a beeline for Bogey.

He grinned and gave me a sideways glance. "Works every time, kid." He passed the treat to the tiny cat and gave us a round, too.

The kitten put the treat in her mouth, and her eyes suddenly went wide. "Oh . . . my goodness," she said in a whisper. "That is the most delicious thing I've ever tasted. Could I have another one?"

Bogey grinned. "Sure, knock yourself out. First cat treat?"

"Uh-huh." She stuffed the second treat in her mouth and ate at the speed of a runaway mouse. When she was finished, Bogey gave us each another round. And another.

Finally, he raised an eyebrow. "Take it easy there, Short-stuff. Better pace yourself."

She downed her treats and began to dance around the room again. "I want to be a cat detective just like you guys so I can have cat treats every single day. And I'm going to be a really great cat detective. A really, *really* great cat detective. I already know how to do cat karate!"

"You do?" I asked as she practically bounced off one wall and then over to the other.

For the second time since I'd met her, I had to say, I found her information to be pretty surprising. After all, she was so young. When did she have time to learn something like cat karate? *I* didn't even know cat karate, and I was a lot older. Lil Bits once told me that she knew cat karate, and she'd learned it when she was about a year old. Though I'd never seen her use it.

"Watch me, Buckley! I'll show you my best cat karate move!" the kitten hollered. Then she raced up six steps, slipped between two spindles, and launched herself off the edge of the staircase. She went flying through the air sideways, with one back foot leading the way. "Hi-yah!" she shrieked as she soared across the room and ran right into a tall vase on the floor.

The vase fell over and the fake flowers inside went sliding out. Thankfully, the vase didn't break and the kitten didn't seem to be hurt, either. She got up, shook her head, and strolled away. Like nothing had ever happened.

Now I had to wonder, did the tiny kitten mean to hit that vase? It seemed more like she'd run in to it by accident. To tell you the truth, I'd never actually seen a cat do cat karate before. So I didn't really know if this kitten was doing it right or not.

But *she* sure seemed to think she was.

Without a word, I glanced at my brother, ready to ask him what he thought. But he raised his brows and shook his head.

All the while, Gracie just kept on staring at her cell phone. Staring without even blinking. I was starting to get worried about her, since it seemed like she was hypnotized. Plus, I was really hoping she would take care of the little kitten who was now flitting around the room. Even faster than before. All that bouncing around sure made it hard for a guy like me to think straight.

Thankfully, the kitten suddenly ran out of steam and trotted back to me. "Buckley, why don't I have a name?" Her eyes filled with tears and her little face fell. "How can I ever be a cat detective if I don't have a name? Everyone else has a name. How come I don't?" Then before I knew it, she started making a sad kind of *mew-mew-mew-mew* sound. It sounded like . . . crying?

And it went on and on and on. For some reason, it made my stomach go all mushy. Plus it made me even more nervous than the thunderstorm that was booming and flashing outside. More than anything, I just wanted that mewing sound to stop.

"Um . . . well . . ." I stuttered. "Don't you know? You *do* have a name."

Her tears stopped and her eyes went wide. "I do?"

Bogey crinkled his brow as he stashed the cat treat bag under the stairs again.

"Well, um . . . yes," I told her, trying to think on my paws. "Your name is . . . your name is . . . um, well . . ."

Right at that moment, I really didn't have a clue what to say next. Because this tiny kitten didn't have a name at all. And even if I *could* give her one, I had no idea *what* name to give her. Yet if I didn't hurry up and come up with a name, I knew she was going to be really upset. Then she would probably start that pitiful mewing sound again. Plus, she might even feel worse than she already did.

Lightning flashed outside and I glanced at the doorknob on the front door. That's when I noticed the doorknob plate. Imprinted at the bottom were a whole bunch of numbers and then finally the letters *M* and *T*. This was followed by a dash and then the letter *Z*. Bogey would have told me it was the part number. But I didn't give it another thought and I quickly blurted out, "M-m-m-i-i-t-t . . . z-e-e." It was the only thing I could come up with on short notice.

"Mitzi?" she repeated with a smile that filled her face.

"Umm . . . yes. Uh-huh. That's it," I nodded and gave her a pat on her little back.

She sat up nice and straight. "Oh, that's so pretty. I love it! Mitzi, Mitzi, Mitzi. Thanks for giving me my name, Buckley! You're the best!" Then she stood on her hind legs, reached up as far as she could go and gave me a hug.

I put one of my big arms around her and hugged her back.

A half a second later, she went back to dancing around the room. And she kept saying her name over and over again. "Mitzi, Mitzi, Mitzi, Mitzi!"

Bogey gave me a grin. "I gotta hand it to you, kid. That was some pretty quick thinking."

"Thanks," I said and tried to smile.

I only hoped I'd done the right thing. Because now that I'd given her a name, there was no taking it back.

Bogey waved to get the kitten's attention. "So . . . Short-stuff . . . Mitzi . . . Since you want to be a cat detective, maybe you'd like to see our latest clue."

Her eyes went wide. "Wow, oh, wow! This is the best! Not only did I get a name, and a place to stay, but now I get to see a clue."

Bogey nodded toward the dining room. "Then let's get a move on."

With that, we made a beeline for the potted plant that I'd used as a hiding place.

Mitzi did her best to keep up with us. "What is the clue?" she chirped. "Diamonds? Fingerprints? Footprints?"

"Nope, it's a little jar with wooden squares," I told her.

Then I used one of my big paws to slide the jar out from behind the plant. Just far enough for us to get a better look. Of course, I was careful to keep it out of Gracie's line of sight. She was still sitting on the bottom step of the staircase, and we didn't want her to see the clue by accident. As always, we thought it was best to keep our cat detective activities hidden from our humans. For their sake and ours, too.

Bogey extended the sharpest claw on his right front paw. "Time to take a look-see at this paper on top."

Then with one smooth swipe, he cut through the tape that held the paper on the lid. He slid the paper to the floor and opened it so we could all see it. And there, in big black letters, were the words, "Ready to play, BBCDA?"

I barely finished reading the message when lightning flashed and thunder boomed. This time it was so loud it made our whole house rattle. Just like before, I nearly jumped to the ceiling.

Gracie glanced up for half a second and went right back to staring at her phone. Much to my amazement, she didn't even notice that it had started to rain. Hard. In fact, the huge, angry raindrops made quite a racket when they pelted the windowpanes. I even got the feeling those raindrops wanted to break right through the glass and get us.

More than anything, I wanted to run straight under our Mom and Dad's bed. And I wanted to stay there until this loud storm was long gone.

But I stayed put instead. After all, I was supposed to be a big, brave cat detective. And I sure couldn't go running off when we'd finally gotten a chance to look at our clue. Plus, I really didn't want to look like a big scaredy-cat in front of this tiny kitten. So I took a really deep breath and kept my eyes glued on the message before us.

I crinkled my forehead. "Somebody sent us a poem?"

Bogey shook his head. "Not sure that was the point of it, kid."

I scooted closer to the paper. "Oh, then I wonder what it means. What do they want us to play?"

"Beats me," Bogey murmured. "But I don't like the looks of this. Somebody has figured out where we are. Makes me wonder if they've figured out *who* we are, too."

I blinked a few times. "You mean, they might have figured out that the BBCDA is run by a couple of cats?"

Bogey frowned. "Could be, kid. But I don't know how. Think you could help me get the lid off this jar? You've got the right size paws for the job."

"Sure," I told him.

So I sat on my haunches and squeezed the lid of that jar between my paws. Then I slowly unscrewed it. Seconds later, that shiny black lid dropped to the floor. It spun around a few times until it stopped with a *thud!* I had to say, it was nice that my huge paws had come in handy twice in one day.

Mitzi's eyes went wide. "Wow, you guys really *are* good cat detectives!"

"We've had a little practice," Bogey told her with a nod.

Funny, but when I thought about it, I knew my brother was right. Sure, compared to Bogey, I was still a rookie. But compared to a young cat who wanted to be a cat detective one day, well, maybe I even looked kind of smart.

With that in mind, I tipped the jar on its side and pulled out the four little squares. Bogey turned each one face up so we could see all the letters. The letter *G* was the first one, then came the letters, *E, M,* and *A.*

"*G-E-M-A*?" I said out loud.

Bogey shook his head. "Nope, kid. Let's try switching the *A* and the *E* around." And so we did. Until the letters spelled out the word, *G-A-M-E.*

Holy Catnip!

I leaned over for a closer look at the squares. "Well, I guess that's what someone wants to play. A game. It's strange, though. They put part of the message in the note and the rest in the squares."

Bogey nodded. "You got that right, kid. It's a lot of drama for a little message. Somebody wanted to get our attention. And they did a pretty fine job of it."

I sat back and stared at the jar. "I wonder what kind of game they want to play?"

"Good question." Bogey glanced at the storm raging outside. "Like I said before, I don't like the looks of this. Any of it."

I was about to agree with him when we suddenly heard a racket coming from *inside* the house. It was Mitzi, meowing and screeching at the top of her lungs.

Was she hurt? Had she been captured or catnapped?

"Buckley! Bogey!" I heard her scream. "Quick! Come here! I caught him!"

She caught him? The person who had left the clue? The person who wanted to play the game?

My heart started to pound as I turned to my brother. "Where is she?"

He jumped to his feet. "It's coming from the kitchen, kid."

Then without another word, we both took off running just as fast as we could go.

"Hurry!" Mitzi hollered again.

And so we did.

We made a beeline for the kitchen. We were zooming so fast that we skidded right around the corner. But once we got inside the room, we put on the brakes and came to a screeching halt.

Because there, right in front of us, was a sight that made my mouth fall open. In fact, my chin nearly hit the floor. I had to blink a couple of times, because I could hardly believe my eyes.

In all the time that I've been a cat detective, I've never seen anything like the scene I saw before me!

Holy Catnip!

CHAPTER 3

Holy Mackerel!

I blinked some more and shook my head. Just to make sure my eyes weren't playing tricks on me. "Is this for real?" I asked my brother. "Am I really looking at what I think I'm looking at?"

Bogey grinned and let out a sigh. "'Fraid so, kid."

Before we could say another word, Mitzi squealed with excitement and meowed at the top of her little lungs. "I got him, Buckley and Bogey! I got him! See, I caught the crook. I'm already a good cat detective! Don't you think so?"

Then she beamed down at us, from high atop her perch.

On our Dad's head.

As near as I could tell, he'd probably just gotten home from work.

He glanced up and then looked at our Mom with a twinkle in his blue eyes. "I see we have a new cat."

Our Mom laughed. "She's a foster kitten, Mike. We're just keeping her until Mrs. Bumble can find a permanent home for her."

"Good thing she's so tiny," our Dad said as he reached up and untangled Mitzi from his blond hair. "I see she's finding her way around the house okay."

Our Mom glanced at the clock. "Gracie was supposed to be watching her."

"Well, I'll say this much . . . she's got some excellent

climbing skills." Our Dad held Mitzi face-to-face, so he could get a good look at her. Then he chuckled, ruffled the fur on her head, and put her on the floor.

She held her tail high and trotted right over to Bogey and me. "See, Buckley and Bogey? See, see? I caught him!" she meowed as she started to dance around the room.

Bogey grinned. "Well, you caught somebody, all right."

Mitzi's eyes suddenly went wide. "*Somebody*? Oh, you mean . . . you mean . . . that's not . . ."

"Nope," Bogey said with a shake of his head. "He's no crook."

"That's our Dad," I explained.

"Oh," she whispered. "You mean . . . I messed up?" And with those words, she hung her tiny head and started making that dreadful mewing sound. Just like she had before.

Not this again!

For some reason, that sound made my heart flutter and my stomach turn somersaults. More than anything, I just wanted that noise to stop. Not to mention, I could hardly keep up with all the ups and downs of this little kitten. She went from hyper and happy to sulky and sad in half a second.

My brother, on the other hand, didn't seem to be bothered by it at all.

He just grinned and gave her a pat on the back. "Don't sweat it, Short-stuff. You showed some good get-up-and-go there."

"I did?" she whimpered.

Bogey nodded. "Some of the best I've seen. But why don't you hold off on catching bad guys. Leave that to Buckley and me."

Mitzi was about to say something more when Gracie walked in and picked her up. "There you are, baby cat. I couldn't find you anywhere."

Our Mom glanced at Gracie. "Honey, I thought you were going to watch the kitten. Right after dinner, I think you'd better show her where the food dish and litter boxes are."

"Okay, Mom," came her half-hearted reply. Then she grabbed her cell phone and stared at it while she cuddled Mitzi.

Our Dad crinkled his brow. "Gracie, weren't you supposed

to set the table?"

"Oh yeah, right . . ." she said as she looked up and glanced around. It was almost like she was seeing the table for the first time in her life. "I'm not sure how I forgot that."

"I have a good idea why," our Mom said gently. "I think you've been spending too much time on your cell phone. It's time to put it away, honey."

And then Gracie did something I've never heard her do before — she started whining like a really little kid. "Oh, Mom, can't I just have it for a few more minutes?"

What was going on? First the kitten made that crying noise and now Gracie was whining. What would happen next? Would Bogey throw a temper tantrum or something?

Our Mom shook her head. "Gracie, this isn't like you. And you know the rules — no phones at the dinner table. Besides, we gave you that phone mainly so you'd have it in case of an emergency. It's not supposed to be something that takes up your whole day."

"All right, all right," she moaned.

She was about to put her phone down when a bright bolt of lightning crackled outside. It was followed by a gigantic boom of thunder.

Then the lights went out.

This time I wasn't taking any chances. I jumped straight into our Dad's arms and tucked my head in.

Though to be honest, I didn't really care so much that the lights had gone out. After all, cats can see in the dark. But what I didn't like was all that flashing and banging going on outside.

Our Dad chuckled. "Take it easy there, big fella."

He gave me a nice hug, which made me feel a whole lot better. Let me tell you, there are times when a guy just needs a good hug. Especially in the middle of a loud, scary storm.

"Our house is safe, Buckley," he told me as he put me back on the floor. "And since you're a housecat and you don't have to go outside, you'll be just fine."

I have to say, it was on nights like this when I was extra happy to live in a house at all. Before I was adopted into my family, I had been living in a cage in a cat shelter. And before that, I was out on the mean streets and didn't even know

where my next meal was going to come from. I sure didn't
have a chance to stay warm and dry like I was now.

And I sure didn't have a family of people and cats. Or a big
brother like Bogey.

I turned and made my way back to where he sat with Mitzi,
just as a flashlight suddenly lit up the room. Or, at least, I
thought it was a flashlight. But then I realized the light was
coming from Gracie's phone.

"See, my phone has a flashlight built in," she declared. "I
guess it really *is* good in case of an emergency. Should I leave
it on during supper?"

Our Mom laughed. "Why don't we eat by candlelight
instead?"

"That sounds like fun," Gracie agreed.

Our Mom grabbed some plates from the cupboard.
"Would you like to get the candles?"

"Sure thing," Gracie replied, sounding like her old self
again. "And I'll set the table, too. Right away." She leaned
over, put Mitzi on the floor, and got to work.

"Thank you," our Dad told her as he grabbed a box of
matches from a drawer.

While our humans went into action, two of the other cats
who live in our house came trotting into the kitchen.

The first was Princess Alexandra, a small, white cat with
big, green eyes and medium-length fur. She's a kind of cat
called a Turkish Angora and she moves like a little ballerina.
She used to be a cat show cat who always had to act prim and
perfect whenever she performed for the judges. That was,
until we rescued her from her abusive owners.

Following the Princess into the room was Lil Bits, a big,
white cat with black spots. Lil is years older than us, and she's
a kind of cat called a British Shorthair. She's got short legs and
is pretty low to the ground. Gracie always says Lil looks like a
Teddy bear, but to me, she sort of looks like a football player.
Either way, I sure wouldn't want to be tackled by her! Lil was
once known as being one of the best cat detectives in the
business. But then she suddenly quit one day and went into
retirement. Though no one knows why for sure. Thankfully,
she still helps Bogey and me with our cases sometimes.

And tonight Lil was all business. She had a grim look on

her face, and right away I could tell something was wrong.

She made a beeline for my brother and me. "Detectives Buckley and Bogey, I'm afraid we've got a situation."

She almost always addressed us by our titles. Out of respect. Lil was just really nice like that. And for a guy like me who was still a little new on the job, I sure appreciated the way she talked to me.

But before she could say another word, the Princess spotted Mitzi. "Oh, my gracious!" she said with a sweet smile. "Where are my manners? I didn't know we had a visitor!"

I put my arm around the kitten's shoulders. "Mitzi, meet Detective Lil Bits and Princess Alexandra. Mitzi is going to be staying with us for a while. Until Mrs. Bumble can find a forever home for her."

"That's right," Bogey added with a nod. "Our house is just a pit stop for Short-stuff here."

"Well, welcome to our home," the Princess said as she sidled up to Mitzi. "We're very pleased to have you, no matter how long you stay." Then she turned my way and glimmered up to me.

And I made the mistake of looking right into her big, green eyes. That's when my heart started to thump and the room started to spin. Just like it always did when I stared into her eyes. But like Bogey would have said, now was not the time to get all dizzy over a dame. Especially since Lil hadn't even told us the whole story about her "situation" yet.

So I took a deep breath, turned my head, and made myself focus on what Lil was about to say.

Bogey gave her a nod. "What's got your dander up, Lil? I'm all ears and then some."

Lil's mouth formed a worried line. "I just got a message on Gracie's laptop up in her room. From an old friend of mine. She's in trouble. Very big trouble. So I'm hoping we can do a rescue. Tonight."

Bogey immediately tilted his ears toward her. "Who's this pal of yours? And what kind of a pickle is she in?"

"She's an old cat detective friend," Lil told us. "Her name is Beatrix. Or Trixie, for short. Her human Mom was a sweet, little old lady. The lady passed away, and then her son and his wife took Trixie into their home. But they don't really want her. At all. So they've shut her away in a room. They feed her now and then, but mostly they just forget about her."

Bogey clenched his jaw and shook his head. "Out of sight, out of mind."

"Exactly," Lil agreed. "Poor Trixie hasn't had water in days. And her food dish has been empty for a while. She won't last much longer. She got her paws on an old laptop in the room and sent me an SOS."

"Lousy way to treat a cat," Bogey said, flexing his claws. "Sounds like a job for the BBCDA. And we don't have a minute to lose."

I gulped. "A rescue? Tonight?" I glanced outside as lightning lit up the sky once more. "But . . . but . . . it's pouring out there."

I shuddered at the thought of going out into that mess. After all, humans knew better than to go outside in a really bad thunderstorm. Shouldn't us cats be just as careful?

Bogey shook his head. "It's gotta be done, kid. Storm or no storm."

Lil nodded. "If we don't save her pretty quick, she might not make it."

And that's when I knew they were right. We didn't have a choice. We had to do whatever we could to save that poor, starving cat. Even if it meant going out in that horrible storm.

"Then let's go save her," I said in a voice that sounded a whole lot shakier than I wanted it to. "Because a friend of Lil's is a friend of ours. Does she live far from here?"

Lil shook her head. "No, not far at all. I've got the route all mapped out. If we stick to the backyards, we've got about a block and a half to run."

Little Mitzi sat up as straight and tall as she could. "I'll help!"

"So will I," the Princess put in.

"Oh, there's one other thing," Lil told us. "Once we get her out, Trixie won't be easy to hide. Even though she's a calico, she's mostly white, like me. So she can't hide under the cover of darkness. And she's a Maine Coon Cat."

That made me smile. "Like me."

"She's even bigger than you are, Buckley, if you can believe it," Lil told me. "She makes plenty of dogs look tiny."

I'm sure my eyes went pretty wide right about then. A cat who was bigger than me? This I had to see.

Bogey glanced at the kitchen table, where candles now flickered with light as our Mom set their dinner on the table. "Well, no matter what size she is, we'd better get this show on the road. So let's hash out the particulars. As near as I can tell, we've got three main obstacles. The first is getting out of our house."

I was already nodding, picking up on his train of thought. "And the second is getting Trixie out of *her* house."

"That shouldn't be a problem," Lil added. "Since no one has been watching her, she's managed to get the window unlatched. But she's pretty weak, and she can't open the window by herself. So she'll need our help. It's the kind of window that slides from side to side."

I raised one of my big paws. "That'll be my department."

"You're perfect for the job, kid," Bogey said with a grin. "Now, for our last obstacle. After we rescue her, we'll need to get *back* inside *our* house. And I've already got a plan in mind."

Right then, Lil motioned for us to all scoot in closer. So we did. Ready to hear every detail of Bogey's plan.

"We'll start with you, Princess," Bogey said with a nod to her. "I want you to stay here and sneak Gracie's phone away from her."

"Got it," she answered and raised her little chin in determination.

Next Bogey turned to the kitten. "Mitzi, I want you to stay with the Princess and . . ."

"But . . . but . . . but . . . I don't want to stay here!" she protested. "I want to go with you and Buckley." And then she started to make that awful mewing-crying noise again.

Bogey shook his head. "Turn off the waterworks, Short-stuff. Cat detectives don't start crying when they draw the short straw. So change that tune and show me your fiercest cat detective face."

And just like that, she quit making that awful mewing sound. Her tiny face took on the glare of a tiger. "How's this?"

"Very good," the Princess said as she sat low on the floor beside Mitzi. "You and I will stay here and carry out our part of the plan. Every part is important, you know."

"That's right, Short-stuff," Bogey told her. "Now here's your part — when the Princess is in place, I want you to create a distraction. Get the attention of our Mom and Dad and Gracie. So the Princess can sneak Gracie's phone away."

Mitzi crinkled up her little face. "How do I do that?"

"Um . . . maybe you could make that crying sound again," I suggested. "Or start dancing around the room, like you did earlier."

Mitzi nodded her tiny head really fast. "Okay, I can do that!"

Then Bogey turned back to the Princess. "I'm going to send a message to Gracie's phone before we head out. But make sure you keep the phone away from her until you see us running back to the house. I don't want her to get the message before then."

The Princess took a deep breath. "Got it. I'll be a nervous wreck just waiting for everyone to come back. But I'll make sure Gracie doesn't get her phone, or the message, until I see you headed for home."

Lil pointed a paw to the floor above us and glanced at Bogey. "You'll have to send that message from Gracie's laptop up in her room. Because it runs on battery power."

I nodded. "And the computer in the office is plugged in to the electricity. So it won't work right now."

"Good thinking," Bogey said. "That should cover the plan to get us back *inside* the house. Now we need to cook up a plan to sneak *out*."

Let me tell you, just the *thought* of sneaking out of the house and into this storm made my heart start to pound. But it also gave me an idea. "If we're getting Trixie out of her house through a window, maybe we could do the same thing here. Maybe we could go through one of our windows."

"Nice idea, kid," Bogey said with a quick glance at the table where our human family was now sitting down to eat. "But thanks to our surveillance rounds every night, our windows are all locked up tight. Plus they're the type that move up and down. Not side to side."

"And windows that open up and down are extra heavy," Lil added.

"Hmmm . . ." I murmured and tried to put my paw to my chin.

But this was one of those moments when my paw wouldn't go where I wanted it to go. In fact, it wasn't even close. And I only ended up poking myself in the eye instead.

Not the kind of thing a guy wants to do when he's in a huddle with a cluster of cats.

Even so, getting poked in the eye *did* make me blink a couple of times, and that's when I spotted it — a broom in the corner. And another idea suddenly hit me.

"I know what we could do," I said as I pointed to the broom. "If we could move that broom to the front hall and stand it up, maybe I could push it back and forth and hit the door. To make it sound like somebody's outside knocking. Then our Mom and Dad will open the door to see who's there. Since they won't be able to see very well in the dark, we can sneak out and they won't even spot us."

Yet I'd barely spoken the words when I realized my paws weren't the only things I had trouble controlling. Apparently I was having trouble controlling my mouth, too. Because I'd just blurted out my big idea without giving it *any* thought at all. And, well, the truth was, I had no idea whether I could actually make a broom swing back and forth. Five seconds ago, I couldn't even make my paw go where I wanted it to go. So could I really pull off a trick like banging a broom against a door?

And what if I couldn't do it? Would we still be able to get outside and go save Trixie? Or would it mess up the whole rescue?

Yet for some reason, Bogey seemed to believe that I could do it, because he gave me a big pat on the back. "Way to go, kid," he said with a grin. "You're really using your noggin. Let's go with your idea. You and Lil move that broom to the front hallway while I run upstairs and send my message. Wait till I get back downstairs before you start swinging."

I gulped. "Sure thing."

The Princess smiled at me as she gracefully rose to all fours again. "Then I'd better go get Gracie's phone right now."

"Sounds good, Princess," Bogey said before he gave Mitzi a nudge. "Short-stuff, I want you to start your distraction the second the Princess is in place."

Mitzi's eyes sparkled in the dim light. "Okay, Bogey! I'll do a really good job! I'll be the most distracting kitten you've ever seen in your whole life."

Bogey nodded at her. "I'm counting on you, Short-stuff."

To tell you the truth, I could hardly believe how much Mitzi seemed to be enjoying herself. Especially since I *wasn't* enjoying myself *at all*. Mostly because I couldn't stop wondering if I could really move that broom. And I couldn't stop thinking about what it would be like to run outside — smack dab into that huge thunderstorm.

And I was still thinking about it when Bogey said, "Okay, everyone. Let's get a move on!"

Which was our signal to go into action!

So we did just that.

Bogey raced for the stairs, while Lil and I ran to the broom. The Princess made a beeline to the kitchen table and jumped up on the extra chair. Mitzi skipped to the other side of the table and started to make quite a racket. She cried and hollered and carried on like a kitten who was pretty scared. I'm not sure I've ever heard so much noise in all my life! With all that commotion for a cover, I scooted my body under the brush part of the broom. That made the handle part slide down from the wall and hit the floor. But I was pretty sure our Mom and Dad didn't hear it. Not after thunder rumbled above us and Mitzi turned up the volume on her caterwauling. I have to say, she suddenly had a pretty big voice for such a little cat.

It was enough to make our Dad drop his fork and our Mom raise her eyebrows as they both turned to stare at Mitzi. Gracie immediately jumped up from her chair and reached down to get the little kitten. But Mitzi bounced away, just out of Gracie's reach. And with all our humans watching Mitzi, the Princess stretched her arm up to the table. In one quick swipe, she had Gracie's phone down on the chair. Then she dropped it to the floor when thunder boomed again, so I was pretty sure no one heard it hit the wooden floor.

The last I saw, the Princess had batted the phone under a china hutch.

In the meantime, Lil slipped in next to me, and scooted toward the handle of the broom. She kept going until it rested right on her back. Then together, she and I slowly and carefully moved that broom out of the room. I carried the brush part on my back and she carried the handle on hers. It took some doing, but we finally got it to the front door.

Just in time to see Bogey come running down the stairs.

"Did you get the message sent?" I asked my brother.

"You know it, kid," he said with a grin. "Now let's get that broom upright and start knocking."

So we got right down to business. I slid out from under the brush end and let it drop to the floor. Then Bogey and I moved under the handle next to Lil. And together, we all scooted closer and closer to the brush end, pushing the handle up as we went.

Then came the moment of truth. It was time for me to grab onto that handle and move it back and forth. Could I do it? Or would I just let everyone down?

That's when Lil touched my arm with her paw. "We all have things we're afraid of, Detective Buckley. Sometimes we have to muster up courage we don't even know we have. It helps if you remember *why* we do what we do."

"To save a big cat who's starving to death," I said with a nod.

And Lil nodded back. "That's right. A cat who probably won't live unless we save her. Now take a deep breath and focus on the task at hand. You can do this, Detective."

So I did exactly what Lil told me to do. I took a nice, big breath and I kept my eyes on that broom handle. I didn't look away and I barely even blinked. When the handle was up straight enough, I stood on my hind legs and grabbed it with my big paws. They didn't go exactly where I wanted them to go, but it was close enough. Thankfully, that broom handle was pretty long so I had lots to aim for.

"Okay, kid," Bogey said to me. "Make that thing hit the door like someone is out there knocking."

"Aye, aye," I told him. Though I sure didn't risk giving him a salute. Not right now, anyway.

Instead, I sat on my haunches and pushed that broom handle back and forth. With all the strength I had. The first few "knocks" were kind of quiet. But then I figured out how to swing that broom so it hit the door pretty hard. Hard enough to make it sound like someone was knocking.

Bogey gave me a huge grin. "Way to go, kid! You're doing it!"

And sure enough, I was. I was so excited that I just kept on banging that broom against the door.

It wasn't long before we heard our Dad's voice from the kitchen. "It sounds like someone's at the door."

"Probably one of the neighbors checking to see if we're all right," our Mom added. "That, or maybe someone needs help."

And the next thing we knew, we heard footsteps headed our way.

"Drop the broom," Bogey commanded. "And scoot it away from the door."

Well, he sure didn't have to tell me twice. I lowered the broom handle until it was pretty close to the floor. Then I let it fall. And together, we pushed it away from the door. Toward the office.

"Get ready to zoom," Bogey meowed quietly.

Just as our Dad and Gracie walked in.

Our Dad put his eye to the door's peephole. "Hmmm . . . It's so dark out that I can't see a thing." Then he swung the door open wide and took a good look outside. At the dark front porch.

And that's when we made our move. Bogey led the way as we zoomed past our Dad's legs and took a sharp left, just to make sure we weren't spotted. We hugged the wall of the house as we went single file down the whole length of the porch. Once we reached the end, we didn't waste a single second before we jumped off to the grass below.

And smack dab into the dark, wet night.

Rain instantly pelted my fur and plastered it to my body. Just as another bolt of lightning flashed across the sky. I jumped behind a shrub while thunder rumbled all around us. If I had thought it was loud inside, well, it was nothing compared to how loud it sounded *outside*.

In fact, it was so loud that I could barely even hear the voice coming from right beside me.

The voice that said, "I'm here, Buckley. All ready to go."

Funny, but that voice didn't sound a thing like Bogey or Lil's. And if I didn't know better, well, I would have said that voice sounded a lot like . . .

I swung my head around to see the tiny, little head of Mitzi. She looked even smaller than she did before, now that she was soaking wet.

"Mitzi, what are you doing here?" I gasped. "You were supposed to stay inside with the Princess!"

She wiped water from her whiskers. "But I didn't want to stay there. I wanted to go with you and Bogey."

I closed my eyes and cringed. As if being out in a scary storm wasn't bad enough, now we had Mitzi to worry about, too. What in the world would we do with such a little kitten tagging along on a rescue mission? How could she possibly keep up with us as we ran? Her legs were so short that I was pretty sure she couldn't go very fast at all.

To make things even worse, the storm was getting scarier by the second. Raindrops fell like little pebbles from the sky, hitting us hard and drenching us completely. And reminding me how much I hated being in water. Most cats do. To us, the idea of getting a bath was one of the worst things in the world.

And with so much water falling on me, I was getting the biggest bath of my life. More than anything, I wanted to be back inside our house, where I'd be warm and safe and dry.

But I knew I couldn't go back inside. Not now. Not when a cat was in danger and needed our help.

That meant I just had to tough it out. And if there was one thing that I knew for sure, the going was about to get a whole lot tougher!

Holy Catnip!

CHAPTER 4

Holy Mackerel!

The rain started to fall in big, giant sheets, and I started to wonder if we might have to swim over to rescue Lil's friend. Yet even with all that water, I could still see the frown on Bogey's face. And I had a pretty good idea what was on his mind right at that moment. Especially since he was staring at the little kitten who had followed us outside. Even when we told her not to come with us. So as near as I could guess, Bogey was probably trying to figure out what to do with her.

Of course, it would have been best if she simply stayed on the porch and waited for us to get back. But since Mitzi wasn't very good at taking orders, it was a pretty good guess that she wouldn't just stick around until we came back home. And who knew what kind of trouble she could get into? She might decide to wander off and get lost for good. Or, since she was so small, she could even get stuck somewhere. Like under the porch or in a big tree.

That meant we really only had one choice — we had to take her with us. Like it or not. So we could keep an eye on her. And with the storm raging on and soaking us to the skin, we didn't have time to sit around and chat about it.

"All right, Short-stuff," Bogey said to Mitzi. "You can come with us. But we'll be flying along pretty fast. Think you can keep up?"

She sat up tall and pointed her little nose straight into the rain. "Uh-huh, Bogey. I can keep up. I can run really fast."

I sure hoped she was right. But with her short legs, it was going to be a very tall order.

"Then we'd better get this show on the road," Bogey said before he shook his fur. "Lil, you lead the way."

And with that, we all took off. Lil ran in front, with Bogey right behind her. I came after him and Mitzi followed me. And though I wanted to catch up to Bogey and Lil, I held back, just to make sure Mitzi was still behind us. Much to my surprise, she did a pretty good job of keeping up with us.

For a while, anyway.

We raced around the side of the house, past the garage, and through a hole in the back fence. Then we ran through the yard behind ours and around that house, until we reached the street. There wasn't a car on the road and the houses and streetlights were all dark.

By now Mitzi had fallen behind, so we stopped for a second to let her catch up. When she did, I could see that she was panting pretty hard. She'd come a long way on those little legs, and I wasn't sure she could go much farther.

Lil blinked and shook the water from her face. "It's a straight shot from here," she told us, pointing to the end of the block.

"Got it," Bogey said.

Only seconds before another bolt of lightning flashed across the sky. It lit up the world around us for a moment or two. Normally, I would have jumped as high as the nearest tree. But at that moment, I was just too weighed down with water to go airborne.

Even when thunder boomed all around us.

Mitzi, on the other paw, *wasn't* too wet to jump. She went straight up in the air and landed right on my back. Which, as near as I could tell, was probably a *good* place for her. After all, it turned out she didn't weigh very much. And if a big cat like me could carry her for a while, well, that also meant I didn't have to worry about her.

"Hang on tight," I hollered back to Mitzi. "And keep your head low."

For once, she *did* take orders and hung on for dear life.

So off we went, with Lil still leading the charge, Bogey next, and me and my passenger bringing up the rear. In fact, we made even better time now that I didn't have to keep looking back and watching for Mitzi.

Yet in all the days I'd been a cat detective, I never dreamed I'd be doubling as a horse. But I guess there are times when a guy just has to improvise. So I kept it up as we all ran clear to the end of the block. Then we crossed the street and stood in front of a gigantic, three-story house. It was built with stone blocks and it had round towers with pointy roofs on either end. To tell you the truth, the building almost looked like a small castle. Though our Mom probably would've called it a mansion.

And the more I looked at it, the more it gave me the shivers.

"This is the place," Lil said quietly.

I turned to my brother. "Is it just me, or does that house look kind of, um . . . well . . . creepy?" Even the dark windows looked like big eyeballs staring at us.

Bogey squinted his eyes and stared right back. "It doesn't exactly scream 'cheerful', does it, kid? Not with the power out and the whole place being pitch-black. Except for that front room with the fireplace."

I glanced at the very window he was talking about. Sure enough, I could see a couple of people sitting around the bright light of a fireplace. I couldn't quite make out their faces, but I could see they were laughing and talking. Almost like they were having a little celebration. And as near as I could tell, they didn't notice us cats outside at all.

Much like they obviously didn't notice Trixie on the inside, either. Instead of having her with them as they celebrated, she was locked up without anything to eat or drink. Just the idea of a cat being neglected like that made me hopping mad. Even though I'm not the kind of guy who gets mad very much. And it was funny, but being mad kind of warmed me up, and all of a sudden, I didn't mind being out in the rain so much. Not when I knew we were about to rescue a helpless cat and take her away from this awful place.

Bogey crinkled his brow and kept on staring at the house. "Do you have a roadmap to reach this pal of yours, Lil? We'll follow your lead."

Lil nodded toward the side of the house. "We have to go around to the back and climb up to the second story. That's where Trixie's room is. She told me she'd be sitting in the window, so we could see her."

Then, without wasting another second, Lil and Bogey took off running. I followed them, with Mitzi still riding on my back. We quickly reached a fence on the side of the house. A wooden fence that we would have to climb.

"Okay, this is where you get off," I told my passenger.

Mitzi did as she was told, and then she stared up at that tall fence. Her tiny mouth was set in a firm line, and I could tell she was trying to be brave. But I could also see that she was nervous about doing something new and probably scary to her. Gee, how many times had I felt that way in my life? I couldn't even count the number on all four paws.

So I gave her some pointers while we watched Lil and then Bogey go up and over the fence. "Did you see how they went?" I asked Mitzi. "I want you to do exactly what they did."

She nodded and bit her lip. "Okay, Buckley. I can do it! I can go really fast, too!"

And sure enough, she scurried her way up like a pro. Then I climbed up after her, only to find her sitting on a board that ran across the top of the fence.

"Buckley, I'm scared," she said with a little whimper. "It's a long way down to the ground."

And she sure had a point. It *was* a long way down, especially for a tiny kitten who'd probably never climbed a fence before. Funny, but it was always a whole lot easier to climb up than to climb down.

"Watch me," I told her. "And run right behind me. When you get close to the ground, kick off and jump down. Ready?"

"Ready!" she squeaked in a fierce, little voice.

Then I pointed my nose toward the ground and ran straight down that fence. Halfway there, I kicked off and jumped into the yard. She followed me the whole way and stayed just a few inches behind me. I landed on all fours and kept running, while she slipped and rolled in the mud when she hit the ground. But she quickly bounced back onto her feet. She shook off the mud in great droplets as the rain quickly washed her clean.

"That was kind of fun, Buckley," she said with a smile.

Did she say *fun*? I'm sure my eyes would've gone pretty wide right about then, if I didn't have so much water running into them.

"We'd better hurry," I told her. "So we can get Trixie out of there."

Then off we went. We caught up to Bogey and Lil as they stood in the backyard, looking up at the second story of the house. Sure enough, there was a huge, mostly white cat sitting in one of the windows.

And I do mean huge! In fact, I did a double take when I saw her. If I thought I was a big cat, well, I almost looked sort of small compared to her.

She raised a shaky paw to wave at us, and I could tell she was feeling pretty weak.

Let me tell you, just seeing that big cat suffering stirred something deep inside of me. It bothered me so much that I took off running without even thinking. To save her. Without waiting for Bogey and Lil. Because more than anything, I wanted to get that poor cat away from those awful people who were treating her so badly. I wanted her to be safe and full and happy. Like I was. Like all the cats in my family were.

I zoomed across the yard so fast that rain droplets flew right off my fur! Then I shimmied straight up the trunk of a huge tree that was next to the house. When I reached a big branch, I pulled myself up and walked across it very carefully, putting one paw directly in front of the other. One step at a time. I had to be extra careful not to slip, or I would have fallen straight to the ground.

The branch led to a small, shingled roof that was just below Trixie's window. A really steep little roof. And once I was close enough, I kicked away from the branch and jumped right onto that roof. From there I walked straight up the steep slope to Trixie's window.

Or, at least, I *tried* to walk straight up that slope.

But I hadn't realized just how slippery those shingles were when they were dripping wet. And with rain pelting me harder than ever, I soon started to slide backward instead of going forward.

Which probably wasn't the best way to rescue a cat in danger. Especially when I started to wonder if *I* was about to become another cat who needed to be rescued. Because no matter how hard I tried to stop, I just kept on sliding down, down, down, until I could see the edge of that roof. Right about then, I realized I probably should have waited for Bogey and Lil. And maybe even come up with a plan.

"Turn around, kid," came Bogey's voice from somewhere to the left of me.

"Huh? Turn around?" I repeated, wondering if the rain had affected Bogey's eyesight. And my hearing.

"Yup, kid," he said. "Turn around. Dig your back claws in and walk your front legs up. Then switch. Dig your front claws in while you push your back legs up the roof. Keep it up until you reach the window."

"Um, okay," I answered him.

And even though it was pretty terrifying, I did just what he told me to do. Then little by little, I went up that roof. Like a reverse inchworm. All the while, my heart felt like it was going to pound right out of my chest. It didn't help that I was staring straight down into the backyard. Below me, Mitzi bounced around and waved to me, like she was trying to direct me. Lil stood near her, and glanced from me to the house and then back to me again. I figured she was also on the lookout for any humans who might suddenly show up.

"You're doing great, kid," Bogey coached me. "Just a few more inches and you're there."

That's when I realized he'd climbed up a whole different way. And he was now on a little roof just above me.

He jumped down onto my roof and met me at the window. "Now let's get this poor cat outta here."

At long last, I made it to the window. Then I turned around and got a good look at Trixie for the first time. My mouth fell open so wide that I sputtered and choked on rainwater. Because, even though Trixie was a huge cat, she was also very thin. And I do mean thin. In fact, I'd even say she looked downright skinny. She had fur that was twice as long as mine, but it was matted into huge clumps all over her body. As near as I could tell, it had been a long time since someone had brushed her hair. That made me extra sad, since our Mom and Gracie brushed us all the time.

I nodded to her and tried to smile, just to cheer her up. But the truth was, I really didn't feel much like smiling at the moment.

Though Bogey managed to flash her a grin. "Howdy, ma'am. Lil called in the cavalry and here we are. I'm Bogey and this is Buckley. Now hang tight while we slide this window open."

I took a closer look at the window, and I could see that Trixie had gotten it unlatched on the inside. Just like she'd told Lil in her message.

"Okay, kid," Bogey said to me. "I'll hook my claws around the outside edge and pull. You push from the middle."

"Aye, aye," I told him as I got into position.

Then we both gave it everything we had. With a little work, we finally slid that window open.

And set off the burglar alarm.

Right away, my heart started to pound about a million miles an hour. Especially since that alarm screeched so loud that I wanted to cover my ears. But I knew I couldn't.

Trixie shook her head. "I'm so sorry. I didn't know the alarm was on."

Bogey darted a quick glance inside the room. "No problem, ma'am, but we'd better pick up the pace." Then he held out his paw to give Trixie some support. "Watch your step, Trix. It's as slick as the marble floor at the museum out here."

Trixie put her two front paws on the roof just outside the window. "Thank you," she murmured. "Lil told me she worked with some of the best cat detectives in the business. And you two are tops."

"Always happy to help a dame in distress," Bogey said as he kept one eye on the bedroom where Trixie had been held captive. "Now the trick is not to get caught. So let's all step lively out here."

With our help, Trixie was soon standing outside on the roof. Of course, the rain immediately drenched her long fur and plastered it to her sides. And that's when I saw that she was even thinner than she'd looked before. In fact, she was kind of a skeleton cat under all that fur.

Which probably accounted for the way she wobbled.

Bogey glanced at me. "Let's get this window shut again, kid. It won't turn off the alarm. But if anyone checks this room, it'll take 'em a while to figure out that Trixie is gone. It could buy us some time."

"Sure thing," I told him.

So we went right to work. With some tugging and some pushing, we had that window shut in a hurry. But even with it closed, I could still hear the alarm ringing, ringing, ringing.

"Good job, kid," Bogey told me. "Now let's all amscray."

"Amscray?" I repeated.

"It's an expression, kid," he said. "It means 'scram'. Skedaddle. Vamoose. In other words, let's get out of here."

"Sounds good to me," Trixie said in a shaky voice.

And we were about to do just that when it happened — a big gust of wind came up and sent us all slip-sliding down the roof.

Bogey and I held on and managed to stay standing. But poor Trixie was no match for that gale. Much to my horror, her legs buckled and she flopped over onto her side. Right away, I put out a big paw and managed to grab her. So she didn't go sliding off that roof. Then I held onto her with all my might and glanced at my brother.

Now I had to wonder, how in the world would we get Trixie back on her feet and safely down to the yard below? Without all three of us getting caught by her abusive owners?

Especially since it was becoming harder and harder to see, thanks to the rain that was now coming down sideways. Not to mention, the lightning that flashed all around us, even more than before.

Holy Catnip!

CHAPTER 5

Holy Mackerel!

There we were, up on that roof, trying to rescue Trixie and get her away from this awful place.

The only problem was, Bogey and I were having a pretty hard time hanging on to those slick shingles. And trying to hang on to Trixie at the same time just made things a *whole* lot harder. To tell you the truth, I wasn't sure if we could hang on much longer. Especially since Trixie was still lying on her side and starting to pant. Worst of all, I had no idea what to do next.

So I was pretty happy when I saw Lil race up the same tree that I'd used to get onto the roof.

"She's probably just dehydrated," Lil hollered over to us.

"De . . . what?" I hollered back.

Bogey tilted his head in my direction. "De-hy-drated, kid. She needs water."

Lil scooted a little closer. "Open your mouth and take a drink, Trix."

For a moment, I wasn't sure if I'd heard Lil correctly. Did she really want Trixie to take a drink? But how could she, when there wasn't a water dish nearby?

Then I looked cross-eyed at the water dripping down my nose, and I realized, well, there was water all around us. *Everywhere*, you might say.

I held up my arm so Trixie could see the droplets falling from my paw. "Lil is right, Trixie. Just open your mouth and let the raindrops fall in. There's plenty of water and you'll have a nice drink."

Without a word, she did just that. She opened her mouth and drank and drank and drank and drank. Then she drank some more. I don't think I've ever seen a cat who was so thirsty before. Sure, I'd been thirsty myself a time or two, but never like that!

In the meantime, Bogey kept an eye on the window of the room where Trixie had been held prisoner. The burglar alarm was still ringing, but thankfully, no one had shown up at the window and spotted the three of us out on the roof.

Yet.

Once Trixie had finished drinking, she perked up right away. "I really appreciate all of you coming out to save me like this. I don't know what I would have done without you."

"We're happy to help, my friend, but we're not home free," Lil replied as she glanced around. "And the faster we get out of here the better."

Bogey shook the rain from his eyes. "Think you can stand up again, Trix?"

I scooted closer to her. "You can lean on me while we get you off this roof."

Lil was already nodding. "Then you can lean on me when you get out to this branch. And we'll all help you get down the tree."

Trixie plastered a wobbly smile on her face and struggled to her feet. "You cats are spoiling me. First I get rescued and then I get treated like a queen. This must be my special day."

I had to say, I was pretty impressed by the way she kept her spirits up. For a cat who was practically dying of thirst and almost starving to death, she wasn't complaining one bit. When I thought about it, I wasn't sure if I'd be so upbeat if I were in her paws!

And speaking of paws — ones with claws — I dug mine in extra deep, just to make sure I could support her. Before long, Lil and Bogey and I had her off that roof and safely down to the ground. I was so happy that I even thought about giving that ground a big, giant kiss.

But only for half a second. Especially now that I was standing in all that water and mud in the yard.

Trixie looked pretty happy herself as she sat for a quick rest. "What a team! You cats are terrific."

Lil nodded. "You won't find a better bunch. And there are more back at our house."

"That's right," I told Trixie. "Princess Alexandra is playing her part to make sure we get back inside. Plus we have Miss Mokie, a really old cat who gives us lots of good advice. You'll be amazed at how wise she is. We also have a human Mom and Dad, and our human sister, Gracie. You're going to love them all."

"They sound wonderful," Trixie murmured.

Now Mitzi started to bounce around with the same speed that raindrops were hitting the grass. "Tell her my name, Buckley! Tell her I'm Mitzi. Tell her I'm going to be a cat detective, too!"

Trixie let out a little laugh. "Nice to meet you, Mitzi. And for that matter, it's been a real pleasure to meet you all."

"The feeling is mutual, Trix," Bogey told her. "But let's save the niceties until we've finished rescuing you first."

He had barely spoken the words when sirens sounded in the distance. And we had a pretty good idea where they were headed — straight for the big, creepy house in front of us. So we didn't waste another second before we vamoosed. Or, in the words of Bogey — amscrayed.

Once we got to the fence, Mitzi looked up at Trixie. "Watch me, Trixie! I'll show you how to climb this fence. Going down is the hard part. But if you do what I do, you'll be okay." Then Mitzi immediately raced all the way up to the top board. She gave us a wave before she ran down the other side.

Well, I had a pretty good idea that Trixie had climbed a fence or two in her lifetime. But because she was so weak, we had to give her a little boost this time. Even so, she made it down the other side with almost no effort at all.

"See, Trixie!" Mitzi said when we were all in the front yard. "That wasn't hard, was it?" But she didn't even wait for an answer before she started to dance around again.

For some reason, this made Trixie smile as she turned to Lil. "The CDITs seem to get younger every year, don't they?"

"CDITs?" I repeated.

"Cat Detectives in Training," Lil explained to me. "But I'm not sure if Mitzi is really in training. I think she's more of a tagalong."

Tagalong was right. Though she didn't tag along so much as she "rode along." In fact, she jumped on my back the second we started for the street. I had to say, it sure would have been nice if she had asked me first. I didn't mind her weight so much on the way over. But now it seemed like she was getting heavier and heavier as we ran through the yard and crossed the street together in the pouring rain.

It took all the strength I had to keep up my speed. Thankfully, we weren't exactly running at top speed anyway, not with the way Trixie was wobbling along. We were halfway up the block when we looked back to see two police cars pull up in front of the stone mansion. The flashing lights on the patrol cars lit up the dark night and practically blinded me. But we didn't stay to watch. Instead, we just kept on moving, so we could get back home.

And get out of the rain.

By now, I was starting to drag my paws. But little Mitzi just seemed to gain more energy by the minute, and she kept on talking and talking and talking. Mostly to Trixie.

"We don't have much farther to go," she told the big cat. "And don't worry, it won't be hard to walk the rest of the way. You can make it. Look at me — I'm not even tired at all! Wait till you see the house where you'll be staying. It's so pretty. And all the people and the cats are so nice. Did you know I'm a foster cat? I guess you'll be a foster cat, too . . ."

And on and on it went. It was a good thing we weren't on a top-secret mission. Or going undercover on a case. Because this kitten would have given us away long before we started.

Still, I liked the way she encouraged Trixie to keep going. Especially since Trixie looked so weak that I was beginning to wonder if she would even make it the rest of the way. I could see she was starting to shiver, much like Bogey and Lil were shivering now, too. So the five of us sort of huddled together to keep warm. And to help Trixie stay on her paws.

It seemed like it took forever before we finally reached the hole in the fence. We went through it one at a time until we were all in our own backyard. Right at that moment, I almost felt like jumping for joy. I couldn't remember ever being so happy to get back home. I even smiled as we passed the windows, especially when I noticed that candles were still lit in the kitchen.

That meant the power was still out.

Bogey shuddered, and I could tell he was a lot colder than he was letting on. "Time for the final part of our plan," he said. "Let's hope the Princess kept an eye out."

Thankfully, we spotted her when we ran around to the front of our house. She was looking out the dining room window and watching for us. Just like she was supposed to do. She jumped when she saw us, and her eyes went wide. Probably because she didn't recognize us at first. Then again, we weren't exactly recognizable. Not with fur plastered to our bodies and whole rivers of rain practically running off of us.

The Princess gave us a quick wave and ran off in a streak of white. I was so tired that I didn't even have the strength to wave back. My legs felt like they weighed a ton each as we all dragged our dripping bodies up the porch steps and sat in front of the door. If nothing else, at least we were finally out of the pouring, pounding rain. Even so, the water kept on rolling off of us, and I had a pretty good idea that it would be days before my fur was completely dry.

That is, if anyone *ever* opened the front door. I glanced at Trixie, who was really shivering hard now, and I wondered what was taking so long.

Mitzi jumped off my back and cuddled up to Trixie, trying to keep her warm. But Mitzi's little body wasn't nearly enough to warm up Trixie's huge body. Especially since Trixie was at least five times her size.

At long last, we heard the thud of footsteps coming from inside the house. They sounded heavy, which probably meant it was our Dad who was headed our way. I could also hear Gracie talking, so I knew she was headed to the door with our Dad.

"Okay, everyone, look alive," Bogey said. "Trixie, you wait out here. Lil, Buckley, and Mitzi — be ready to shake a leg when the door opens."

I wiped water off my forehead. "Shake our legs? Shouldn't

we run inside instead?"

"Just an expression, kid," Bogey said with a grin. "It means hurry up. We've gotta get in and make it look like Trixie is the only cat out here."

Trixie's chin dropped. "That doesn't sound like a very good plan to me."

Lil put her paw on Trixie's shoulder. "You have to trust these cats, Trix. They won't let you down. After all, they rescued you once, right?"

Trixie took a deep breath. "You're right, Lil. And I do trust you. All of you."

Bogey shook himself, so that water ran off his slick fur and formed a big puddle on the porch. "Don't worry, Trix. My plan is already in place. You just wait here until our Dad and Gracie have eyeballed you. Then stroll on in like you own the place."

Trixie's eyes went wide for a moment. "All right. Whatever you say."

I did my best to smile at her, though it was probably kind of shivery. "Welcome to our house."

"Thanks, Buckley," she said. "Thank you all again. You're such a great bunch." For a moment, I couldn't tell if those were raindrops or tears rolling down her big cheeks.

But I didn't get a chance to find out, since the footsteps sounded closer and closer, and Gracie's voice became louder and louder.

Little Mitzi started to bounce around the porch. "When you said 'bunch,' you meant me, too? Right, Trixie? I'm going to be a great cat detective one day, just like Buckley and Bogey! I already know cat karate! Watch me!" She jumped onto a porch chair and launched herself into the air. "Hi-yah!"

Just as our Dad opened the door.

Mitzi went flying into the house, spraying water as she went. She barely missed Gracie's legs by a few inches. The force of her jump even scooted the porch chair back just a little.

But "a little" was all it took to expose something that had been right underneath that chair. For sitting there on our front porch was another glass jar with a shiny black lid. It was exactly like the one we'd found earlier. Only this one had something different inside.

"Bogey . . ." I murmured as I blinked my eyes. "Those look like . . ."

Bogey raised his brows. "Yup, kid. They do look like . . ."

"Diamonds?" Lil and Trixie both blurted out at the very same moment.

"No time for this now," Bogey said as he pointed a paw toward our front hallway.

Then he and Lil zoomed inside. In the darkness, they raced right past Gracie's legs, kicking up water as they went. As for me, well, I used one of my big paws to bat that little jar right into our house. Kind of like I've seen hockey players on TV when they smack a hockey puck with a stick. I could hardly believe it, but my big paws went exactly where I wanted them to go. If I had been playing hockey, I would have scored a perfect goal. I raced in after the little jar, only seconds before our Dad shined a flashlight right onto Trixie.

"So Mrs. Bumble just sent this poor cat over to our house? To be a foster cat?" our Dad asked. "All by herself in the pouring rain? That's really odd."

"I know, Dad," Gracie said with a shrug. "But that's what my phone message said. It's a good thing little Lexie found my phone under that buffet. I still don't know how it got there."

Hearing that made me smile. It meant the Princess had played her role in our plan perfectly. She'd hidden the phone on time, and then gotten it back to Gracie just like she was supposed to. At the exact, right moment.

Our Dad shook his head. "I think Mrs. Bumble should have waited until the storm was over and then brought the cat over herself."

"And maybe asked us if we could take in another foster cat," our Mom said with a chuckle from the other end of the room. "It's a wonder this cat could even find her way over here. Thank goodness she didn't get lost out there."

Gracie gasped. "Oh, this poor kitty, she's all wet! And look how huge she is. She's even bigger than Buckley. The message on my phone said her name is Trixie."

"She's skin and bones," our Dad said in disbelief. "It looks like she hasn't eaten in a week."

As Gracie took Trixie into her arms, I batted the little jar behind the potted plant in the dining room. Then I looked up to see Gracie give Trixie a nice, gentle hug. The big cat closed her eyes, probably exhausted from the journey. Not to mention, relieved to be somewhere safe.

"I'll get her some food and water," Gracie said softly. "Right after I get her dried off." She didn't seem to mind one bit that she was getting wet, with Trixie dripping water all over her.

And our Mom and Dad didn't seem to mind, either.

That is, until the lights suddenly went back on, exposing us all. Our Mom and Dad and Gracie all gasped at the exact same moment. But Bogey just grinned and wiped more water from his face while Mitzi shook her whole body.

"Oh, my goodness," our Mom said under her breath. "These cats are all soaking wet! What in the world . . .? Do we have a leak in the roof somewhere?"

Our Dad shook his head and shut the front door. "I don't know how they got so wet. We just got a new roof last spring. We've never seen a leak during any other thunderstorms."

"It almost looks like these cats have been . . . out in the rain," our Mom added with wide eyes. "Because they're muddy, too."

"I don't know how they could have been outside," came our Dad's reply. "I thought they were inside the whole time."

Our Mom shook her head. "Well, one thing's for sure, regardless of what happened — they all need a bath."

That's when my breath got stuck in my throat. A bath? Did she just say a *bath*?

Apparently so. Because the next thing I knew, Lil, Mitzi, Trixie, Bogey and I were all being carted to the upstairs bathroom. Gracie and our Mom shut the door and started to fill the huge claw-foot tub with warm, sudsy water.

I could hardly believe what was happening. Of all the things I hated the most, a bath was probably smack dab at the top of my list. It came right after running around outside in a thunderstorm and being drenched by rain. Okay, maybe there were a few other things on my list that were higher, but a bath was still pretty high up there. As far as I was concerned, we'd had enough water for one night. Maybe even a whole year.

To top it off, Bogey and I hadn't even had a chance to look

at the second clue we'd found. Specifically, the jar that looked like it had diamonds in it. Instead, we were locked in a bathroom with no chance for escape.

Helplessly awaiting our doom.

Holy Catnip!

CHAPTER 6

Holy Mackerel!

There I was, staring at a huge, claw-foot tub that was being filled with water. Okay, maybe it wasn't actually being filled *full*. The truth was, our Mom didn't put a lot of water in the tub for a cat bath. But still, a bath is a bath, no matter how you looked at it. And I could not stop shaking in my paws at the very thought of being lowered down into that tub. Worst of all, I seemed to be the only scaredy-cat in the whole bunch.

Mitzi was so excited that she would've happily leaped into that tub on her own. If she'd been big enough to get up and over the sides. As it was, she jumped right out of Gracie's hands and into the water when Gracie lowered her in. And Lil didn't mind one bit when our Mom gently lifted her in. Trixie was so happy to be away from her old house that she didn't care, either. In fact, I think she enjoyed getting some attention for a change. Because she went into the tub right beside Lil.

While all this was going on, Bogey grinned and nudged me in the ribs. "Don't sweat it, kid. It'll be over before you know it."

Funny he should say that. Because, as far as I was concerned, a bath was something that usually went on *forever*.

And ever.

My brother pulled a bag of cat treats out from under a cabinet. He glanced to make sure no one was looking before he passed me a couple of treats and then took some for himself.

"Here you go, kid. This'll take the edge off," he said before he hid the bag again.

"Thanks," I told him. "I needed that."

And those were my final words before our Mom took Bogey and put him in the tub with the others.

That left me as the only cat still sitting on the tile floor. And wouldn't you know it, but Gracie leaned down and picked me up, too. All ready to set me into the water. But I had other ideas. In fact, I decided this might be a *really* good time to give her a nice, big hug. After all, a cat should show appreciation to his humans every day. And when I thought about it, I realized I hadn't shown her as much love lately as I should have. So I wrapped my arms around her neck and hung on for dear life.

She started to giggle right away. "Buckley, you have to take a bath. How did you get so wet and muddy, anyhow? I sure hope you didn't go outside. You know I would be lost if anything ever happened to you."

Just like I would be lost if something ever happened to her. And to show her how much I cared, I gave her a big, wet kiss on the nose.

She giggled again. "Buckley, you have to let go now." Then she pried my arms away from her.

And before I knew it, there I was, sitting right in the middle of that tub. I let out a loud yowl and tried with everything I had to scramble my way up and out of there. But the more I tried to escape, the more I just slipped around.

I glanced over to Bogey and Lil, and I could hardly believe my eyes. The two of them looked downright calm. And if *they* were calm, I knew I had to do my best to be brave, too. Sometimes there's a lot of pressure on a guy to be a big, tough cat detective — especially when he was facing down a bathtub full of water.

Holy Catnip!

But being brave was easier said than done, especially when Mitzi started to bounce around and play with the bubbles. She even splashed water in my face a few times, right before she jumped on my back. Just like she'd jumped on my back when we were running back and forth to rescue Trixie. And even though she didn't weigh much, it was still enough to knock me over in the slippery tub. That meant we both landed in the sudsy drink. But instead of saying she was sorry, she just laughed and scampered off.

And let me tell you, I did not appreciate it one bit! I knew she was just a little kitten, but she was starting to get on my nerves. I tried to say something to her, but my words just came out like, "*blub, blub, blub*." Probably because I now had suds in my mouth, thanks to all the splashing.

At least I managed to make my way to the faucet and rinse my mouth out. After that, we all got scrubbed and rinsed until we were squeaky clean. It seemed like an eternity passed before I was back in Gracie's arms and wrapped up in a fluffy towel. More than anything in the world, I wanted to take a nice, long nap while Gracie cuddled me. Especially since it was so comfy and warm right there in the bathroom. In fact, all of a sudden, my eyelids felt like they weighed about a hundred pounds each. I could even feel them starting to droop.

Only seconds before Gracie's cell phone rang. Then without so much as a "Here you go, Buckley," she plopped me on the floor and answered her phone.

"Uh-huh, Sophie," I heard her say. "That's right, our lights went out, too . . ."

Our Mom wrapped Lil in a big, blue towel and waved to get Gracie's attention. "Please tell Sophie that you'll call her back later. Right now I need you to go get some food for the cats and bring it up here."

Gracie's eyes took on kind of a funny, glazed look, like she didn't know where she was for a moment or two. But then she snapped out of it.

"Oh, okay, Mom," she said before she got off the phone and dropped it in her pocket. Then she left the bathroom and shut the door behind her.

Our Mom picked up Trixie and dried her off, too. Without hesitating, the big cat leaned into our Mom and started to purr. Very, very loudly. As loud as a lawn mower. In fact, I've never heard a cat purr like she did. I thought Bogey and I purred loudly, but ours was nothing compared to hers.

"There you go, big girl," our Mom murmured as she set

Trixie carefully on the floor again.

Trixie looked right up at our Mom and meowed her thanks.

Mitzi, on the other hand, didn't want to hold still when it was her turn to get dried off. Despite all that, our Mom had everyone toweled off by the time Gracie returned with six plates and a couple of cans of tuna fish.

The Princess pranced right into the bathroom behind Gracie and joined us. "Welcome to our home, Trixie," the Princess meowed graciously. "I'm so glad the rescue went well. I was once rescued from a bad situation myself, so I know what it's like to be in your paws. Just know that you are safe now and you couldn't be staying in a better home."

"Thank you," Trixie meowed back with tears in her eyes. "I can't even begin to tell you how grateful I am. To all of you. I wish there were some way I could repay everyone."

The Princess waved her off. "You don't owe us a thing. And who knows? Maybe you'll end up rescuing another cat in danger some day. But right now, please just enjoy a nice meal and don't worry about a thing."

I found myself smiling at the Princess. She was always so kind and thoughtful. Just looking at her and hearing her words was enough to make my heart go *thump*, *thump*, *thump*. Really loud. So loud I was afraid someone else might hear it. Thankfully, none of the other cats were paying attention to me. Because Gracie didn't waste any time dishing out our dinner and putting the plates in front of us.

Let me tell you, I took one good whiff of that tuna fish and I suddenly realized how hungry I was! As near as I could tell, everyone else was, too. Because we all dug into our dinners and barely came up for air. I couldn't remember when food ever tasted so good.

I could only imagine how Trixie must have felt.

Though I was starting to get a pretty good idea when I saw her eat and eat and eat some more. Like she hadn't had any food in a year.

I was so glad she was here with us. And I couldn't help but feel proud when I played back the whole rescue in my head. It took more courage than I knew I had to run through that scary thunderstorm. Not to mention, climb up onto that slippery roof and get her down. But now that I saw her looking so happy, I had to say — going out in that awful storm and saving her was one of the best things I've ever done.

And I'd do it all over again if I had to.

Especially since I knew our Mom and Dad and Gracie would take really good care of her. And of course, us cats would help out plenty, too. I only hoped the people at that creepy mansion wouldn't try to find her and take her back. Just thinking about it made a shiver run up and down my spine.

But I didn't have time to think about that now. Not with such good food in front of me. And not when all the other cats were having so much fun.

In fact, the whole thing turned into quite a party before long. Bogey pulled out his hidden bag of cat treats and passed around plenty for everyone. The Princess and Trixie kept on chatting away, like they were old friends. Lil watched as Mitzi showed off her "cat karate" and hit a stack of toilet paper rolls with a loud "Hi-yah!" The rolls tumbled in all around her, but that didn't seem to bother Mitzi one bit. She just grabbed the end of one roll and ran. Seconds later, she had that whole roll of toilet paper wound around the room.

Gracie giggled and giggled while our Mom laughed, too. Then she started to gently comb out the tangles in Trixie's fur.

Bogey raised a brow to me. "Better enjoy this while you can, kid. We'll have to put our nose to the grindstone the minute we get out of here."

"Nose to the grindstone? Won't that hurt?" I tried to cover my nose with my paw but I only ended up poking myself in the ear instead.

Bogey grinned. "Just an expression, kid. It means we've got to get right to work. We need to give this latest clue the once-over. Maybe even a twice-over. But any way you look at it, we need to give it a good going over."

I was already nodding at my brother. "So we officially have a new case for the BBCDA?"

"Looks that way, kid," Bogey meowed. "This is the second clue that appeared from out of thin air. And I have a funny feeling the sender is just getting warmed up. So we might as well make this investigation official. Let's check out that second jar before we run surveillance tonight."

I was about to say more when our Mom stood up and looked from one cat to the next. "I think everyone's clean and dry enough now. And my, what a good-looking bunch they are!"

Beside her, Gracie nodded and smiled. "They all look so pretty and their fur is so shiny."

For some reason, all that praise made me sit up extra straight. Because the truth was, I liked how I felt after a bath. Sometimes it was really nice to have such shiny, clean fur. I only wished I didn't have to go through the horror of a bath to get that way.

Our Mom reached down and petted Trixie's head. "Trixie's long hair looks so lovely now that it's all combed out. Wherever she came from, I don't think she was well cared for. We'll have to be sure to brush her a lot so her hair doesn't mat up again."

Trixie glimmered up to our Mom, saying thank-you with her bright eyes.

If only our Mom knew the truth about how we had rescued Trixie. Because one thing was for sure — she wouldn't be too happy if she knew how badly Trixie had been treated!

Our Mom turned to Gracie. "Honey, would you mind showing Trixie and Mitzi around the house? And let them know where the food and water dishes are?"

Gracie's dark eyes sparkled and she scooped Mitzi up in one hand. "Sure thing, Mom. I'd love to."

And the next thing I knew, the door to the bathroom was open and we all went into the hallway. While the girls trotted off with Gracie, and our Mom headed to her room to change clothes, Bogey and I zoomed down the stairs. Straight to the dining room. We heard our Dad cleaning up in the kitchen, so we figured we had a little time to ourselves without being spotted.

Of course, we made a beeline for the little jars that someone had left on our doorstep. The first one was exactly where we had left it, with the wooden squares right next to it. So I scooted the second jar closer to the first one. Then I unscrewed the lid on the second jar and dropped it to the floor. At long last, we got a good look at the jewels inside. There were ten small stones that sparkled in the light.

"Do you think those are real diamonds?" I asked my brother.

"Near as I can tell, kid. But we'll need the Princess to take a look and tell us for sure. That dame knows her diamonds."

I had to say, she sure did. In fact, it was thanks to the Princess that we were able to identify some gems on another case. She even came to us with a diamond collar. One that our Mom kept locked up in a safe.

I glanced from the diamonds to the four wooden squares and then back to the diamonds again. "Why would anyone leave this stuff on our front porch?"

Bogey arched an eyebrow. "Looks like a trail of breadcrumbs to me."

"Breadcrumbs? I don't see any breadcrumbs." I scooted closer to the diamonds for a better look.

"Just an expression, kid. It means someone is trying to lure us into following a trail." Bogey used a claw to snag the bag of cat treats that he kept stashed behind the potted plant.

I glanced outside the window. "Oh, okay. I wonder where this trail starts?"

My brother pulled the bag open and handed me a treat. "I'd say this last jar gives us a pretty good clue."

I munched on the fish-flavored treat. "We've got too many clues, if you ask me. All in one night. Because I'm still not sure where any of this leads."

Bogey took a couple of treats for himself. "I think the wooden squares and the note were meant to get our attention. But I'm betting those diamonds are supposed to lead us straight to Garnet's Jewelry Store."

I felt my eyes go wide. *Really wide.* "They are?"

"That'd be my guess, kid. "

I nodded. "We've had a couple of cases that involved jewels."

Bogey gave us each another round of treats. "Some people just can't keep their paws off. Not when it comes to something shiny."

"And Garnet's Jewelry Store probably has lots of shiny stuff," I said before I ate another treat. "That store is really close to our Mom's antique store."

Bogey stashed the cat treat bag behind the plant again.

"You got it, kid. It's just a few doors down. We could go to work with our Mom tomorrow and sneak out when the coast is clear."

I nodded my head. "And then sneak into the jewelry store. Without anyone even knowing we're there."

"You read my mind, kid. But now we've got to decide if we want to play along with this 'game' or not. And follow this trail of clues that someone left us."

"But Bogey . . . could we be walking into a trap?"

Bogey glanced out the window for a moment, and his ears perked up. "Could be, kid. Could be. We'll have to think on our paws. Like we always do."

All of a sudden, my heart started to pound really hard. "Maybe we should just stay home. And not even risk it."

Bogey shook his head. "Then we might miss another clue. And we'll never get to the bottom of this. I think it's a risk we've gotta take. But what do you say, kid? Are you in?"

I gulped and stared at my brother. Somehow I knew he would want to investigate. In spite of any risks. But as far as I was concerned, I'd been through enough risks tonight to last me for a long, long time.

Even so, in my heart, I already knew what my answer would be. After all, what kind of a cat detective would I be if I didn't go out and investigate?

So I took a deep breath and nodded to my brother. "Okay. I'm in."

"Good deal, kid," Bogey said with a grin. "I knew I could count on you."

Now I had to wonder, what were we getting ourselves into? And exactly how risky was this case that already seemed to have too many clues?

Holy Catnip!

CHAPTER 7

Holy Mackerel!

For the rest of the night, I couldn't stop thinking about our plan to sneak into Garnet's Jewelry Store the next day. And I couldn't shake the feeling that we might be stepping smack dab into a big trap. After all, somebody sure seemed to be baiting us. They had even sneaked right up on our front porch to leave us those clues. And I really had to wonder why.

I also wondered if they might be back again tonight.

Worst of all, my mind just *kept on* wondering and wondering. No matter how hard I tried to make it stop. All that wondering made me pretty nervous as we ran our first surveillance round of the night. I even had a hard time keeping my mind on the job. Thankfully, I'd been running surveillance with Bogey since the day I'd become a cat detective. So now I kind of did it automatically.

Of course, I didn't even know what the word surveillance meant until I met Bogey. So if you've never heard of it before, well, like Bogey would say, don't sweat it. Surveillance is just a big word that means "checking the place out." To make sure all the doors and windows are locked. And to make sure the whole house is safe and sound.

It's part of our jobs as cat detectives. We do it as a way to pay our family back for all the things they do to take care of us. Sort of as a way to earn our keep, you might say. Of course,

Bogey and I are always happy to help our family, especially when it comes to keeping them safe. And with them now tucked away in bed, it was our time to be on patrol. The lights were all off, but that wasn't a problem for us cats. Like I said before, we can basically see in the dark.

Normally, I enjoyed running surveillance rounds. But tonight it felt like my heart was racing even faster than my legs. And every little noise I heard sounded about ten times louder than normal. Plus all the shadows looked like big, giant monsters ready to pounce on me. I was so frazzled by the time we passed the big upstairs window that I went straight up like a rocket when an owl suddenly hooted outside.

Bogey grinned when I landed back on all fours. "A little jumpy tonight, kid?"

I let out a huge sigh. "Uh-huh."

"Those clues got you rattled?"

I nodded. "Usually I'm pretty happy to find clues. But I don't like these clues. And I don't like it when people leave things like this on our doorstep."

Bogey glanced toward the staircase. "It's a little too close to home, isn't it, kid?"

"It sure is."

Now he arched an eyebrow. "Let me guess. You're wondering if the person who left them might come back."

I gulped. "I really am. Do you think they will?"

"Take a deep breath, kid," Bogey told me. "I doubt we'll hear from them again tonight. They probably got their message across and now they're waiting for us to make the next move. I think we can rest easy for a bit. Why don't you get some shut-eye when we're done here."

As if I would actually shut *both* of my eyes at the same time tonight. To tell you the truth, I planned to sleep with one eye open.

If I *even* slept at all.

And apparently I wasn't the only one who wasn't going to sleep tonight. When we ran past Gracie's room, we saw her staring at her cell phone. It glowed with a bright light in the dark of the room. It was enough for me to see that her poor eyes looked red and tired. And sore.

"Isn't she supposed to be asleep?" I asked my brother

quietly.

"Yup. She should be sawing logs by now."

"Sawing . . . what?" I asked.

Bogey grinned. "Just an expression, kid. For snoring."

"Oh," I murmured. "Well, whatever it's called, she's going to be really tired in the morning. And she's supposed to help our Mom at her antique store tomorrow."

Bogey tilted his ears in her direction. "You got that right, kid. Too bad humans haven't figured out how to take catnaps."

I nodded to my brother. "If she keeps this up, she'll be so tired tomorrow that she'll need a whole bunch of naps." I tiptoed closer to her bed. "So maybe I should step in and help her out."

"Knock yourself out, kid," came Bogey's reply.

And so I did. Well, sort of, anyway. I had a pretty good idea that Bogey didn't really want me to knock myself out. And I figured that was just another one of his expressions.

So I jumped up on Gracie's bed and gave her a kiss on the nose. She giggled and turned her head away from me. And that was all the time I needed to give her phone a really good *swack*! Of course, I planned to hit the side of the phone and send it flying out of her hands. But my huge paw didn't go exactly where I wanted it to go. And instead, I hit the phone smack dab in the middle of the screen. That's when I heard a weird *blurp* sound.

Gracie gasped. "Buckley, you just sent a reply to a message that Sophie sent me!"

I did? How did I do that? I crinkled my brow and glanced at her phone. The thing sure was sensitive.

Gracie gasped again and *thunked* a hand to her chest. "And you sent it to Jackson! That's the boy that Sophie likes. Oh, Buckley, she's going to be so mad at me! I'm going to be in so much trouble!"

Well, I really didn't mean for *that* to happen. I only wanted Gracie to get off her phone and get some sleep. But now I felt pretty bad, just hearing that Gracie was going to be in trouble. I hung my head as Bogey jumped up beside me. Then he put his paw on the top of the phone and pushed it to the bed. Of course, *he* never had any problem getting his paws to go where he wanted them to go.

Gracie sighed. "All right, all right, boys. I'll get off my phone. Especially since I have no idea how to explain this to Sophie. I guess I'll have to try to sort it all out in the morning. If I can . . ." With that, her tired eyes fell shut and she went right to sleep. She didn't even pull her covers up, which was strange. She never went to sleep without her covers in place.

I glanced at my brother. "Gracie sure has changed a lot since she got her cell phone."

"I hear ya, kid," Bogey said as he shook his head.

I reached down and used my claws to snag the top of her covers. For once, it didn't matter whether my big paws went where they were supposed to go or not. I pulled the covers up to her shoulders as she started to snore softly. She'd been up way too late for a girl her age.

Then Bogey and I jumped off her bed and ran back into the hallway. Now, not only did I feel nervous, but I felt sad, too. I really didn't mean to cause problems between Gracie and her friend.

I was still feeling bad when we headed for the final room on our run — the sunroom. Of course, since it was nighttime, there was no sun in there at the moment. Instead, I saw plenty of stars twinkling in the dark sky when I glanced through the windows. That meant our bad thunderstorm was completely gone.

Which was probably one of the reasons why all the other cats in the room looked so happy and relaxed. Because we found Lil, Trixie, Mitzi, and the Princess all chatting away and resting on chairs when we trotted in. Thankfully, I also noticed the big, gray cat relaxing on a purple velvet couch.

Miss Mokie.

I bowed to her right away, and Bogey did the same. Bogey once told me that she is a kind of cat called a Norwegian Forest Cat. She has long, thick fur that forms a big ruff around her neck. It kind of makes her look like a lion. And believe me, she is just as majestic as any lion.

She waved her paw above us like a queen on her throne. "Good evening, Detectives Buckley and Bogey. Please arise and carry on. From what Lil and our guests have told me, I understand that you've had a rather eventful evening. I've also been told that you and the rest of the team performed admirably. And, I might add, with great courage."

For some reason, her words suddenly made me feel a whole lot better. "Umm . . . thank you, Miss Mokie," I managed to get out.

Though Miss Mokie is her real name, the rest of us cats simply know her as the Wise One. And let me tell you, the name fits! Paws down, she has got to be the wisest cat in the world. Probably because she's so old and she's seen so many things in her lifetime. Bogey once told me that she's lived in five different states and two different countries. And, it's been said that she even flew on an airplane back when she was my age. But that was a long, long, *long* time ago.

Now, none of us actually know just *how* old she is. I once heard Gracie say that Miss Mokie was over a hundred in human years. I wasn't sure how old that made her in cat years, but it still sounded pretty ancient to me! I only hoped I would be as old and wise as she was one day.

Yet even though Miss Mokie is very wise, her joints are another matter. I guess they're kind of stiff and achy, and it makes it really hard for her to get around the house. So she mostly just stays in the sunroom. She likes to feel the warmth of the sun as soon as it comes up in the morning. The heat makes her aching joints feel better.

But if you looked at the sparkle in her green eyes, you'd never know she had any problems at all.

She pointed a paw in the direction of her private water dish. "Please partake of a drink, Detectives. You must be parched after your long day."

"Don't mind if I do," Bogey said as he touched his forehead, like he was tipping a hat.

And so we sidled up to her water dish. Of course, I wasn't going to mention that we'd probably seen enough water for one night. No, that would've been really rude, since she'd just graciously offered us a drink. And nobody, but *nobody*, is rude to Miss Mokie. So instead, we both took a nice drink before we checked the windows in the room. Just to make sure everything was locked up tight.

On the way out, Bogey nodded to the Princess. "Mind taking a look-see at one of our clues downstairs? We could use your eye for jewels."

She smiled her sweet smile. "Why, certainly. I'd be happy to."

"Jewels?" Lil repeated with a tilt of her head. "Sounds like an interesting case."

Bogey rubbed his head with his paw. "It's like nothing I've ever seen before, Lil. So far, anyway."

Though he didn't add that it was a case that had landed right on our doorstep. I couldn't help but shiver when I thought about it.

"You two look beat," Lil said quietly. "Need an extra cat to take your rounds tonight?"

Trixie sat up straight and towered over everyone. "I'd be happy to lend a paw if you'd like Lil and me to run a second surveillance team."

But Bogey shook his head. "Another night, Trix. First, you need to get your strength back. So why don't you and Lil sit back and keep talking about old times. Then maybe you could get some shut-eye. We'll see how you're doing tomorrow."

Trixie responded with a tired smile, and I knew the big cat really wanted some sleep. As near as I could tell, she was pretty worn out. Mitzi, on the other hand, was another matter. In fact, she was still bursting with energy. Even after the big rescue and a big bath.

"I'll go, I'll go, I'll go!" she insisted. "I'm going to be a cat detective. I'll be as good as Buckley. Maybe I can use my cat karate tonight."

Then she bounced onto a chair and was about to launch herself into the air — straight at the Wise One.

The rest of us all shouted "*Noooo . . .!*"

Just in time to make her pause. She crinkled her face in confusion. But then she shrugged and bounded out into the hallway.

I let out a long, slow breath. *Whew.* I had to say, that was a close one. I couldn't imagine what would've happened if Mitzi had cat karate-chopped herself on a collision course with Miss Mokie!

And I wasn't the only one.

I glanced over to see the Princess' eyes had gone just about as wide as our food dish. But she quickly blinked a few times, shook her head, and pulled herself together. And she jumped down from her chair like a feather floating on the air. Then the three of us jogged into the hallway and barely caught a glimpse of Mitzi before she raced down the stairs in a flash. In fact, she went up and down, and then back up and down again, before Bogey and the Princess and I even got to the first floor.

"Do you think we'll catch any bad guys?" Mitzi hollered as she ran around in circles. "Do you, Buckley? I'll bet you'll catch a *whole* bunch of bad guys!"

If only she were right.

But first things first. So without another word, we made a beeline for the little jar with the diamonds.

The Princess didn't waste any time in looking at those gems. "They're real diamonds, all right," she told us. "Ten nice little stones."

Bogey raised an eyebrow to her. "Are they worth much?"

The Princess nodded. "Oh yes. They would be worth a lot. Where did they come from?"

"Somebody put them on our front porch," I explained. "In that little jar."

Her chin nearly dropped to the floor. "I wonder why someone would do that. People usually steal diamonds. They don't usually *leave* them on someone's porch."

It was one of the questions that Bogey and I had been asking ourselves. And any way we looked at it, there wasn't a good answer.

Bogey shook his head. "It's a real head-scratcher, all right. Hopefully we'll get to the bottom of this tomorrow."

Mitzi suddenly stopped moving, though her eyes were still dancing. "Where are you going tomorrow?"

"On an investigation," I told her.

"I'll go!" she announced and started to bounce around again.

Bogey put a paw on her shoulder to get her to hold still. "Sorry, Short-stuff. Not this time. Because we don't know what we're walking into. Could be a trap. And we might have to do some pretty fancy footwork to get out of there. So you're staying home."

I gulped when I heard his words. Just talking about walking into a trap suddenly made a chill race up and down my spine. On top of it all, having to do any "fancy footwork" made me even more nervous. After all, for a big guy like me who couldn't get his paws to go where he wanted them to go, "fancy footwork" wasn't exactly something I was good at. And if we had to rely on that to get us out of a bad situation, well . . . we just might be in a whole lot more trouble than I thought.

Holy Catnip!

CHAPTER 8

Holy Mackerel!

The next morning, I was really dragging when we set off for our Mom's antique store. But I wasn't the only one. Gracie had slept through her alarm and our Mom had to wake her up. Twice. And Bogey had to do plenty of stretching before he could even crawl out of his cat bed.

Our Mom was the only one who seemed to be awake and raring to go. But if nothing else, at least Bogey and I were waiting at the back door by the time she and Gracie were ready to leave.

"I guess the boys are going with us today," our Mom laughed as she picked up Bogey. "Honey, could you please take Buckley?"

"Sure, Mom," Gracie said in a sleepy voice. Then she picked me up and gave me a nice hug. "I love you, Buckley. But I'm still a little mad at you."

So I gave her a big kiss on the nose. Just to tell her I was sorry. And to let her know that I loved her, too.

Then the next thing I knew, we were in our soft-sided pet carriers and in our Mom's car. And we were headed to downtown St. Gertrude, where our Mom ran the best antique store in the whole town.

But oddly enough, I couldn't get comfortable in my pet carrier. I wasn't sure if I was just tired, or if I'd grown some more overnight. For some reason, the space seemed smaller than usual. And the floor and the rear even felt sort of lumpy. I tried and tried to wriggle into position. Yet no matter what I did, I couldn't settle down and relax.

"You okay over there, kid?" Bogey asked from his pet carrier next to mine.

"Something's not right here," I told him. "And I can't figure out what's wrong."

Then I used a claw to pull up the bottom mat of my carrier. And that's when I finally figured out the source of my problem. In fact, I could hardly believe my eyes. Especially when I saw a little face staring right up at me.

Mitzi.

She blinked twice and stretched.

I gasped. "How in the world did you get in here?"

She rubbed her sleepy eyes. "I sneaked in here last night. So I could go with you today!"

"But . . . but . . . but . . ." I blathered on. "How did you even know about the pet carriers?"

She smiled. "That's easy! I asked the Princess how you would get out of the house today. And she told me about the pet carriers."

I felt my eyes go wide. "Did the Princess know what you were up to?"

"Nope," Mitzi said with a shake of her head. "I kept it a secret. And after you went to sleep, I climbed into one of the carriers and hid under the mat."

Bogey tilted his head and looked down at her. "So you became a stowaway, huh, Short-stuff?"

"That was pretty sneaky . . ." I murmured. For some reason, the whole situation kind of irritated me.

"Yup," she said as she sat up and stretched. "I figured out what to do all by myself. See, Buckley? I really am going to be a great cat detective some day. Just like you."

Bogey nodded. "Not sure if I like your method, Short-stuff. But I have to give you credit for figuring things out."

Okay, when it came right down to it, so did I. She was pretty smart for such a young kitten. Even so, I thought she should have followed Bogey's orders from last night. And I thought she should have stayed home. Though mostly, I didn't want her to get in the way while we investigated.

My brother must have been thinking the same thing. "All right, Short-stuff, but don't get any ideas about tagging along with us today. I want you to stay at our Mom's store until we go home tonight."

Her lower lip started to tremble. "But, I want to go with you and Buckley . . . I want to catch some bad guys . . ."

Bogey shook his head. "Sorry. Not this time."

Just hearing that made me feel better as we drove past the big sign in front of our Mom's store. The one that said "Abigail's Antiques." As always, our Mom turned at the corner and headed for the back alley. She parked near the back door, and then she and Gracie carried us inside and opened our pet carriers. Bogey and I stepped out right away.

Our Mom's two employees, Merryweather and Millicent, were waiting there to greet us. Millicent had short, curly gray hair and dark-framed glasses that she wore on the end of her nose. Merryweather was dressed in a pink, polka-dotted dress with a big skirt. A dress she once said was from the 1950s. Her dress went really well with her red hair and her pink glasses. Our Mom called them "cat-eye" glasses. And I have to say, I liked them a lot!

Bogey grinned and purred up to both the ladies, while I rubbed around Merryweather's legs.

"These two are especially sweet today," Millicent said with a smile.

Merryweather picked up Bogey and gave him a nice hug. "Oh, Bogey, you are such a handsome guy. If only I could find a man like you."

But Millicent was already shaking her head. "I don't know, Merryweather . . . I think these two are up to something today. Mark my words. They always lay on the charm when they're cooking up some kind of scheme. One that usually involves them sneaking out of the store."

"Which they're not supposed to do," our Mom said as she rubbed behind my ears. "Last night we found them dripping wet, just inside the front door. We have no idea how they got that way. If I didn't know better, I'd say they'd been outside."

"We still don't know how they got so wet," Gracie chimed in. "Because we thought they were inside the house with us the whole time."

"Hmmm . . ." Millicent murmured. "Sometimes I wonder if there's more to these boys than meets the eye . . ."

"Maybe they're great detectives who secretly go around solving big mysteries," Merryweather said. Then she laughed and plopped a kiss on Bogey's forehead.

Millicent laughed, too, and so did Gracie. And they kept on laughing while Bogey just grinned up at them and purred away.

But the strange thing was, our Mom didn't laugh at all. Instead she just tilted her head, put a finger to her chin, and looked from me to Bogey. And then back again.

Millicent picked me up. "Well, Buckley won't be going anywhere today. He's pretty easy to spot, since he's so big. So I'll be keeping my eyes on him . . . " she started to say.

Just as Mitzi came strolling out of my pet carrier.

And everyone gasped, except for Bogey and me.

The next thing I knew, Bogey and I were back on the cold, hard cement floor. Without so much as a "See you later, boys." And Mitzi was now in the arms of Merryweather.

Then we heard all kinds of *oooohs* and *aaaahs* from Millicent and Merryweather. And when they started in on a chorus of "She's so cute," Bogey and I made a beeline for the front door.

Okay, maybe it wasn't a beeline exactly. Maybe it was really more of a zigzag route. Because we ran into the front room of our Mom's store and immediately hid under an old dresser. From there we ran behind a cabinet full of pretty vases and glasses. We kept as low to the floor as possible, so we wouldn't be spotted. Then we zoomed behind some bookshelves and under another little table. We know our Mom's store like the back of our paws, and we were at the front door in a hurry.

Just as a couple of customers strolled on in. Thankfully, the man and the woman stood there with the door wide open for a good full minute. It was plenty of time for Bogey and me to slip on out. Without them even knowing it. By the time the lady called out, "Yoo-hoo, Abby," Bogey and I were already outside and halfway up the sidewalk.

Bogey gave me a quick grin. "That was pretty slick.

Wouldn't you say, kid?"

"Uh-huh," I told him with a nod.

To tell you the truth, I could hardly believe how easy it had been to sneak on out. Usually it took a lot of planning and finagling on our part. Even then it might be iffy. But today things were definitely going our way. Now all we had to do was get into the jewelry store, investigate, and then sneak back into our Mom's store. All without anyone knowing we'd even gone anywhere. And since things were going so smoothly, I had a good idea that the rest of the trip was going to go that way, too.

For once.

So I wasn't exactly surprised when Garnet Gabinski herself opened the door to her store. She held it open wide while she smiled in the sunshine and breathed in the fresh air.

"Ah, what a perfectly lovely day," she said out loud.

As near as I could tell, she was talking to herself. Because I was pretty sure she didn't see Bogey and me when we slipped inside and then hid behind a cabinet. Once we were in place, I peeked out to get a good look at Garnet. She had fluffy, bright red hair that went down to her shoulders. She was wearing a black dress with a huge diamond necklace. And really, *really* big diamond earrings. I had to say, those diamonds sure sparkled in the sun! They were almost kind of blinding.

Before long, a short, round man strolled into the store.

"Good morning, Mr. Pennypacker," Garnet greeted him in a sing-songy voice. "I believe I have the perfect gift for your wife's birthday. And we're having a big sale today."

"Ah, excellent," he answered and removed his bowler hat to reveal his bald head.

She followed him inside and started to show him some jewelry. "I think your wife would love this ruby bracelet."

Mr. Pennypacker shook his head. "I'm not so sure. I believe she prefers pearls and emeralds. Do you have anything like that?"

"Why, yes, I've got several to choose from. I've got a stunning pearl and emerald pendant in the far display case. And I've got a couple of bracelets and a ring or two in there as well."

"Splendid," came his reply. "My goodness, you certainly have an excellent selection."

Which made me take a glance around. And sure enough, she did have lots of jewelry in her store. All of her cabinets and display cases were positively packed with jewelry. She even had some things sitting on the top of the glass cabinets, too. And with the sun shining in, the whole place sparkled.

In fact, it was so sparkly that it even made me blink a couple of times. Thankfully, Bogey nodded toward the back room, and I knew it was time for us to sneak off and investigate. But just when I thought he was about to slink out of there, he suddenly froze. His eyes darted to a spot just behind me and his brows shot up his forehead. Like something had completely shocked him.

For as long as I've known Bogey, I don't think I've ever seen him react like that. To anything. He was a true pro when it came to being a cat detective. So it took something pretty serious to make him act that way.

So what had Bogey seen? Was there a snake or a spider right behind me? Did Garnet have a gigantic dog that had spotted us? Or had Garnet herself figured out that we were there?

Without even looking behind me, I started to shake in my paws. A very big part of me wanted to run away and then look back from a nice, safe distance. But as long as *Bogey* didn't take off running, well, then I couldn't, either. Because I sure didn't want to be a total scaredy-cat. So I decided to face the music instead. Or, rather, I decided to face whatever big, scary thing had caught Bogey's attention. So I took a deep breath and turned around.

And that's when I saw a sight that made my heart skip a beat. Not only did my *jaw* drop, but my chin almost hit the floor, too.

For standing there, just a few inches away from me, was Mitzi.

Right away I had a bad feeling that our investigation was doomed. A very bad feeling.

"I'm here!" she meowed. "I'm going to help you catch the bad guys!"

I quickly clamped one of my paws over her mouth and gave her a "*Shhh!*" Thankfully, my big paw went right where it was supposed to go for once.

Still, I could hardly believe my eyes. How in the world had Mitzi gotten here? She must have followed us somehow. But we sure hadn't noticed her coming behind us. Now I only hoped that Garnet and Mr. Pennypacker hadn't seen her, either.

Especially when they suddenly went silent.

"What was that?" Garnet asked. "Did you hear something?"

Mr. Pennypacker wheezed. "I did hear something. But I don't hear it anymore. Perhaps it came from outside."

Garnet trilled with laughter. "Oh, I'm sure it was nothing at all. Now, how much jewelry would you like to buy today? As I said, everything is on sale."

"Oh, I haven't decided yet," Mr. Pennypacker said. "Let me keep looking."

Then while the two of them talked, Bogey and I slipped into the back room. Thankfully, Mitzi followed us.

Bogey frowned and turned to Mitzi when we were safely out of earshot. "I'm not tickled that you decided to join us, Short-stuff. Buckley and I are on an important case. But now that you're here, I want you to stick close and keep a lid on it."

She crinkled up her tiny face. "Keep a lid on it? What am I supposed to keep a lid on?" She glanced up at me.

And I glanced at Bogey. To tell you the truth, I wasn't sure where that lid was supposed to go, either.

"Just an expression," Bogey said. "It means I want you to keep quiet."

"Oh, okay," she chirped and then started to dance around.

Bogey waved a paw. "And there'll be none of this dancing business on a case, either. If you want to help us, you've gotta be serious. And play by our rules."

With that, her eyes went wide and she sat up straight. "Okay, Bogey. Whatever you say. I want to be just as good a cat detective as Buckley."

Bogey gave her a nod. "All right, then. Stick close, pay attention, and stay out of sight. Don't let the people in the store see you."

She nodded her head and her eyes practically bounced with excitement. I was pretty sure her little body wanted to do the same.

"I won't let them see me at all," she announced with a flick of her tiny tail. "After all, I sneaked up on you and Buckley. Twice."

Much as I hated to admit it, I knew she was right. She had sneaked up on us. And she'd done a pretty good job of it. We didn't even see her coming.

Bogey raised a brow. "Yup, Short-stuff, you're a natural when it comes to stealth. But you've gotta learn to take orders."

I was pretty sure Mitzi didn't hear the second part of Bogey's comment. Because she bounded up onto the desk with a, "Woo-hoo! Bogey said I was a natural!" Though if nothing else, at least she kept it to a whisper. A really *loud* whisper.

Unfortunately, she also landed on a stack of papers that was leaning over the edge of the desk. Her paws barely touched the papers when the whole pile came tumbling down to the floor. Mitzi came down too, but she bounced back up on her feet and jumped out of the mess right away.

Bogey raised his paw for silence and we all froze in place. Then Bogey and I pointed our ears toward the outer room and listened for signs that someone had heard us. Thankfully, we could still hear Garnet and Mr. Pennypacker talking about jewelry.

I breathed with relief and then glanced at the papers scattered on the floor. As near as I could tell, they were Garnet's bills. The bill on top looked like it was from her insurance company. And I could see that she used the same company for her store that our Mom used for hers.

But now I wondered how we would get those papers back in place. So she would never know that we'd been in there.

As always, Bogey practically read my mind. "Don't sweat it, kid. She'll just think the wind knocked them over. Now, I want you to use your big paws to pull those drawers open and look inside. See if there's anything fishy in there."

I crinkled my brow. "You think she keeps fish inside her desk? Like canned tuna?"

Mitzi's eyes went wide and Bogey shook his head. "Just an expression, kid. For anything that seems out of place."

"Um . . . okay," I told him as I glanced at the lowest drawer.

Bogey jumped to the top of the desk. "While you've got

your paws full, I'll snoop around up here. And Short-stuff, I want you on the floor. Look behind the furniture and all around. Put your nose into it."

"Okay, Bogey," she said as she went to work on her own little part of the investigation.

In the meantime, I grabbed the handle on the bottom drawer and pulled it open. There was nothing inside but a bunch of store catalogues. So I kept on going.

Thankfully, it wasn't long before we were all finished. Bogey was back on the floor and I'd shut all the drawers. But none of us had found anything that looked the least bit suspicious. And we sure hadn't found a little jar with a black lid.

Bogey shook his head. "Maybe the clue we're supposed to find is out in the main room. Let's go take a look." But before we took off, he nodded to little Mitzi. "Remember, Short-stuff, you've gotta be quiet as a mouse. Can you do that?"

She nodded and clamped her mouth shut. Even so, her eyes went wide. Really wide. For a moment, I thought she was going to explode. Because she looked like she wanted to bounce off the walls. Still, I had to hand it to her, for once she was doing a pretty good job of keeping herself under control.

And she kept on keeping herself under control as we all tiptoed to the outer room. This time, we ran behind the far display case, just as Garnet was ringing up Mr. Pennypacker's purchase.

And that's when we spotted it. Sitting in a corner.

Another clear jar with a shiny black lid. One that looked exactly like the others we'd found on our porch. Needless to say, we made a beeline for it.

Above us, we could see Mr. Pennypacker's reflection in a mirror. Thankfully, he couldn't see us as he put his bowler hat back on his head.

"He's getting away!" Mitzi meowed in a whisper.

"Who?" I asked, keeping my voice really low.

Mitzi started to bounce around. "Him! The bad guy!"

"What bad guy?" I asked as Bogey took a good look at the jar.

"That one!" She pointed a paw at Mr. Pennypacker's reflection.

I crinkled my brow. "What makes you so sure he's a bad guy?"

Fire burned in her eyes. "I just know he is. Because I'm a cat detective."

"You're not a cat detective yet, Short-stuff," Bogey murmured. "So sit tight while Buckley opens this jar."

Let me tell you, I didn't waste any time doing just that. I had that lid off and quietly on the floor in a split second. In the meantime, Mitzi kept on bouncing around, faster and faster. She was positively bursting with energy. As near as I could tell, any attempts to keep herself under control had gone right out the door. And if she didn't calm down in a hurry, I was afraid she would give us away.

"I have to catch him, Buckley and Bogey! I have to go now!" she insisted.

"Hang on, Short-stuff. I don't want you going anywhere," Bogey cautioned her.

Then Bogey and I turned our attention to the jar. We looked inside, and I could hardly believe it — the whole thing was completely empty! But instead of moving away, we just kept on looking at it. Almost like we were hoping some clue might magically appear if we stared at that jar long enough.

"I have to go. Now!" I heard Mitzi say. "I've got to catch that bad guy."

"Put a lid on it," Bogey said.

I wasn't sure if he was talking to Mitzi or me, so I put the lid back on the jar anyway.

Bogey frowned at Mitzi. "That goes double for you, Short-stuff."

"But I can't wait anymore," she whined.

"A good cat detective keeps their cool," Bogey told her.

But she just kept on bouncing around. "Can I go now?"

I shook my head. "Nope. We don't even know if he's a bad guy."

"But I *know* he is. And he's getting away! Look!" she gasped. "How about *now*?"

"No," I whispered.

"Okay, what about now? Can I go now? I'll use my cat karate!" She jumped against the wall and just missed the door of a display case.

Then before either Bogey or I could say another word, she hollered, "I'm going in!"

And with those words, she raced right into the middle of the room and made a beeline for Mr. Pennypacker. She shot straight up his back and landed right on top of his bowler hat. Then she dug in her claws and hung on with every ounce of strength she had.

"I've got him! I've got him! Buckley and Bogey, I caught the bad guy!" she yowled at the top of her lungs. "He can't get away!"

If nothing else, at least she remembered to stick to cat language.

Garnet shrieked and stared at Mitzi for a moment. Then she stomped over and glanced behind the counter to where Bogey and I were hiding.

"What on earth . . .? There are cats in here!" she shouted. "And I recognize those cats! They're Buckley and Bogey! They belong to Abigail down the street. What are they doing in here?"

Honestly, I don't think I've ever seen another human being so angry in my whole life!

And since there was no use trying to hide anymore, Bogey and I crept out from behind the counter. Right away, I started to shake in my paws. Because I had absolutely no idea what was going to happen next.

But one thing I did know for sure — we were in trouble.

Very big trouble.

Holy Catnip!

CHAPTER 9

Holy Mackerel!

Seconds after we'd been discovered, Garnet was on the phone to our Mom. "Get over here immediately and remove Buckley and Bogey from my store! And take that other little pip-squeak of a cat," she yelled into the phone. "I will not have such rodents running around here!" Then she hung up.

I'm pretty sure she didn't even give our Mom a chance to speak.

I glanced at my brother. "Rodents?" I meowed. "We're not rodents. We're cats. Felines."

Bogey gave me a slight grin. "Don't I know it, kid."

In the meantime, Mr. Pennypacker removed his hat from his head. Mitzi was still attached, since her claws seemed to be stuck in his hat. She had a ferocious look on her tiny face and I was pretty sure she wanted to take a swipe at him. Only she couldn't get her paws loose.

Mr. Pennypacker smiled at her. "My, what a fun little game you're playing, little one. Are you a cohort of Buckley and Bogey over there? You seem rather petite to be running around with the likes of them. Shall I unlatch you from my hat?"

Mitzi only responded with a hiss. It was pretty clear to me that she wanted to get her hooks into *him* — instead of just his hat. Even though he was being pretty nice to her.

He set his hat on the counter, with her still attached. "Perhaps I'll simply let you wait here, young calico."

Thankfully, we didn't have to wait long. Because our Mom and Gracie came through the door seconds later. Our Mom looked from us to Mitzi and then to Garnet. Gracie had walked in with her cell phone in front of her, and even now she barely glanced up from it.

Our Mom sighed. "How did you two boys get out? And what are you doing in Garnet's store?"

Mr. Pennypacker smiled at our Mom. "What about this little one?" he said with a flourish of his hand. "She seems to be clamped onto my hat. Is she with your bunch as well?"

"Yes, she is for the moment," our Mom said with a feeble smile. "She's a little foster kitten who is staying with us."

"My, but she is a feisty little thing," Mr. Pennypacker said with a chuckle. "Perhaps you might disengage her from my hat?"

Our Mom turned to Gracie. "Could you please get the kitten, honey? While I round up the boys?"

"Just a minute, Mom," Gracie muttered. "I have to finish my message to Sophie. She's mad at me, and I've been trying over and over again to explain what happened. I don't think she'll ever forgive me."

That's when I felt a twinge of guilt. After all, it was partly my fault that Sophie was mad at Gracie.

And speaking of mad, Garnet crossed her arms and started to tap her foot. "Apparently you can't control your child or your animals, Abigail. So you certainly have no business bringing them to work with you."

"I realize you're upset, Garnet," our Mom said firmly. "But my daughter is a very bright and usually thoughtful young woman. And Buckley and Bogey are wonderful cats. They're just more curious than most. As near as I can tell, they have done no harm to you or your store. So I'll be taking my family — both human and feline — and we'll get out of your hair."

To which Garnet let out a loud, "*Harrumph!*"

Our Mom turned to Gracie. "Honey, I'm not going to ask you a second time. You can contact Sophie when we get back to our store. Now please put the phone away and get the kitten."

"Oh, all right, Mom!" Gracie moaned. But instead of getting off her phone, she kept on tapping on the screen as she walked forward. And instead of heading for Mitzi, Gracie walked right into a display case.

Jewelry and boxes clattered straight to the floor.

And that's when Gracie finally did put her phone down, and her eyes went wide in horror. She gasped, and our Mom gasped, and Mr. Pennypacker wheezed, and Garnet . . . well . . . Garnet's face turned so red that it practically matched her hair. And I was pretty sure she was about to explode.

"You clumsy girl!" she shouted. "Look what you've done!"

Tears formed in Gracie's eyes. "I'm so sorry, Garnet. It was an accident. I didn't mean to knock that over. I'll pick it all up."

"You'd better believe you will!" Garnet shouted some more.

Gracie kneeled down on the floor, and tears slipped down her cheeks. "I'm so sorry, Garnet," she said over and over.

"You should be!" Garnet told her. "If you had stayed off your phone, none of this would have happened. You'll pay for any damages."

And that was all my brother and I needed to hear before we raced right over to take a good look at the jewelry that had fallen to the floor. Because we wanted to see what damage — if any — had *really* been done. We got there only seconds before our Mom did. And we got up really close so we could investigate it thoroughly. Sure, some of the jewelry might have landed a little funny, but we could see that nothing was broken. Or dented or scratched or bent. Or hurt at all.

"Of course we will pay for any damage," our Mom said as she helped Gracie. "But it doesn't look like anything was harmed."

"I'll be the judge of that," Garnet said while she examined all the jewelry that Gracie put on a counter. "It appears that everything is all right. But I assure you, I will take a closer look. And if I should find anything broken later on, I will bring you a bill for the damages!"

"That's fine," our Mom said. "And I'm sure you won't mind if I take a quick photo or two. Of anything that landed on the floor. Just so we have proof from our end of things."

She nodded to Gracie. "Could I please borrow your phone,

honey?"

"Sure, Mom," Gracie said meekly.

Then while she passed her phone to our Mom, Mr. Pennypacker handed his hat to Gracie. With Mitzi still attached. Gracie carefully unlatched Mitzi's claws while our Mom took several pictures of the jewelry.

"Would you like me to help you set up the display again?" our Mom asked Garnet politely.

She shook her head. "No, Abigail. I'd really just like you and your bunch to leave my store."

Our Mom nodded. "Then we will. Again, I apologize for the bother."

Mr. Pennypacker returned his hat to his head and reached down to pick up Bogey. "Allow me to assist you and your gaggle back to your own store, Mrs. Abernathy."

Our Mom smiled at him. "Well, thank you, Mr. . . . ."

"Pennypacker," he supplied. "You may not remember me, but my wife and I bought a dining room set from your store. A year ago. And I've bought an old train set from you as well."

"Yes, of course," our Mom nodded. "I do remember you. So nice to see you again." She picked up little Mitzi, and Gracie reached down for me.

Right away I could feel that Gracie was shaking. And I could tell that she was pretty upset about what had happened. So I wrapped my paws around her neck and gave her a nice hug. Then I held on tight as she followed our Mom and Mr. Pennypacker outside.

When we got back to our Mom's store, she carried me to the back room. Then she sat down, with me still in her arms. And that's when big, warm tears flowed freely down her cheeks.

"You know, Buckley," she whispered into my fur. "Ever since I got that cell phone, it's caused me nothing but trouble. I wish I'd never gotten it."

I purred into her ear to make her feel better, and before I knew it, she was sound asleep. Probably because she'd been up so late the night before.

That's when I slipped out of her arms and ran to the front room to join Bogey. I found him sitting on an old dresser by the front window. His eyes were squinted and he was watching something outside.

"How's she doing, kid?" He gave a nod toward the back room, and I knew he was talking about Gracie.

"She's really upset," I told him. "And it makes me upset to see her so unhappy."

Bogey nodded and pulled a bag of cat treats from a vase. "I hear ya, kid. Here, have a treat or two. This'll take the edge off." He passed me a couple of treats and took some for himself.

"Things sure went wrong at Garnet's store," I said before I munched on my treats. "I feel sort of responsible for Gracie getting into trouble."

Bogey finished his treats. "I hear ya, kid. One thing led to another. There's no denying it."

I nodded. "Uh-huh. And if we didn't go over there to investigate, then Gracie wouldn't have bumped into that display."

Bogey shook his head. "But we had to do our job, kid. Because we don't know who left those jars on our porch. And this whole setup is starting to feel a little sinister to me. So we've got to get to the bottom of this. That new kitten was the wild card. We didn't plan on her showing up."

"You can say that again," I mumbled. "Speaking of Mitzi, where is she now?"

Bogey glanced in the direction of the cash register. "She's riding around in the pocket of Merryweather's apron. It's keeping her out of trouble."

As far as I was concerned, that seemed like a very good place for Mitzi to be — out of trouble.

Bogey passed us one more round of treats and then hid the bag in the vase again.

I sighed and ate a treat. "I'm not even sure what we found on our investigation. And I don't understand that clue at all. Why was there an empty jar? Just sitting there?"

Bogey shook his head and downed a treat himself. "Your guess is as good as mine, kid. I've never seen anything like it."

"Do you think it was the wrong jar?" I suggested.

"I doubt it, kid," Bogey said as he stared outside again. "I can't imagine too many of those little jars just lying around town. And this one was on the floor, where we'd spot it. Plus, we covered most of the store and didn't see another jar. So I'm betting that jar was meant for us."

"That's so odd," I told my brother. "If somebody wanted us to find that jar, it seems like they would have put something inside it."

Bogey raised his brows. "That would make more sense, kid. But any way you look at it, there's not much we can do now. We'll have to wait for whoever is leaving these clues to make the next move."

For some reason, the thought of it gave me the shivers.

After that, Bogey and I ran surveillance in our Mom's store. Then we had a bite of lunch and took a good long nap. And before we knew it, it was time to go home. Mitzi joined me once again in my pet carrier. But instead of bouncing around and chattering away, she fell sound asleep. In fact, she didn't even mention our trip to the jewelry store at all.

Which let me listen in on the conversation between our Mom and Gracie.

"Mom, I will save my allowance and pay for any damage that I did to Garnet's jewelry," Gracie said quietly. "I'm so sorry. I don't know how I walked into that display case."

Our Mom pulled the car over and turned to Gracie. "Honey, I wonder if you're really ready for that cell phone. They can be very, very distracting. Let's face it — when a person is paying attention to their phone, they're not paying attention to anything else around them."

Tears rolled down Gracie's cheeks. "I really thought I could do both things at once. I thought I could help with the kitties and send messages to Sophie at the same time. The strange thing was, I didn't even realize that I was sort of . . . sort of . . ."

"Impaired?" our Mom suggested gently.

"Impaired?" Gracie repeated. "What does that mean?"

"That something has made it so you can't function safely, like you normally would," our Mom explained.

Gracie nodded. "Well, then I guess that would be the right word. And it was scary. Because I really thought I was just fine. I didn't realize I *wasn't* until I hit that jewelry display. Then I felt like I'd been sleepwalking or something. And when I hit that display, it was like I woke up and didn't even know where I was for a few seconds."

Our Mom put her hand on Gracie's shoulder. "Well, you're not alone. Lots of people have problems with cell phones. Sometimes a phone can put a person in kind of a trance. And plenty of people get hurt because of it. Some people even fall down stairs or walk right in front of a car while they're on their phones. And believe me, I don't ever want something bad like that to happen to you."

"I already walked into a display of expensive jewelry," Gracie said with a sniffle. "Guess I'm learning the hard way."

"Well, I'm glad *you're* not hurt. And hopefully none of Garnet's jewelry was damaged, either. I guess we'll know for sure in a few days. In the meantime, we'll need to figure out what to do about your cell phone. We can talk about it at dinner tonight."

"Okay, Mom," Gracie said with more tears.

I had to say, our Mom was right. When Gracie was on her phone, she didn't even know where she was half the time. Even so, I could tell that Gracie had learned a hard lesson today. And right at that moment, I really wanted to give her a big hug.

Unfortunately, I was stuck inside my pet carrier. With Mitzi. To top it off, I was a little bit mad at her for not obeying orders when we were at Garnet's Jewelry Store. But I was even more upset at whoever had put those jars on our doorstep in the first place. Because that was the person who had basically directed us to the jewelry store. And like Bogey said, one thing led to another.

I was still fuming a little when we got back to our house. Our Dad was already home, and he was in the kitchen cooking dinner. Gracie barely even said hello to him as she let us cats out of our pet carriers. Then she raced straight for her room.

Mitzi plodded off to one of our cat beds while Bogey and I stopped for a drink of water.

"What's wrong with Gracie?" our Dad asked our Mom.

While Bogey and I took a nice drink, our Mom told our Dad the whole story. It was just as hard to hear it a second time as it was to see it the first.

They were still talking when Bogey meowed to me. "Let's check the front porch, kid. And see if anyone left us another clue."

"Okay," I told him.

But the truth was, I didn't care if I never saw another one of those clues again in my life. They'd caused us enough trouble already, as far as I was concerned.

Still, I kept pace with Bogey as we headed into the dining room. Then we looked out all the windows at the front of the house. Yet no matter where we looked, we didn't see another little jar with a shiny black lid.

Bogey frowned. "Looks like the trail's run cold, kid."

I shook my head. "I don't understand. Why would someone even leave those clues for us in the first place? Where were they going with this?"

"Beats me, kid," he murmured. "Beats me. But I hear Gracie coming down for dinner. Let's go see how she's doing."

And so we did. We ran back into the kitchen just as our Dad was serving up dinner.

He glanced from our Mom to Gracie. "Would you two ladies like some honey to go with the biscuits that I bought on the way home?"

Our Mom nodded to our Dad. "Honey sounds good."

"It's fresh," he explained. "Someone left some for us on the front porch."

Our Mom smiled. "I'm guessing it was Mrs. Bumble. Maybe to thank us for taking in Trixie and the kitten. I know she keeps bees and harvests the honey."

Then our Mom picked up the little jar filled with honey. A little jar with a shiny black lid. A jar that looked exactly like all the other jars that we'd found already.

And just like that, there it was, right at the kitchen table.

Our very next clue.

Holy Catnip!

CHAPTER 10

Holy Mackerel!

I could hardly believe my eyes. There we were, staring at what appeared to be our next big clue. In whatever game this was that we'd been pulled into.

Except we couldn't even investigate our clue, since it was on the kitchen table at the moment. And well, with our family eating dinner there, we couldn't exactly jump up and take a good look. The kitchen table was supposed to be off-limits for us cats, especially at mealtime.

So Bogey and I had to settle for watching the jar carefully from the floor. And believe me, we kept our eyes on it as our humans passed it around and poured honey onto their biscuits. At long last, they set it on the table while they dug into their food.

"We've gotta get a good look at that jar," Bogey meowed quietly to me. "Before everything inside it is gone."

I nodded. "I know. But how?"

"I'm not sure yet, kid," Bogey said under his breath.

Then a few minutes later, a solution accidentally came to me. Right after our Dad asked Gracie about everything that had happened today. That's when Gracie started to cry. Big, gigantic teardrops rolled right down her cheeks. And without even thinking, I jumped up on her lap and wrapped my arms around her neck. She dropped her head onto mine, and her tears went right into my fur. Normally, I hate being drenched by anything wet. But tears are something different altogether.

Our Dad spoke softly. "A cell phone is a lot of responsibility, Gracie. Your Mom and I have talked about it and we're wondering if you're really ready for a phone."

Gracie shook her head. "I don't know. All my friends have them. So I wanted one, too. But now that I have a cell phone, it seems like it's the only thing I ever think about. I'm always waiting to see if someone has sent me a text or an email. So when I'm not looking at it, I *want* to be looking at it. And then when I *am* looking at it, I lose track of everything else. It's really weird."

"I know what you mean," our Dad said with a nod. "Cell phones can really take over someone's time. And life. They can put you in your own little world. So you have no idea what's going on in the real world around you."

Gracie sighed. "That's where I was all right. In my own little world. When I walked into that jewelry display. I can't believe I did something so dumb. I've never, ever, ever done something like that at Mom's store. And I sure hope all the stuff that fell over is okay."

Our Mom glanced at our Dad. "Me, too. As near as I could tell, everything was fine. I took the pictures to prove it. But we'll see if Garnet shows up with a bill or not. I truly doubt she will."

Gracie gulped. "I'll pay for anything that I broke. Out of my allowance. Or when I sell the cat collars that I make."

Our Dad took a deep breath. "If there's any damage, your Mom and I will pay for it right now. But yes, you will have to pay us back. You might have to work at the store, or you might have to weed the neighbors' gardens for money. I'm sure we can come up with a plan."

"Okay, Dad," Gracie sniffled. "I know I messed up and I'm so sorry. And now I'm really wondering about my cell phone. Because I'm not sure if I even like it anymore. But if I don't have one, I might not have any friends. Because none of my friends talk in person since we all got cell phones. Everyone just sends messages instead. Or emails. And nobody talks out loud to each other because everyone is always busy staring at their phones. Or taking pictures of themselves."

"I see it all the time at the store," our Mom added before she took another bite of her dinner. "People barely get off their phones when they buy something. And after they've finished, they don't even say good-bye. They're too busy focusing on the phone in front of them. It's like Merryweather and Millicent and I suddenly become invisible."

I glanced up and gave our Mom a couple of slow eye blinks. Something us cats do to say "I love you" with our eyes. Because I could not have agreed with her more. Ever since Gracie had gotten her phone, it seemed like she hardly noticed us cats at all. And to tell you the truth, I felt kind of invisible when Gracie was on her phone. I missed her spending time with us.

Our Dad reached over and petted my neck. "I remember when we only used cell phones to make phone calls."

This made Gracie's eyes go wide. "Really?"

"Yup," our Dad told her. "That's the reason why phones were invented in the first place. So people could talk. But modern phones don't even seem like phones at all. They're really just computers that we carry around with us."

Our Mom wiped her mouth with her napkin. "And sometimes people need to take a break from their computers."

"That's right," our Dad agreed. "So now, Gracie, we need to decide what to do about your cell phone. Because it's like anything else — if you're not in control of it, then it's in control of you. And that's not a good feeling."

Gracie nodded and rested her chin on my head.

"I've got an idea," our Mom suggested. "Let's see how you do if you try to limit the amount of time you spend on your phone. I think an hour a day total is plenty to start out. There's a place on your phone that keeps track of how much you use it, or screen time, I believe it's called. We can use that to see how you're doing. And, I think it goes without saying, that you shouldn't be on your phone at all when you're supposed to be doing something else."

"Like walking?" Gracie asked with a sigh. "And helping you get Buckley and Bogey out of a jewelry store?" She hugged me tighter.

Our Mom tilted her head. "Uh-huh. *Just* like that. And sleeping."

"That sounds good, Mom," Gracie told her.

"Now I think you'd better let Buckley down so you can eat," our Mom said as she smiled at me.

Gracie kissed the top of my head. "Okay, Mom."

And that's when my brother meowed up to me from the floor. "Quick, kid. Take a look at the jar."

So I did. When Gracie tried to put me down, I latched my arms around her neck and held on tight. Then I turned my head and stared right at that little jar. Even from where I was positioned, I could see it was exactly the same as all the others. And it had the same shiny black lid. But this jar had honey in it, as well as a couple of sparkly bee stickers pasted to the outside. Stickers that looked exactly like the bees that were attached to Mrs. Bumble's glasses, the day she dropped off Mitzi.

Mitzi.

Did she have anything to do with all these clues that kept showing up on our front porch?

Somehow, I found that really hard to believe. After all, Mitzi was only a kitten. And though she was an extra *smart* kitten, I was pretty sure she couldn't arrange to have all these clues secretly sent to us.

Still, she *had* given us away when we were investigating Garnet's store. Which was partly to blame for Gracie being in trouble now. And okay, it probably didn't do any good to keep replaying the whole thing in my mind. But there was one thing I did know for sure — we couldn't have a repeat of what had happened today. I knew we needed to do something about Mitzi. And we needed to do it right away. Yet I had no idea *what*.

But I *did* know *where* I could get some advice on what to do.

And all of a sudden, I couldn't wait one more minute to get that advice. So I let go of Gracie's neck and jumped to the floor. Then I gave my brother a quick wave before I made a beeline for the stairs. I was in such a hurry that Bogey's head practically swiveled when I flew by. I raced up to the second floor and ran straight to the sunroom. Because I knew there was only one cat who could help me out when it came to something like this.

The Wise One.

And even though I was in a hurry, I put the brakes on when I got to the sunroom door. Then I carefully stepped inside.

Thankfully, Miss Mokie was the only one in the room. I found her snoozing in the sun that was still shining in through the windows.

Her eyes flew open when I entered. "Stop and identify yourself," she commanded with a raised paw.

I bowed, just like I was supposed to. "It's me, Miss Mokie. Detective Buckley."

"Ah, yes, young Detective," she said with a nod. "I can see that now. I must confess, you startled me for a moment. Please, partake of a drink from my water dish."

Of course, I did exactly as she told me. I leaned over and took a good slurp. As always, her water was delicious. The best in the house.

When I had finished, she waved her paw above me again. "Please, come closer, young one. Tell me what brings you here today. I can see that you are troubled."

I scooted closer to her purple velvet couch. "I am, Miss Mokie. I am. Something really bad happened today and I'm not sure what to do about it."

"Ah, yes," she said as she sat up nice and straight, like a queen sitting on her throne. "I have endured many an unfortunate event throughout my very long life. Of course, such events can teach us important lessons. That's why great wisdom comes with great age and experience. I am often amused by the way humans fail to see the value and importance of age. Fortunately, cats are much smarter about such matters."

I immediately nodded, because I knew Miss Mokie was right. Once again, I hoped that I might be as old and wise as she was one day.

Using her paw, she fluffed out the huge gray ruff around her neck. "Now tell me, young Detective. What is weighing so heavily upon your mind?"

So I told her. I started with how I came up with Mitzi's name.

At that point, she raised her paw again and interrupted me. "You are to be commended, young one. Every cat should have a name. And 'Mitzi' is certainly a delightful name, no matter how you manufactured it. The young kitten truly seems to be taken with it."

I held my head a little higher. After all, it was always nice to get a compliment from the Wise One.

"Why, thank you, Miss Mokie," I told her. "I thought she needed a name. Because I couldn't imagine not having one."

"Nor could I," she said. "Now please continue your tale."

And so I went on. I told her about the way Mitzi had ridden on my back like a horse. And how she did her cat karate that I was pretty sure wasn't cat karate at all. Then I talked about the way Mitzi tried to *act* like a *real* cat detective, even without any training. Finally, I went on to tell the Wise One how Mitzi had messed up our investigation this afternoon.

I finished with, "I don't know what to do about her, Miss Mokie. Because she sure is wrecking things." I finished with a loud "*Huff!*"

And then I saw something that was so rare, I wasn't sure I'd ever see it again in my lifetime. Kind of like humans talk about things like solar eclipses or comets or blue moons.

In fact, I even blinked my eyes a few times to make sure I'd really seen what I thought I saw.

For Miss Mokie was smiling. And not just any old smile. No, she was smiling from ear to ear. In fact, I'd never, ever seen her smile so big before.

She rubbed her forehead and it sort of looked like she was trying hard not to laugh. "Please excuse my mirth, young Detective. Perhaps I might answer your question best by asking a few questions of my own. I'd like you to think back to when your brother, Detective Bogart, took you under his paw. Do you remember the very first days when you worked as a cat detective? Did you know all there was to know about the business?"

My mouth fell open. "Well . . . umm . . . no . . ."

"And Detective Bogart trained you, am I correct?"

"Well . . . umm . . . yes . . ." I sort of stammered.

"Is it possible that he had a few moments where he felt as though you had hindered an investigation?" she went on.

"Umm . . . well . . . maybe . . ."

Okay, probably.

I crinkled my brow and thought about it some more. "But he never said anything . . ."

Her smile suddenly beamed with warmth. "I believe Detective Bogart is known as one of the most outstanding cat detectives in the field. And he set out to help you become an outstanding cat detective yourself. He has been an excellent instructor. Though every instructor endures moments where they feel much like you do now."

I had to say, I hadn't thought of it like that before.

I turned my chin up and met her gaze. "Have you ever felt that way, Miss Mokie?"

But she didn't say a word, and instead, just kept on smiling.

"So what do I do?" I asked her.

"Well, this young kitten truly does look up to you. In fact, she's rather in awe of you. And she desperately wants to be a cat detective. Perhaps you might train her. Though should you decide to do so, I must advise you — it's quite important to be firm with a kitten. You must let her know when she has behaved correctly. And incorrectly. You cannot be wishy-washy."

"Oh, umm . . . okay," I said just as firmly as I could.

Then I gulped at the idea of training someone else to be a cat detective. After all, I'd always been the student. I was the rookie and Bogey was the pro. I'd never been somebody's teacher before.

Miss Mokie tilted her head. "And if this kitten wants to know cat karate so badly, perhaps you might consider finding a suitable instructor for her. For if young Mitzi were to learn and possess such skills, she might not feel the need for false boasting."

And that's when an idea dawned on me. "I think Lil and Trixie both know cat karate. For real. Do you think I should ask them to teach Mitzi?"

"Ah, yes, young Detective. It's an excellent idea."

But before I could say another word, Miss Mokie's eyelids began to droop.

"Are you tired, Miss Mokie?" I asked quietly.

She raised her paw again. "Yes, young Detective. You must leave me now, for it is time for me to rest."

"Thank you, Miss Mokie," I murmured. "I hope you have a nice nap."

She nodded. "You have done well, Grasshopper."

Okay, don't ask me why she called me that, for nobody in our house ever seemed to know the answer. She called everyone "Grasshopper" whenever we had a talk with her. It was one mystery that we'd never managed to solve. As far as we knew, it was just something she did.

I bowed to her and backed away. Her eyes were already closed by the time I got to the door.

That's where I found Bogey waiting for me.

Right away, I just had to know the truth. "Bogey, did I ever annoy you when I was first learning to be a cat detective?"

Bogey grinned and pulled out a bag of cat treats that he kept stashed behind a little table. "We all have to start somewhere, kid."

I glanced at the floor. "Well, I'm sorry if I ever caused any problems."

Bogey chuckled and handed me some treats. "Don't sweat it, kid. You did the best you could for being a brand-new cat detective. You've come a long way in a short time. And you've even saved my neck a time or two. Having you as my partner in crime-solving has been worth any bumps in the road." He took a couple of treats for himself.

I looked back up at him. "Really?"

He grinned. "Sure thing, kid. It wouldn't be the same without you."

Well, I had to say, that made me feel a *whole* lot better. I munched on my treats and I realized he was right — I *had* saved him once or twice. Plus, I had learned a lot since I'd first become a cat detective. Even so, I still had a long way to go before I was anywhere near as good as Bogey was.

I smiled at my brother. "Thanks for saying that, Bogey."

He passed out a few more treats. "Don't give it a second thought, kid. Instead, tell me about the clue on the kitchen table."

So I got right down to business, since I was more determined than ever to become a better cat detective. "The jar was just like all the others," I told him. "It had the same shiny black lid. It looked like it had been full of honey, and there were even a couple of bee stickers on it. They were just like the bees we saw on Mrs. Bumble's glasses the day she brought Mitzi over."

Bogey frowned. "So this new clue is leading us straight to Mrs. Bumble's place."

I finished off another treat. "That's what I think, too."

"Hmmm . . ." he murmured as he passed out another round of treats. "It's probably worth checking out. Since her place is so close. Hope it takes us to a real clue this time. Instead of another dead end. With nothing but an empty jar."

I nodded and munched on a treat. "Me, too."

Bogey arched an eyebrow toward the sunroom. "I gotta say, kid, I overheard you talking to the Wise One in there. And I think training Short-stuff is a good plan. She's got all the makings of a great cat detective. She could be a big help to us."

"Uh-huh," I told him.

Bogey grinned at me. "She looks up to you, kid. So I think you should be in charge and oversee her training. Asking Lil and Trixie to give her cat karate lessons is a great start."

To be honest, I did think it was a good idea for Mitzi to have cat detective lessons. But I still wasn't crazy about the idea of being the one to teach her. Or even being the one in charge of making sure she got the right lessons. I was about to say so when Lil, Trixie, and the Princess came around the corner.

Bogey grinned and held the open treat bag in their direction. "Good timing, ladies. My associate here has something he wants to ask you." Then he turned to me. "Go ahead, kid. Do your stuff."

Like it or not, it looked like I was stuck with the job of making sure Mitzi got trained.

So I paused for a moment, while everyone took a "paw-full" of treats.

Then I just jumped right in. "Lil and Trixie, I was wondering if you could teach Mitzi how to do cat karate. She seems to think she knows how to do it already. But I don't think what she does now is real cat karate."

Lil was already shaking her head. "I'm afraid it's not."

Trixie nodded and swallowed her treat. "I agree. It's not even close to real cat karate."

Bogey passed us all another round of treats. "So what do you say, Lil? Trix? Can we count on you two to give the little one some lessons?" Then he tilted his head in my direction. "Buckley is going to teach her the fine art of being a cat detective. I'll lend a paw, too, of course."

Trixie smiled and I couldn't help but notice how much better she looked already. Even after only a day of having food and water.

"I'm always happy to help out a new Cat Detective in Training," she told us. "I was a CDIT myself once. A long time ago."

Lil chuckled. "It was a long, *long* time ago for me. And even though I'm retired, I think I could help out a new recruit. That young one truly has the heart for the job."

"And I can teach her about diamonds and gems and jewelry," the Princess added. "Things that bad people like to steal."

Lil and Trixie both nodded. "That would be very valuable for her to learn."

Bogey grinned. "Perfect. Then it's all settled," he said just before he turned back to me. "Guess you should be the bearer of good news, right, kid?"

"Me . . .? Why do I have to . . ." I started to ask.

But then I quickly caught myself. Okay, maybe I wasn't crazy about dealing with Mitzi. Not after what she'd done this afternoon. And well, I was still probably a little mad at her, and I didn't exactly want to talk to her right now. But I'd just gotten advice from the Wise One and an assignment from Bogey. They'd both spent plenty of time teaching and training me, so now it was my turn to step into that role. For Mitzi.

So I took a really deep breath and put a smile on my face. "Sure, I'd be happy to," I somehow managed to say. Though it wasn't exactly easy to get the words out.

And the next thing I knew, I was on my way to find Mitzi. I ran downstairs and checked our cat beds, thinking she might have gone for a nap. When she wasn't there, I looked all over the family room and then in the living room. After that, I searched the home office. She wasn't there, either, so I kept on searching for her throughout the house.

But she was nowhere to be found.

For some reason, I was starting to get a little annoyed as I went along. The funny thing was, she'd practically been glued to me since the second she'd come to stay at our house. In fact, it had been kind of hard to shake her. And sometimes she was there when I didn't even *know* she was there.

But now when I actually *wanted* her around, I couldn't find her anywhere!

And to think, I was a cat detective! Finding clues and missing things was something I was trained to do. Yet it seemed like this little kitten had practically disappeared from the face of the earth. Or, at least, from inside our house.

That's when I suddenly had a thought that sent my heart racing. Had Mitzi gotten out somehow? Was she running around outside where there were plenty of dangers for a tiny cat? I remembered my own days of being out on the mean streets. Before I'd come to live at our forever home. And believe me, there was a reason why they called those streets "mean." The idea of little Mitzi being out there all alone without anyone to care for her made my stomach twist into knots. So I just kept on running and looking and searching. I checked the kitchen pantry and the closets and I finally ran back upstairs. I looked under our Mom and Dad's bed. And I searched every nook and cranny that I could think of.

I finally ran into Gracie's room for a second time. Then I just stopped and tried to think where Mitzi might be. By now I was really starting to panic. More than anything, I wanted to see that tiny little orange and black face. With the little black mustache under her pink nose. I could hardly believe I'd been so upset with her earlier. She was just a little kitten. Sure, she should have listened to us. And yes, she should have stopped when we told her to stop. But she didn't know better. And unless Bogey and I and the other cats taught her a few things, she never would know any better.

But we'd never get the chance unless I found her. Then again, maybe I needed to change the "I" to a "we." Meaning, maybe I needed to form a search party.

Even if it meant sneaking outside to keep on looking for her.

I was just about to race from the room and find the other cats when I heard it. A faint mewing sound. The very same mewing sound that I'd heard the night before.

The mewing sound that Mitzi made.

That meant I'd found her at last!

Well, sort of. Since I could hear her, I knew she must be close by. Now I just needed to figure out where she was exactly.

But how?

Especially since my heart seemed to be pounding even louder than the quiet, little mewing noise that I could barely even hear.

Was Mitzi in trouble? Was she stuck somewhere?

Holy Catnip!

CHAPTER 11

Holy Mackerel!

There I was, standing in Gracie's room and listening for all I was worth, with my ears pointed in the direction of Mitzi's mewing. I could hear her just faintly, but I sure couldn't see her. And no matter where I looked, I couldn't find her anywhere.

So I just stayed focused on that mewing sound.

"Mitzi," I called out. "Where are you?"

"Buckley, is that you?" came her muffled voice.

"Yes, it's me. Would you please come out and talk to me?" I checked under the bed and in the closet again, and I still couldn't find her.

"But I don't know where I am!" she cried. "Help, Buckley! I'm lost!"

I crinkled my brow. "How did you get lost?"

"I don't know. But now I can't find my way out!"

"Um . . . okay," I told her. "Just keep talking. I'm going to follow the sound of your voice."

"Buckley, I'm scared," she whimpered.

Well, I had to say, this was the first time I'd ever heard her admit to anything like that. Usually she just acted really tough.

"It's okay," I told her. "We all get scared sometimes. But don't worry, I'll get you out. Then I've got something to tell you. Something I know will make you extra happy."

"You do?"

By now, I could tell her voice was coming from somewhere around Gracie's bed, and I knew she couldn't be far away.

"Uh-huh," I said. "And I'm going to tell you just as soon as I see you. Can you give me some hints about where you are? And how you got in there?"

"I don't know. I can't remember for sure. I came up here to hide. But then I guess I just hid too well."

I glanced under the bed once more. "Why were you trying to hide?"

She started to make her mewing sound again. "Because I made a bad mistake. I messed up your case. When you were investigating at the jewelry store."

Funny, but I was pretty sure this was exactly what Miss Mokie had been talking about. And while I wanted to tell Mitzi that "everything was okay," I remembered the words of the Wise One. And how I was supposed to be firm and let this little kitten know when she had acted "incorrectly."

So I took a deep breath and did my best to do what Miss Mokie had told me to do.

"Um . . . yes, young one," I said as firmly as I could. "You should have listened to Bogey and me. And you should have stayed put instead of running up Mr. Pennypacker's back."

"I know," she said. "Are you mad at me, Buckley?"

I scrunched up my face, reminding myself not to be wishy-washy. "Well . . . um . . . yes. I was."

Then she started to mew even louder. "I'm sorry, Buckley. I was just trying to be a cat detective. Like you."

"And that's why I was looking for you," I told her. "I wanted to tell you the good news."

"Good news?"

I nodded, even though I was pretty sure she couldn't see me. "Uh-huh. I wanted to tell you that we decided to train you to be a cat detective."

"For real?" she chirped.

"Yup," I told her. "For real. Lil and Trixie even agreed to teach you cat karate."

I heard her gasp. "They did?"

"Uh-huh, they sure did."

"Oh, Buckley! I am so excited! I can hardly stand it."

And that's when the pillows leaning against the headboard of Gracie's bed suddenly fell over. And a lump beneath her comforter started to bounce around.

I couldn't help but roll my eyes. Because it turned out that Mitzi wasn't really all that lost. She'd only been under the covers and the pillows at the top of the bed.

I moved closer to the bed. "Scoot toward the sound of my voice. Okay? I'll keep talking and you keep moving."

"Okay, Buckley. Whatever you say."

And so she did. As I kept on talking and talking, I could see the bump under the covers slowly heading toward me. That was, until it stopped completely.

"Buckley, it's dark in here," Mitzi whimpered. "I'm scared."

For a second or two, I really felt like rolling my eyes again. After all, us cats can see in the dark.

But then I had an idea. "Maybe you should close your eyes. And keep on scooting toward my voice. I'll let you know when you're almost out."

"All right, Buckley," she told me as she started to move again.

Then, little by little, I could see that bump in the bed heading my way once more. When she got close to the edge, I used one of my big paws to hold the covers up.

"You can open your eyes now," I told her. "And come on out."

So she did just that. She slid out head first with her arms stretched out before her. When her front feet touched the ground, she rolled and did a somersault. Then she bounced onto all fours and just kept on bouncing around.

"Oh, Buckley," she cried. "You saved me! From that dark bed." Then she did one of her karate moves and bounced off the side of the bed. With a very loud "Hi-yah!"

I started to say something to her, but she interrupted me before I could even get a single word out. "Did you see how brave I was, Buckley? I went right through those dark covers and I wasn't even scared."

That's funny, because I sure didn't remember it like that.

"I'm going to be one of the best cat detectives ever," she babbled on, still not letting me speak. "You'll see!"

To tell you the truth, right at that very moment, I wasn't half as sure as she was. But one thing I *was* pretty sure about — there didn't seem to be anything I could say that would get her to settle down and listen to me. So I did something I'd seen the Wise One do many times. I raised my paw for silence. And I just kept on holding it up there in the air.

I could hardly believe what happened next. Little Mitzi suddenly stopped talking and sat down at attention. Almost like I'd turned off a switch somewhere.

I was so shocked I *almost* gasped. But thankfully, I caught myself in time and I did my best to look firm and serious. After all, what kind of a teacher would I be if I acted all surprised when my methods worked? Miss Mokie never looked shocked when we bowed to her. No, she commanded respect, and believe me, she got it! So I figured I should probably do the same.

I cleared my throat and put my paw down. "Umm . . . that's better," I told Mitzi. "Now here's the deal. If you want Bogey and me to teach you how to be a cat detective, then you have to settle down. And you have to listen and follow orders. If you don't, then we're not going to train you anymore. Got it?"

And she nodded her little head. "Yes, Buckley. And Bogey."

I turned my head to see my brother standing in the doorway. "Good job, kid," he told me with a grin. "Looks like you're a natural when it comes to teaching a CDIT."

"Thanks," I said, though I sure didn't feel like a natural.

Unnatural was more like it.

Bogey nodded toward Mitzi. "Glad to see you've already started working with Short-stuff here. Because we could use her tomorrow."

I crinkled my brow and looked at my brother. For a moment or two, I wasn't sure if I'd heard him correctly. After all, Mitzi had caused all kinds of trouble for us today at the jewelry store.

"Are you sure . . .?" I asked Bogey.

"I'll go, I'll go, I'll go!" Mitzi chimed in. Her eyes were wild and I could tell she was fighting the urge to start dancing around again. But I had to give her credit — for once she was doing a pretty good job of keeping herself under control.

Bogey strolled on into the room. "Let's face it, kid. Short-stuff here knows her way around the Bumble place. She could give us a leg up, so we're not walking into the place blind. But only if you can give her some more training tonight." Bogey extended a claw and pulled out a bag of cat treats that he kept hidden behind Gracie's desk.

"Umm . . . sure," I said as he handed Mitzi and me a treat.

Mitzi attacked her treat like she was jumping on a bug. She scarfed it down and looked to Bogey for another one. Without a word, he passed out another round of treats.

Bogey raised an eyebrow in Mitzi's direction. "You might start by teaching her how to hold her horses."

My chin nearly dropped to the floor. "Horses? You want me to teach her how to ride a horse?"

Bogey grinned. "Nope, kid. Just an expression. I want you to teach her to be patient. And to wait when she's supposed to. So she doesn't do what she did today."

"Oh, okay," I nodded, though I wasn't exactly sure *how* I was supposed to teach her that.

But before I could ask Bogey for any ideas, he stashed the treat bag behind Gracie's desk. "It's a plan then, kid," he said as he headed for the door. "I'll meet you later when it's time to run our rounds."

I looked at my brother and saluted. "Aye, aye," I told him. But I missed my forehead and poked myself in the ear.

Thankfully, Bogey had already trotted into the hallway and he didn't see me.

And thankfully, neither did the Princess when she waltzed into the room a few seconds later. "Hello, Buckley. I'm here to help. If you need me." She gave me a smile and looked up at me with her big, green eyes. All of a sudden, my heart started to pound and the room started to spin.

As if I didn't have enough to worry about with training little Mitzi.

And speaking of Mitzi, the next thing I knew, I heard a loud "Hi-yah!" Then I felt her feet hit my side and suddenly the room *really* was spinning. Because Mitzi and I were rolling and rolling and rolling across the hardwood floor.

When we stopped, I bounced to my feet and so did she.

Only she kept on bouncing around. At least, I think she did. It was kind of hard to tell for sure since my eyes were still moving in circles.

Once I could focus again, well, I was really pretty mad. I had to say, I didn't appreciate somebody practicing their cat karate on me. Especially when they didn't even know how to do *real* cat karate.

So I did exactly what I'd done before. I raised my paw in the air. And once again, Mitzi sat on the floor at attention.

The Princess gasped and put a paw to her mouth. For a moment, I thought she was going to say something, but she just kept quiet.

But Mitzi wasn't about to stay quiet. "Buckley, I want a treat."

I shook my head. "Not after you just tried to karate chop me."

"But I want a treat," she repeated.

I crinkled my brow. "And that's not even the right way to ask for a treat."

Mitzi tilted her head. "It isn't? How am I supposed to ask for a treat?"

That's when the Princess jumped in. "I'll handle this," she said to me before she turned to Mitzi. "Young lady, you should always use good manners. Especially when you are talking to an older cat."

"Manners?" Mitzi repeated the word like she'd never, ever heard it before in her whole life.

"That's right," the Princess said gently. "You should always say 'please' and 'thank-you.' If you would like a treat, you should say, 'May I please have a treat?'"

Mitzi smiled and glimmered up to the Princess like she was the most beautiful cat in the world. Then again, as far as I was concerned, the Princess *was* the most beautiful cat in the world.

"I want to talk just like you do," Mitzi gushed before she turned back to me. "It sounds so nice. Buckley, may I please have a treat?"

"Yes, you may," I told her and pulled the bag of treats from behind the desk. "As long as you say you're sorry for karate chopping me."

Her little chin drooped. "I'm sorry, Buckley. Sometimes I just get so excited and I don't know how to stop."

"I know," I told her. And for some reason, I wasn't mad at her anymore. I passed her a cat treat and she practically inhaled it.

The Princess scooted closer to Mitzi. "Now you should say thank you."

Mitzi's eyes went wide. "Oh, okay. Sure. Thank you, Buckley."

"Very good, Mitzi," the Princess said as she put her arm around the little kitten. "Cats are known for their manners and it's important that you have manners, too. You won't get very far in life without them."

And that's when an idea hit me like a cat toy flying across the room. "Bogey also wants me to teach you how to have patience," I told the little kitten. "Because a good cat detective figures out when it's time to run in. Or if it's just better to stay put. Or . . . if you should run right on out the door."

Mitzi nodded so fast her chin was kind of a blur. "Oh, wow, Buckley! I think it would be good for me to learn that. Do you think I can? Do you think I'm smart enough?"

I tilted my head. "Well . . . sure. I think you're a very smart kitten. You figure out lots of stuff."

The Princess smiled her brightest smile. "That's right. I just know you'll catch on in a hurry."

Mitzi looked at the floor. "I've never had anyone teach me things before."

That's funny. Because I'd never taught things to anyone before. I guess we were both learning new things today. I only hoped my idea would work.

So I grabbed the bag of cat treats and took them across the room. "Okay, here's what I want you to do . . ." I pulled a treat from the bag and put it on the floor. "I want you to stay right where you are until I count to ten. Then you can run across the room and get your treat."

She tilted her tiny head. "Why can't I just have the treat now?"

"Umm, well . . . because sometimes a cat detective needs to wait for things," I told her. "And that's what I want you to learn — how to wait for things."

The Princess smiled at Mitzi. "That's right. You have to learn how to be in control of yourself."

Mitzi put her paw to her chin. "Oh . . . Okay. I get it."

"Are you ready?" I looked right in her eyes to make sure I had her attention. "Here we go . . . one . . . two . . ."

And the next thing I knew, a blur of orange and black and white whizzed right past me. It was so fast I almost fell over. To make things worse, the treat was gone. And Mitzi was standing in the very spot where the treat had been.

She smiled up at me. "How did I do, Buckley? Did I do good? I got the treat."

I crinkled my brow. "Umm . . . maybe you don't understand how this is supposed to work. You're not supposed to run for the treat until after I finish counting to ten."

That's when she started to bounce around again. "Oh, okay. I've got it. I can do this."

So we tried it again. This time I had barely said the word 'five' when she was already in front of the treat and scarfing it down.

Right away, she started to dance around. "How was that? Pretty good? I did better that time. I did, I did, I did! I know I did."

For a moment, I couldn't even speak, and when I finally could, I wasn't sure what to say. "Maybe we should do this a little differently. Maybe you should wait till I count to ten and then the Princess says 'Go!'"

I glanced at the Princess and she quickly nodded to me. Letting me know she was on board.

Then I looked right back at Mitzi. "Maybe you should repeat the plan back to me. So I know you understand it."

She looked from me to the Princess and then back at me again. After a few seconds, her eyes kind of lit up. It reminded me of a light bulb going on.

"Oh, right," she said. "You're going to count to ten and I'm going to wait until the Princess tells me to 'Go!'"

"That's it!" I hollered. I could hardly believe how happy it made me feel, just knowing she'd figured it out.

So I put a treat down and we tried it one more time. And this time, she did it exactly right. Holy Catnip! After that, there were paw bumps all around, and Mitzi started to bounce around some more.   For some reason, I sort of felt like bouncing around, too.

But I didn't.

Instead, we just kept on practicing. Soon I was counting to twenty and even thirty. And I had to say, she was really getting the hang of it. She could wait for quite a while before going after a treat.

That's when I realized that the Wise One had been right, when she suggested we give Mitzi some training. Because Mitzi wasn't a bad kitten. And she might even be a really good cat detective one day. She just needed someone to train her.

But she couldn't learn everything she needed to know in one lesson. So after a while, I figured she'd had enough for one night.

"Let's stop for now," I told her. "Because you'd better get some sleep."

"But I want to run around with you and Bogey," she whined. "When you run surveillance."

By now, I knew just how to handle this situation. I raised my paw and she quieted down right away. "No, we need you to be rested for tomorrow."

"Okay, Buckley. Aye, aye," she said and then stuck her paw in her ear.

I crinkled my brow. "What are you doing?"

She looked up at me so sweetly. "I'm just saluting you like you saluted Bogey."

I dropped my head to my arm and shut my eyes for a second or two. That's when I realized that I was going to need a lot of patience myself to train this kitten. Being a teacher was really, really hard work. And I couldn't help but wonder if it had been pretty hard for Bogey, too. When he was training me.

I turned to the door and saw him standing there with a grim look on his face. "How'd it go, kid?"

The Princess batted her eyes at me.   "Buckley did a wonderful job! He's absolutely brilliant when it comes to teaching young ones."

Bogey raised a brow. "You might just have a new role at the BBCDA, kid. Training the CDITs."

I tried to say something to my brother, but for some

reason, my words came out like, "*blub, blub, blub* . . ." Because I wasn't really sure if I wanted a job like this one. Not full time, anyway.

Bogey nodded to Mitzi, who sat at attention. She had a huge smile on her face and I could see she was really pleased with herself.

"We've had a change of plans for tomorrow," he told Mitzi. "You'll be staying here and working with Lil and Trixie. On your cat karate."

"We're not going to Mrs. Bumble's house?" I asked my brother.

He shook his head. "Probably not, kid. Because we need to go back to our Mom's store. Without Short-stuff."

I hated to say it, but the idea of spending the day running surveillance at our Mom's store sounded just perfect to me. And a nice afternoon nap or two would be wonderful.

Still, I had to wonder *why* we'd had a change of plans. Especially since it was pretty clear where our newest clue was leading us — straight to Mrs. Bumble's house.

But Bogey answered my question before I could even ask it. "We've got to sneak back into Garnet's store."

That got my attention. Not to mention, made my heart start to thump really loud. I really didn't like the idea of going back in there again. Especially after we'd been caught. And I sure didn't like the way Garnet had treated Gracie.

"Bogey . . . why would we want to go back there?" I asked.

He glanced at the dark night sky outside the window. "I just caught word over the Internet. The burglar alarm went off at the jewelry store. Looks like there was a break-in. And a robbery."

The Princess gasped, and I could see the fear in her big, green eyes.

I fought hard not to gasp myself. Because I could hardly believe it. A break-in at the jewelry store?

"That's really odd," I told my brother. "We were just in that store today."

"I hear ya, kid," Bogey said. "And I can't shake the feeling that this break-in is somehow connected to our case."

That's when my eyes probably went about as wide as our food dish. Because this case just kept getting stranger by the minute!

　　And, it seemed like the more we learned, the less we knew. Holy Catnip!

CHAPTER 12

Holy Mackerel!

Even though I tried my best to stay calm — just like a good cat detective is supposed to do — Bogey's news still made my fur stand on end. Because it hadn't been very many hours before when we were right there in Garnet's Jewelry Store. And now it had been robbed. To make things even worse, we had plans to go right back into that store. The very place where we'd been caught and Gracie had knocked over a jewelry display.

Yet before we could talk about it more, Gracie came up to bed. Apparently, she'd heard the news, too. Because her eyes were wide and she was shaking her head when she walked into her room.

"That's so weird," she murmured to herself over and over again. "I can't believe it! A break-in and a robbery at the jewelry store! And to think, it's just a few doors down from *our* store."

I had to say, she seemed pretty shook-up about it all. Then again, I guess we all were. But if nothing else, I was happy to see that Gracie didn't have her cell phone with her. And instead of tapping away on that phone, she reached down and petted each one of us cats. Plus she talked and talked to us.

She even sat down on the floor with us. "It's funny, but I feel like I haven't spent any time with you kitties lately. Even though I was right here with you in the same room with you. But when I was on my phone all the time, I didn't even know all the stuff that was going on around me. It's so nice to be back."

I reached up and gave her a kiss on the nose. Because it was really nice to *have* her back. So to speak.

She giggled and gave me a hug before she picked up little Mitzi. "My goodness, I hardly even noticed how cute you are, little foster kitten. I sure wish we could give you a name."

Of course, Gracie had no idea that I'd already taken care of that problem. Though she might not be happy if she found out that Mitzi had been named after a doorknob. More or less, anyway. Then again, it turned out to be a pretty good name. If I ever had to find a name for someone again, I might just check out the other hardware around our house.

Gracie put Mitzi on the floor and leaned over to give the Princess a kiss on the head. Then she picked up Bogey and looked right into his eyes. "Can you believe it, Bogey? You and Buckley and I were all in Garnet's store today. It really gives me the creeps when I think about it. Especially after my accident in there. What were the odds of all that happening in one day?"

But Bogey's only response was to purr and give her some slow eye blinks.

She cradled him for a moment before she put him back on the floor again. After that, she got ready for bed, climbed between the covers, and fell fast asleep. That's when Lil wandered in and said hello to us all. She jumped up and settled down on the end of Gracie's bed, ready to watch over her. Just like she always did. Mitzi hopped up, too, and curled up next to Gracie's pillow. Seconds later, she was out like a light.

I had to say, I was glad to see Mitzi was going to get some sleep. Not only did she need it, but she was also doing what she'd been told to do. For once.

And believe me, we were careful not to wake her. Or Gracie. Bogey and the Princess and I all quietly waved goodnight to Lil and then tiptoed out the door. The Princess headed to the sunroom while Bogey and I went downstairs to run our first surveillance round of the night. By now, our Mom and Dad were in bed, too, so the whole house was dark. Except I noticed they'd left the porch light on for a change, which sort of surprised me. Maybe it had something to do with the news about the break-in.

And maybe that was why Bogey and I both seemed to be on full alert tonight as we checked all the doors and windows. I had to race to keep up with my brother after he started us out running twice as fast as we usually went. We even doubled-back to the front door and paused there for a moment.

I turned to my brother. "Bogey, what do you think is going on? First we get all these clues on our doorstep. Then one of those clues leads us to a store that gets robbed later on. Doesn't that all seem strange to you?"

Bogey set his mouth in a grim line. "You got that right, kid. I'd bet a case of cat treats that it's all connected somehow. And that someone is trying to send us a message."

"A message?" I repeated. "What do you think that message is saying?"

"I don't know yet, kid," Bogey said under his breath. "Could be they're trying to tell us that our Mom's store is next."

I gulped at the thought. Especially since I knew our Mom would be really upset if someone tried to rob her store. Or our house, for that matter.

I stretched up to the knob on the front door and double-checked to see that it was locked. All the while, I couldn't shake the idea that somebody had been right out there on our doorstep, only a few inches away from where we were now. Three times. Just to leave some little jars for us.

Bogey raised his brow and motioned to the dining room. "Time for a quick break, kid."

So we made a beeline for the potted plant, and Bogey grabbed the bag of cat treats he kept stashed there. But much to my surprise, he gave me a couple of treats and only took one for himself. Then he stashed the bag right back where it had been.

I felt my eyes go wide. "Aren't you hungry tonight?"

Bogey shook his head and grinned. "Just trying to cut back, kid. If Gracie can ease off her cell phone, then I can cut back on the treats."

"Oh, okay," I told him.

He patted his belly. "Think I've been stress-eating, kid. Too much work and not enough play."

Well, I had to say, that made plenty of sense to me. "We've had a lot of cases lately for just the two of us at the BBCDA."

Bogey nodded. "You can say that again, kid. This new case didn't help, either. It's really got us chasing our tails."

I glanced back at my own huge tail. "I haven't chased my tail since I was a little kitten. Well, okay . . . maybe there was that one time when I was really happy because our Mom was about to give us tuna fish for dinner."

Bogey grinned. "Relax, kid. It's just an expression. It means we're doing a lot of busy work and not really getting anywhere."

"Oh . . . well, that sounds about right," I told him. "Because we sure don't seem to be getting anywhere with this case. Not so far, anyway."

"Don't I know it, kid," Bogey said with a nod toward the stairs. "Don't I know it."

Then without another word, we took off to finish our rounds. When we were done, we headed for our beds in the family room. We got a little shut-eye before our early morning surveillance run. And after that, we took our final nap of the night. Luckily, everything was quiet and nobody left us any new clues on our front porch.

Even so, I couldn't fall asleep for a long time because I was busy listening for footsteps outside. But I must have dozed off at some point. Because the next thing I knew, it was morning and we were dragging ourselves out of bed. Gracie fed us all breakfast, and she even gave each one of us a quick hug before she put our food down. I had to say, I sure didn't miss her cell phone one bit.

Then it wasn't long before Bogey and I were in our pet carriers and headed for our Mom's store. Mitzi had promised she would stay home today for her cat karate lessons. But I checked the back of my pet carrier anyway. Just to make sure she wasn't hiding in there and riding along.

Thankfully, I was the only one in my carrier.

Once we got to our Mom's store, I couldn't believe how packed the place was. There were people standing around in bunches all up and down the block, and lots of them had wandered into our Mom's store. Plus, plenty of those people were shopping and buying things as well. So our Mom and Millicent and Merryweather sure had their hands full.

Gracie got right to work, too. She wrapped small items in newspaper and put them in bags for customers. "I wonder why it's so busy today," she said to Merryweather.

Merryweather pushed her cat-eye glasses up higher on her nose. "It's because of the lookie-loos."

"Lookie-loos?" Gracie repeated. "What are those?"

Merryweather taped a box full of antique dishes. "Whenever something bad happens and it's big news, some people want to get a good look at it. And today people are coming into your Mom's store so they can catch a glimpse of the scene of the crime."

Gracie grabbed another sheet of paper. "You mean, Garnet's store?"

Merryweather nodded. "That's right, honey. They aren't allowed to go inside. And they need a good excuse to hang around and see what's going on. So they came down to your Mom's antique store."

"Oh . . . " Gracie said.

Millicent brought a glass vase to the counter. "Garnet gets robbed and now we're making out like bandits with all these sales."

"Don't you feel sorry for Garnet?" Gracie asked.

"Yes and no," Merryweather said. "She's not the nicest person around. In fact, you might even say she's downright mean."

"Very mean," Millicent added.

Merryweather lined another packing box with bubble wrap. "But that doesn't mean I'm happy that her store was robbed. Though maybe it's the reason why someone decided to break in and steal her jewelry. Maybe she was nasty to them and they decided to get even."

She had barely spoken the words when Bogey caught my eye and nodded in the direction of the front door. Of course, I knew exactly what he meant. And let me tell you, if there was ever a day when no one would notice a couple of black cats sneaking out of a store, well, this was it. So I followed him as we went from dresser to cabinet, and from table to wing chair.

Without anyone even seeing us at all. Then we slipped right out the front door while people stood talking to each other.

Of course, the robbery was the *only* thing that anyone wanted to talk about. And we heard more and more about it as we slinked along the sidewalk to Garnet's store. Thankfully, no one even looked down at all. And nobody seemed to notice what was going on around their feet.

Namely, Bogey and me running by.

Then it was just a matter of minutes before we were inside Garnet's store again. Though I barely even recognized the place. It looked completely different from the way it had yesterday. All the cabinets were bare and all the valuable jewelry was gone! Not to mention, the glass cabinets had been smashed and little pieces of glass were everywhere.

And I do mean everywhere!

I almost froze in shock when I saw the whole mess.

But I managed to stay focused, and I followed my brother as we tiptoed behind a cabinet. We had to be extra careful wherever we stepped, so we didn't cut our paws on any bits of glass. If nothing else, at least we knew our way around this time. So we stayed low to the ground as we crept past some more cabinets. We finally stopped when we found the perfect hiding spot. One that was nicely out of sight but where we could still see what was going on.

Right away we spotted a couple of police officers who were busy dusting for fingerprints. Then there was another one who was picking up bits of evidence from the floor. Believe me, with all those little pieces of glass around, he had plenty to choose from.

In the meantime, our old friend, Officer Phoebe Smiley, was talking to Garnet. They were both sitting in chairs across from each other. And let me tell you, I would not have wanted to be in Officer Phoebe's shoes for anything in the world at that moment. Because Garnet was mad. *Really* mad. And she was being extra nasty to Officer Phoebe.

"The police in this town are a joke!" Garnet said as she practically shot laser beams from her eyes. "If you had been doing your job, this crime never would've happened. And my store never would've been robbed."

"We got here as quick as we could," Officer Phoebe said.

"We made it in five minutes."

"Yeah?" Garnet went on. "Well, it was long enough for the crooks to wipe me out! Just look at this place! It's completely empty."

Officer Phoebe shook her head. "They were pretty fast, all right. Can you think of anyone who would want to do this to you? Do you have any enemies?"

"Not a one!" Garnet yelled. "Everyone loves me," she screamed.

I felt my eyes go wide and I glanced at my brother. Because I had a pretty good idea that not very many people — or cats, either — liked her at all. In fact, I guessed she probably had *lots* of enemies.

"She takes the cake," Bogey whispered to me.

"She took a cake?" I repeated. "Somebody's birthday cake? That's the meanest thing I've ever heard!"

Bogey shook his head. "Just an expression, kid. It means she's the worst example of something. In her case, she's the nastiest dame around."

Well, he could sure say that again. I especially didn't like the way she was talking to Officer Phoebe. Nobody deserved to be treated like that. Miss Mokie never would've put up with that kind of treatment. Maybe Officer Phoebe should have tried raising her hand, just like Miss Mokie raised her paw. And just like I'd learned to raise my paw when I was talking to Mitzi.

Unfortunately, Officer Phoebe didn't try that.

Even so, she still managed to keep her cool. "Did you see anyone around here acting suspicious lately? In the days before you were robbed?"

For once, Garnet was quiet. But only for a second or two.

Then she suddenly jumped up from her chair. "Yes, there *was* something suspicious that happened yesterday. Gracie Abernathy ran right into one of my displays! She knocked over some jewelry and probably even scratched or dented some. She and her mother weren't too happy when I told them they'd have to pay for any damages."

I could see that Officer Phoebe was really struggling to keep calm. Probably because she is our Mom's friend, and she knows Gracie pretty well, too. Not to mention, she's always been very nice to us cats.

"Come now, Garnet," she said through clenched teeth. "Do you really believe that a twelve-year-old girl could set up a jewel heist like this?"

"Sure she could," Garnet shot back. "She has a cell phone, doesn't she? She could send messages to all her friends and they could help her out. She and her bunch could have robbed my store in a matter of minutes. The door to the alley was broken into, and she would know all about that door. She's probably been by it a million times when she's gone to work with her mother. Plus, she probably wanted to get even with me!"

By now, I was really starting to get mad. Because I knew Gracie would never rob a jewelry store! She wouldn't even think of doing something so awful. She sure wasn't a crook. So how could Garnet even say such a thing?

"I find it pretty hard to believe that a young girl would steal all your jewelry," Officer Phoebe said. "Especially if that young girl was Gracie."

Garnet put her hands on her hips. "Why? Because Abigail is your friend? Maybe you should be taken off this case. Maybe you can't be objective about it."

"Objective?" I whispered to Bogey.

He tilted an ear in my direction. "Not letting your personal feelings cloud your judgment, kid."

I nodded. "Oh, okay."

"Where would Gracie even put all that jewelry?" Officer Phoebe said with a laugh.

"Why, that's easy!" Garnet went on, fuming even more by the minute. "She'd simply move it all to her mother's store! Maybe they did it together. Just to get even with me!"

"Neither one of them would steal your jewelry," Officer Phoebe said through clenched teeth. I could tell she was finally starting to get upset.

"I insist that we go over there and see for ourselves. Immediately!" Garnet hollered.

Then before Officer Phoebe could say another word, Garnet jumped up from her chair. She raced right out the door and turned in the direction of our Mom's store.

Officer Phoebe bounced to her feet and ran after her. "You

can't search Abby's store! Not without her permission!"

I sat bolt upright and turned to my brother. "Should we go after them?"

"Yup, kid, but first we need to check something out." And with that, he ran around the corner of a cabinet.

I raced after him as he zoomed past a few more cabinets and made a beeline for the back wall. To the very place where we'd found our clue the day before. Or maybe I should say, the lack of a clue. Because the empty jar with the black lid that we'd found yesterday was gone! Had the crooks taken it, too?

Then again, maybe the crooks were the ones who had put it there in the first place. My head started to spin just thinking about it.

"Let's get out of here, kid," Bogey said to me. "We know everything we need to know. Plus we got an earful. We'd better get back to the store before the fur starts to fly."

For once, I knew exactly what his expression meant.

So we vamoosed right on out of there! Bogey took the lead and I raced to keep up. We ran single file and low to the ground. Just as fast as we could go. Soon we were out of that awful place and back on the sidewalk.

Then we ran straight for our Mom's store.

That was, until Bogey stopped for a second or two and glanced across the street.

Naturally, I stopped with him, though every inch of me was dying to get back to our Mom's store. "Um . . . Bogey, don't you think we should hurry up and get back? So we don't get caught?"

He tilted his head. "Hold on a second, kid. Take a look across the street and tell me what you see."

So I did just that. And that's when my chin practically hit the pavement. Because there, staring right at us, was Mr. Pennypacker. He tipped his bowler hat to us and smiled.

"It's . . . it's . . ." I barely managed to stammer.

"Yup, kid," Bogey said. "It is."

Now I had to wonder, what in the world was he doing there?

Holy Catnip!

CHAPTER 13

Holy Mackerel!

Shivers ran up and down my spine as we watched Mr. Pennypacker staring at us from the other side of the street. And I do mean staring! He didn't even blink. Not once. Worst of all, for some strange reason, I couldn't seem to look away as we watched him watching us.

Bogey touched my shoulder. "Don't let him rattle you, kid. Let's get back to our Mom's store. Garnet and Officer Phoebe are probably there already. And Garnet's probably raising a ruckus."

"A ruckus?" I repeated. I was still having a hard time turning away from Mr. Pennypacker's gaze. It was like he had hypnotized me or something.

"Yup, kid. A ruckus. A commotion. A hullabaloo. A very big fuss with a whole lotta noise."

"Oh . . . that," I said, nodding.

And I was finally able to turn away. Then I followed Bogey as we ran around the legs of the people on the sidewalk.

Getting back inside our Mom's store was easy, since a customer was standing there with the door wide open. The older lady was practically frozen to the spot, just watching the "ruckus," as Bogey had put it. So I guess I wasn't the only one who had trouble turning away from something that had caught my attention. Then again, I had to admit, this time it was

extra hard to look away. Because my brother had been right —
Garnet *really* was raising a *very* big commotion. She was
yelling and waving her arms and accusing Gracie of robbing
her jewelry store.

Poor Gracie was in tears. Thankfully, Merryweather had
put her arm around Gracie's shoulders and pulled her close.
Like she was protecting her.

Then our Mom planted herself solidly between Gracie and
Garnet. "If you think for one moment that you're going to get
away with this, Garnet . . . accusing my daughter of a crime she
couldn't possibly commit . . . and for that matter, wouldn't
even *think* to commit . . . then you're about to have much
bigger problems than just a robbery! Because you're going to
have to deal with me. And my husband. And the St. Gertrude
Police Department."

"Your daughter is a crook!" Garnet hollered. "She's a crook
and a liar!"

Our Mom put her hands on her hips. "She certainly *is*
not!"

Officer Phoebe pulled out her handcuffs. "Garnet, you
either calm down or I'll have to arrest you."

"But I'm the victim here," Garnet wailed. "I'm the one who
was robbed."

"I know you are upset," our Mom said firmly. "Now, if you
will just settle down, I will allow you to look through our store.
With Phoebe watching over you, of course. Then you'll see that
we did not steal your jewelry. And after that, I fully expect you
to apologize to my daughter. In a very big way. Because you're
way out of line to accuse her of a crime like that."

"Fine. I agree," Garnet said, practically chomping on her
words.

All the while, my heart was pounding so hard it felt like a
bouncy ball inside my chest. When Bogey said Garnet would
raise a ruckus, commotion or hullabaloo, well, he wasn't
kidding. I turned to my brother, thinking he'd be pretty mad
about the whole situation.

But he just arched an eyebrow and grinned. "Gotta love
our Mom. She's a real champ when it comes to protecting our
family."

I nodded. "She sure sticks up for us all. No matter what."

"You got that right, kid," Bogey said as he motioned to the scene before us. "Now it looks like we're up. We've got security detail."

Well, he sure didn't have to tell me twice. Without another word, we made a beeline for our Mom. Though I took a quick little jog over to Gracie first and rubbed around her legs. Just to let her know that *I* was sticking up for *her*.

Our Mom sighed and turned to Officer Phoebe. "Would you mind being a witness, Phoebe? And watch Garnet while she looks around? That should prove to her that we don't have her jewelry."

Phoebe frowned. "Of course, Abby. But you have nothing to prove. Everyone in town knows you and Gracie would never rob a jewelry store."

"Thanks," our Mom told her. "But this way there'll never be any question about it."

So off they went. Officer Phoebe followed Garnet as she searched through antique china hutches and dressers and shelves. Of course, Bogey and I tagged along, too. And believe me, we kept a close eye on her.

A *very* close eye.

Needless to say, Garnet wasn't especially happy about Bogey and me being there. In fact, she got upset whenever she turned to see Bogey staring at her from the top of a bookcase or a dresser. Or when she caught me sitting right next to her on a chair or a stool.

"Can't you call off the dogs?" she demanded of Officer Phoebe. "Maybe lock them up somewhere?"

"Dogs?" I meowed to my brother. "I don't see any dogs. Doesn't she know we're cats?"

He grinned and meowed back. "Just an expression, kid. She thinks we're coming on a little strong."

I crinkled my brow. "Are we?"

"Absolutely," Bogey meowed and scooted a little closer to Garnet. "Just like any good cat detective would."

"Make them stop all that meowing!" Garnet hollered.

Officer Phoebe laughed and petted me on the head. "I wouldn't dream of telling Buckley and Bogey what to do. They're Abby's cats. And believe me, they have minds of their own."

Garnet squinted at me and sneered. "Oh, I believe it, all right."

In the meantime, our Mom's store became even more packed with people. It seemed like everyone who had been out on the sidewalk now decided to come inside and shop. Probably so they'd have a front-row view in case Garnet caused another ruckus. And all those people also started to buy things. Lots and lots of things. Before long, our Mom, Millicent, Merryweather, and Gracie were so busy they could barely keep up with it all.

Bogey and I stayed on the job, too. As we trotted along behind Garnet and Officer Phoebe, we heard people in the crowd talking.

"Do you think that little girl robbed the jewelry store?" one man asked.

"How could that be?" his wife answered. "She's just a child."

"Maybe that's her disguise," someone else suggested. "If so, it's a good one. No one would ever suspect a child of such a complicated crime."

"I've known Abigail and Gracie and Mike for years," another lady added. "They are good, upstanding citizens of St. Gertrude."

Then several other people chimed in with things like, "That's right," and "I agree."

At least most of the people in town knew better than to believe something bad about our family. And much to my amazement, Garnet herself even came around. She raced back to our Mom and Gracie right after she'd finished searching.

Then Garnet burst into tears. "I'm so sorry Abigail. And Gracie. I don't know what came over me. I guess I was just upset about the robbery. I never should have said the things I said." She tilted her head back and cried and cried and cried.

Really loud.

Bogey squinted his eyes. "Seems a bit thick, doesn't it, kid?"

I nodded. "Like she's trying to make everyone feel sorry for her. Even though she was so mean to Gracie and our Mom."

And let me tell you, people sure did feel sorry for her. Someone jumped in with some tissues so Garnet could blow her nose. Someone else patted her hand, and our Mom even gave her a hug. Finally, Garnet reached over and hugged Gracie, too.

All the while, I caught a glimpse of Mr. Pennypacker walking around our store with his bowler hat in his hands.

For some reason, I shivered again. Then I scooted closer to my brother.

Not long after that, Garnet blew her nose one last time and smiled a shaky smile. She seemed to be feeling better when she walked out of our store with a whole bunch of people around her. People who were all saying really nice, cheerful things to her.

But nobody was saying things like that to poor Gracie, and she still looked pretty close to tears. So I ran over and stretched up her side. She picked me up and held me tight, and I gave her a kiss on the nose. But this time she didn't even giggle. Instead, she just put her face in my fur.

"Oh, Buckley," she whispered. "I don't think I've ever been so scared in my whole life. How could anyone think I would rob a jewelry store? If Garnet hadn't searched our store, she would have accused me of committing a crime. A really bad crime."

I knew it was true. And sure, Garnet had said she was sorry, but it hadn't made Gracie feel much better. So I gave her another kiss on the nose before she put me down and went back to work.

The crowd had started to thin out a little by now, and as near as I could tell, Mr. Pennypacker had gone, too. Still, I kept my eyes peeled for him as I joined my brother. Then together, we trotted to the front of the store and jumped up onto a dresser in the big, picture window. Right under the huge "Abigail's Antiques" sign. So we'd have a good view of what was going on outside.

I immediately glanced across the street to the very spot where Mr. Pennypacker had been standing when we'd first seen him. Again, I couldn't help but wonder what he'd been doing there. Was he just another one of the lookie-loos that Merryweather had been talking about? Or did he have another reason for being downtown today?

And apparently I wasn't the only one wondering about

him.

Bogey grabbed a bag of cat treats that he had stashed in a vase on the dresser. "Any thoughts on why old Pennypacker was out there, kid?" He handed me a treat and took one for himself.

I munched on my treat. "I was wondering the same thing. And I sure don't know the answer. How about you?"

Bogey ate his treat and glanced down the street. "You know what they say, kid. Crooks like to return to the scene of the crime."

I gulped. "They do? Do you think . . .?"

Bogey passed us another round of treats. "Could be, kid. I think we'd better keep this guy on our radar."

Right at that moment, I'm sure my eyes went really wide. "We have radar now? When did we get radar?"

Bogey shook his head and grinned. "Just an expression, kid. It means we'll have to watch out for him."

I glanced around us. "That sounds like a good idea since he was in our Mom's store today. Just like he was in Garnet's store yesterday. I sure hope we don't get robbed tonight!"

Bogey handed out one more round of treats. "Ditto for me, kid. But any way you look at it, we've gotta be on our paws. Until we figure out who's behind this. And why."

I finished my last treat. "I sure hope we figure it out fast."

Bogey stashed the treat bag back in its hiding place. "You can say that again, kid."

But I didn't have a chance to say another word. Because the next thing we knew, our Mom and Merryweather came to find us.

Merryweather picked up Bogey. "Much as I always enjoy the company of two such handsome fellas, I'm afraid it's time to say good-bye."

Bogey grinned up at Merryweather and started to purr.

Our Mom picked me up, too. "That's right, boys. We're going to call it a day. Gracie's had a rough morning and she's still pretty upset. So we're heading home early."

Just knowing that Gracie was upset made me upset, too. In fact, I meowed to her through my pet carrier as we drove home. And I kept on meowing until she took me out and held me tight. Then I wrapped my arms around her neck and buried my head in her hair.

"I wish I'd never used that cell phone," she murmured into my fur.

A couple of hot tears dropped onto my head.

Our Mom put her hand on Gracie's shoulder. "I know this has all been quite an ordeal. Are you okay, honey?"

Gracie sniffled. "Sort of. But not really. I keep thinking back to when I was on my cell phone and I walked right into that jewelry display. If I hadn't done that, none of this would have happened."

"Well . . ." our Mom said. "That's true enough. But even so, Garnet never should have acted the way she did. She was way over the top. Though I know she wasn't really upset with us. She was really upset about the robbery."

"I know, Mom," Gracie sighed. "But I'm still not sure if I want my cell phone anymore. Not after the mess it's caused."

Our Mom nodded. "Cell phones can certainly cause their share of problems. Even so, they are good to have in case of an emergency. And it was nice to have it the other day to take pictures of the jewelry that landed on the floor at Garnet's store. For proof of what really happened. But it's your choice whether you want to use it now or set it aside for when you're older."

Gracie rested her head on mine. "The only problem is, I'd miss my friends if I got rid of it. Everyone just sends emails and texts these days. Otherwise, they don't talk at all. Not like we're talking now. I wish we could all go back to the way we used to be. Back when we were younger and didn't have cell phones. When we talked and played and just hung out together. It was fun."

Our Mom nodded. "I know, honey."

"I wish there was something I could do about it," Gracie said as she put me back in my pet carrier. "I'm not sure my friends even know *how* to talk to each other anymore."

"Well, you're a very bright girl, Gracie. And I know you've solved problems like this before. I'll bet you can come up with a solution."

I knew our Mom was right. Because Gracie wasn't just a nice girl — she was a smart girl, too. And I could tell she was thinking hard about her problem when she suddenly got very quiet. She stayed that way until we got home. Then she went straight to her room right after she let us out of our pet carriers.

That's when Bogey pulled me aside. "Why don't you go on up with Gracie, kid. Make sure she's okay. I've gotta take care of something on the computer first. Then meet me upstairs in the guest room."

"In the guest room?" I repeated.

"Yup, kid. That's where Lil and Trixie planned to set up their cat karate school. We'll run in and grab Short-stuff before we head over to Mrs. Bumble's place. To check out that latest clue."

"Aye, aye," I told him with a salute. This time my huge paw went almost exactly where I wanted it to go. It was close, but still a little high on my forehead.

Bogey gave me a quick nod before he zoomed off. And I didn't waste any time taking off after Gracie. I was glad Bogey wanted me to check on her, because I was afraid she might be upstairs crying into her pillow. Especially after the way Garnet had treated her.

But thankfully, Gracie wasn't even close to tears when I found her in her room. She'd gone straight to her computer, and I could see that she'd searched the words, "How to get people to talk to each other." And for the first time all day, Gracie even smiled. Then she pulled out a notepad and started to take notes.

I couldn't have been more proud of her. Just like our Mom had said, she was trying to figure out a way to solve her problem. Plus, she was staying off her cell phone, exactly like she'd planned. I had to say, when Gracie put her mind to something, well, she sure stuck with it.

I glanced out to the hallway and saw the Princess motioning to me. So I ran right out to join her.

"Everyone is home early," she said in her sweet voice. "Is anything wrong?"

I sighed. "Plenty. Lots of bad things happened today." And then I filled her in on the details.

The Princess' green eyes went even wider than ever. "Poor Gracie! She's been through so much."

I nodded. "She sure has. And it really upset her a lot. But

now she's trying to do something about her situation. She always tries so hard to make things better."

The Princess smiled. "We couldn't have a better human sister. And I think I know just the thing to help her out. Gracie needs to host a party. A good, old-fashioned party. One where everyone has to make conversation."

"I think Gracie would like that," I told her. "She's had parties before."

The Princess nodded and stepped into Gracie's room. "I can take it from here, Buckley. When Gracie turns her back, I'll just type in my own Internet search. Then she'll end up reading about the kind of party she should host."

I nodded. "That sounds like a really good idea."

Just the thought of it made me smile. The Princess always knew what to do when it came to things like that.

"Mitzi is looking for you," she added. "She's been absolutely dying for you to get home. She wants to show you what she learned today."

Right away I was concerned. "Did she do okay?"

The Princess' eyes sparkled. "Mitzi did *very* well. She is a natural when it comes to cat karate. *Real* cat karate, that is."

This I had to see for myself. So I said good-bye and made a beeline for the guest room. Much to my surprise, I barely even recognized the place when I strolled in. Little pillows were scattered all over and long twigs had been pulled out of our Mom's dried flower arrangement. And a whole lot of those twigs looked like they had been snapped in half.

Bogey was leaning against the doorframe, while Lil and Trixie stood on either side of little Mitzi.

Mitzi's eyes went wide when she spotted me. She immediately sat back on her haunches, put her front paws together like she was praying, and bowed. "*Oooss*," she said to me.

I wasn't exactly sure what I was supposed to say to that. And I sure didn't know what it meant. Plus, I could hardly believe this was the same out-of-control kitten I'd been dealing with for days. She acted so calm and in control.

But a split second later, she glanced up with a wild gleam in her eyes. "Do you want to see, Buckley? Do you want to see?" And like someone had flipped on a switch, she started to bounce around again. "I did *soooo* good today! Watch me do my cat karate!"

Trixie stood in front of her. "Settle down, young one, and show us what you have learned." She sat back and used her front paws to hold a twig firmly before her.

"Yes, Teacher," Mitzi said, becoming serious again.

Then Mitzi took a deep breath and made a very sudden kick. A lightning fast kick. I heard the twig make a loud *snap!* And the next thing I knew, Trixie was holding a twig that was now in two pieces. I could hardly believe my eyes.

"Buckley, did you see me break the stick?" Mitzi meowed excitedly.

"Umm . . . yes," I told her. Though to be honest, the whole thing was such a blur that I didn't actually see Mitzi's foot even touch the stick. It had all happened so fast.

After that, she did some really quick punching moves with her front paws. And finally, she jumped up, turned a circle in the air and kicked high at the same time. Really, really fast. Scary fast.

She finished it all off with the same bow and by saying, "*Oooss.*"

Right about then, I'm pretty sure my chin practically hit the floor. I had to say, it sure didn't take Mitzi very long to learn all that! And well, I sure wouldn't want to be on the other end of all that kicking and punching.

She glanced up at me with a huge smile on her face. "How did I do, Buckley? Did I do good? Did I?"

For some reason, I couldn't speak for a second or two, so I just nodded and nodded. I finally managed to say, "You did great, Mitzi. You did really, *really* great. I can tell you worked hard on this all day. I am very proud of you."

Bogey grinned at Mitzi. "That's some pretty fancy footwork there, Short-stuff."

"She's a very talented student," Trixie added with a big smile. "But I think we've had enough for one day."

Bogey nodded to Lil and Trixie. "In that case, we'd like to borrow Short-stuff here. We need her to come with us to Mrs. Bumble's place and show us the lay of the land."

I crinkled my brow. "Plus, we'll need a plan to get outside."

Bogey grinned. "Already got it covered, kid. Our Mom was

supposed to get a big package delivered to the store today. But I got on the computer and had it rerouted to our house. It'll be the perfect cover for us to sneak out."

"Oh, umm . . . sounds like a good plan," I said with a nod before I turned to Mitzi. "Okay, little one, you stick with me. We'll have to hide near the front door and wait until our Mom opens it. But we can't run out too soon or we'll be spotted. So we'll have to be very patient. Do you think you can wait with me?"

For a moment, I thought she was going to say that "*Oooss*" word again. But instead, she just nodded her head. Really fast. "I can do it, Buckley. I know how to wait. Just like you taught me last night." Then she bowed.

"We'll have to be on our paws," Bogey said. "One misstep and we could get stepped on. Or worse yet, not even make it out the door."

I nodded and looked back at Mitzi. "So stick really close to me, okay? And you'll have to run as fast as you can when we finally zoom outside."

Before she could answer, we heard the rumble of the delivery truck as it came up the street.

"That's our cue," Bogey hollered before he flew out into the hallway. "It's show time!"

So Mitzi and I raced after him, doing our best to keep up. We all got to the front door only seconds after our Mom did.

She pulled the door open and sort of gasped in surprise. "Hello, Chester. I thought you would be taking this to my store."

Bogey hid behind the potted plant. And I motioned for Mitzi to hide with me just inside our Mom's office.

"Can we go now?" she whispered.

"Not yet," I whispered back. "Wait till I say go."

The deliveryman rolled a crate on a cart up to the door, blocking our escape route. "Well, I don't understand it myself, Mrs. Abernathy. It's addressed to your store and that's where I thought I was supposed to take it. But I got a last minute notice that said the delivery address had been changed. And I was told to bring it to your house instead."

"I wonder how that happened," our Mom replied.

"Beats me," Chester said. "What would you like me to do

with it?"

"Well, I think you'd better take it down to the store," our Mom told him. "It's too heavy for me to haul down there myself. And it won't fit in my car."

The man shrugged his shoulders. "As you wish. I'm still not sure how things got so messed up." He turned and started to roll the huge box away with him.

And that's when Bogey signaled to me.

Then I whispered to Mitzi, "Let's go! Follow me!"

Bogey darted a glance back at us before he raced for the door. I fell in line right behind him with little Mitzi bringing up the rear. One by one, we slipped through the opening between the box and the doorway, just as the deliveryman moved the crate down the porch to the stairs. Our Mom walked with him and helped him to steady the big box.

And neither one of them had seen us at all.

While they went straight, we took a right turn and ran to the edge of the porch. Then we jumped into the yard below. And the next thing I knew, we were running along the front of the house. We stayed close to the bushes and out of sight. Seconds later, we were on our way to Mrs. Bumble's house just a couple of doors down.

All in search of a clue about our latest clue.

Holy Catnip!

CHAPTER 14

Holy Mackerel!

Just as soon as we reached the edge of Mrs. Bumble's yard, I stopped and turned to Mitzi.

"Good job!" I told her. "You waited for me to say go!"

She smiled and started to dance around. But then she quickly stopped. And I knew it probably wasn't easy for her to control herself. But she was learning, that much I could tell. Plus she was trying extra hard.

Bogey paused just ahead of us. "I agree with Buckley, Short-stuff. You handled yourself like a pro back there. Now we need you to show us around the Bumble place. Think you can do that?"

She smiled and nodded really fast. "Uh-huh. I can do that."

Then we all glanced up at the mansion where Mrs. Bumble lived. Her house was probably just as old as our house was. But hers looked like it needed some paint and a little fixing up in spots.

Bogey squinted as he looked from one end of the place to the other. "Let's start in the backyard and go from there."

My mouth fell open wide. "Wait a minute. The backyard? Isn't that where the bees are?"

Mitzi nodded. "Uh-huh. That's where Mrs. Bumble keeps the bee houses."

I gulped. "Don't bees sting?"

Mitzi's eyes went wide. "Oh, yeah! They sting, all right. Especially if you chase them and catch them."

"I'm not sure this is such a good idea," I said as I glanced behind me, in the direction of our house. Our nice, safe, cozy, happy house. Our house that I wouldn't mind returning to at any moment. Especially since I usually tried really hard to stay away from anything that wanted to sting me.

Bogey licked his paw and held it up to check the direction of the wind. "It's gotta be done, kid. We've gotta follow that last clue and get to the bottom of this case."

All of a sudden, my heart started to pound. "But we might be walking into a big, giant trap. For *real* this time. A trap where we could all get stung."

Bogey shook his head. "Not to worry, kid. Just like us, bees have an important job to do. They're busy, and we're not going to bother them. Or chase them like Mitzi here did. They'll only put up their dukes if they think someone is after them. Or their home."

I crinkled my brow. "Put up their dukes? Bees have dukes?"

Whatever *dukes* were.

"Just an expression, kid. It means they'll fight. In the case of bees, if you hit one or two, the rest might swarm and attack. So as long as we don't swat at 'em, they won't think we're a threat. And if we leave them alone, they'll probably leave us alone."

Probably? To tell you the truth, I sure didn't like the sound of that. But what could I do? Bogey was already motioning for us to move on. And little Mitzi was raring to go. How would it look if I acted like a scaredy-cat and held back?

That meant I had to go on. Like it or not. And I had to make it look like I wasn't scared one bit. So I took a deep breath and put one paw in front of the other. As fast as I could go. Then I kept up with Bogey and Mitzi as we all ran toward the house. Once we got closer, Mitzi directed us down the driveway and past the garage.

She pointed to a big hole in the fence. "That's how I got in. The first time I came here."

"Thanks for the directions, Short-stuff," Bogey told her.

He ducked through the hole, Mitzi followed, and I was the last to go through. We all came out in the backyard not far from a big tree.

A big tree with lots of flowers.

But those weren't the only flowers in that yard. Oh, no! I glanced around and saw lots more flowers. Lots and lots more flowers. Everywhere. There were shrubs with flowers, and vines with flowers, and regular flowers growing in the gardens. There were pots with flowers and even more trees with flowers hanging from them.

And as near as I could tell, all those flowers had bees on them.

Buzzing, buzzing, buzzing bees.

In fact, the whole place seemed to be buzzing. Loudly.

But the loudest noise of all came from the bee houses that were smack dab in the middle of the big yard. I sort of gasped when I saw them, but I could barely even hear myself over all that buzzing.

Right away, I looked around to find a hiding place from those bees. Just in case we needed one.

And that's when I glanced up at Mrs. Bumble's house and saw a whole bunch of cats on the screened-in porch. I guessed they were Mrs. Bumble's foster cats — the cats she took care of until she found forever homes for them. Well, I had a pretty good idea what those cats were going through, since there was a time when I didn't have my forever home or family, either. So I sure hoped those foster cats ended up with real homes soon. Because it was awfully sad for a cat not to have a home. Not to mention, it was pretty sad when *humans* didn't have a cat in their home, either.

I gave the cats a wave, just to say hello. And to cheer them up. Most of them were out sunning themselves and didn't even notice me. But a few of them were sitting on their haunches and suddenly started to wave. Frantically.

"Help!" I heard a couple of the cats meow. "Please save her!"

Save her? Who exactly did they want me to save?

I crinkled my brow and looked in the direction they were pointing. And sure enough, there was a tiny kitten hunched down close to the ground, right below the bee houses. She was about the same size as Mitzi and had the same colors. Only her colors were in different places than Mitzi's. Her whole face was white, with orange and black marks at the top of her head that looked sort of like bangs.

But mostly she just looked really, really scared.

And for a *very* good reason!

Because the bees were starting to circle around her, and she was busy trying to swat them away. As near as I could tell, she was crouched down just as low as she could go. And she was sitting right next to a clear glass jar with a shiny black lid.

Holy Catnip!

It was the same kind of jar that we'd found on our porch and at the jewelry store. I could see this jar had something in it, too, though I couldn't tell *what* for sure. From where I stood, the most I could see were some little red-brown things.

But the clue wasn't nearly as important as the safety of that kitten!

"Look!" I hollered to Bogey. "Over there! That poor little kitten is surrounded!"

Bogey sprang to attention. "Those bees are about to swarm her. She doesn't stand a chance."

"She doesn't stand a chance?" I repeated, right before I realized what he was really saying. And let me tell you, what he was saying wasn't good.

"We've got to save her!" I shouted.

"You got that right, kid!" Bogey hollered back.

Just then, Mitzi started her mewing sound. And she began to dance around. Though this time her dancing wasn't an excited kind of dancing. Instead, it was a *scared* kind of dancing.

"That's Magnolia Belle! She's my friend," Mitzi cried out. "We've got to save her! Those bees will get her!"

"We'll save her, Mitzi!" I told her. "Don't you worry."

"I'm going in!" Mitzi hollered. "I've got to save Magnolia! Right now!"

And the next thing I knew, Mitzi tried to take a big leap toward her friend. Thank goodness I caught her and held her back.

"Oh no you don't," I said. "You stay right here. We have to come up with a plan before we go in."

"But those bees will hurt her!" Mitzi cried.

"That's why we've gotta do this right, Short-stuff," Bogey told her. "And you're no help unless you can be a team player. Can you follow orders?"

Tears rolled down her little cheeks and she swallowed hard. "Um . . . okay. I can."

"Good," Bogey said firmly. "Now here's the game plan. I'm the fastest, so I'll run in, distract those bees, and get them to chase me." Then he arched a brow in my direction. "As soon as the swarm is after me, kid, you zoom on in. Grab the kitten and bat that clue toward Short-stuff here."

"Aye, aye," I told him with a salute. A salute that finally went where it was supposed to go.

Now Bogey looked right at Mitzi. "Short-stuff, you stay here and . . ."

"But Bogey, she's my friend . . ." Mitzi started to protest.

Bogey shot her a stern look. "That's why you've got to follow orders. So we can save her. Now, you stay here and get the little jar when Buckley bats it to you. Do whatever it takes to push that thing to the other side of the fence. And wait there for us."

"Okay, Bogey." She saluted him, too. Properly.

He returned his attention to me. "When you get the kitten, kid, run all out to the fence. Push the kitten through the hole and get yourself out, too. Make sure Mitzi and Magnolia are both on the other side."

All of a sudden, I could barely breathe. "But what about you? Those bees could get you, too."

Bogey just grinned. "Don't worry about me, kid. If everyone sticks to their job, we'll be fine."

He glanced back at the kitten and the growing cloud of bees above her. They were obviously ready to strike at any moment. She cowered closer to the jar, like she was hoping it might protect her.

But I knew it couldn't, and I guessed she probably did, too.

Bogey stood up and flexed his back legs. "Okay, folks, this is gonna go fast. Everyone ready?"

"Ready!" I shouted.

"Me, too!" Mitzi hollered.

"Then let's get the job done," Bogey commanded before he

took off running.

And the next thing I knew, he flew right straight at those bees. And I do mean flew! He zoomed by so fast that it seemed to confuse them all for a moment or two. Then he made another pass and they spotted him. In a split second, that whole big swarm went flying off after him. But they were no match for his speed. Even though they were flying as fast as they could, they couldn't catch him.

And on they went. With Bogey running ahead and that whole swarm chasing after him.

The last I saw, Bogey and the bees were headed for the back corner of the yard. And that's when my heart really started to pound. Because I knew he'd get boxed in if he went to that corner. And if he tried to jump the fence, he'd run straight into the whole swarm. That meant there was no place for him to hide.

Now I felt just like Mitzi must have felt, when she wanted to race in and rescue her friend. But I knew I had to follow orders, too. Just like we'd told Mitzi to follow orders. Because I had a job of my own to do. So I took off running just as fast as I could go, until I reached the kitten. I grabbed her with one arm and batted the little jar with the other. I was so worked up that I didn't even know my own strength. I hit that jar with so much force that I almost shot it clear to the hole in the fence. If I had been playing hockey, well, I would have hit the puck smack dab into the middle of the goal.

Mitzi's eyes even went wide as the little jar flew right past her. But she was up and on it in a flash. She pushed the jar over on its side, and then she used her head and front paws to roll it through the opening. I was pretty happy that she'd followed orders. Especially since I knew it took a lot for her to do that.

Now I just needed one more kitten to cooperate. And I knew it wasn't going to be easy. Because, if Magnolia had been scared before, well, it was nothing compared to how she was acting right now. Funny, but she didn't even seem worried about the bees anymore. Instead, she looked more scared of me. Judging by the way her eyes were wide and she was shaking all over.

So I knew I had to convince her to go along with our plan.

If I was going to have any hope of saving her.

"Don't be scared, Magnolia," I said quickly. "My name is Buckley and I'm a cat detective. I'm here to save you. Your friend is just on the other side of that fence. I know what it's like to be scared, but I want you to be very, very brave. Just for a little while. Can you do that?"

Without saying a word, she nodded her tiny chin.

"Okay, here we go!" I said with the best smile I could come up with at the moment. "I want you to ride on my back like you're riding a horse."

She gasped right before I practically tossed her up on my back. "Hang on tight, Magnolia!" I hollered to her. "Whatever you do, don't let go!"

"I will, Buckley," she cried. "I will!"

Then I took off just as the buzzing sound got louder again. And I aimed straight for that hole in the fence. I glanced back for a moment to see that Bogey had made an S-turn and completely fooled the whole swarm. Those bees were flying right into each other and they didn't seem to know which way to go.

Then Bogey straightened out and ran full out toward the opening in the fence. The bees recovered quickly and started to chase him. All the while, I raced right for that fence, too. And straight for the opening. I could feel Magnolia on my back, clinging to me for dear life.

Suddenly Mitzi popped her little head into the opening of the fence. "Hang on, Magnolia!! You're almost here!" Then she got out of the way as I zoomed on through and practically skidded to a stop.

Bogey was right behind me, in my dust. He came through that opening in a streak of black. At the same time, he batted the little jar and sent it flying up the driveway, toward the street.

"Keep running," Bogey told us.

Thankfully, Mitzi took off after him, and I ran in the rear with Magnolia still on my back. Behind me, I could hear bees going *whump, whump, whump* as they hit the fence. Obviously Bogey had confused them again, and they probably didn't even see the opening near the ground. Plus, that hole would have been way too small for their entire swarm to fly through at once. Though a few bees did come buzzing up over the top. But they quickly gave up and turned back by the time we made it to the front of the neighbor's house. We hugged the wall for protection, and Bogey batted that little jar the whole way.

Finally, we stopped to let little Magnolia off my back. She was still shaking as she touched the ground.

"Whew!" I told my brother. "That was a close one."

"All in a day's work," Bogey said with a grin.

Mitzi cuddled right up to her friend. "You're coming home with us, Magnolia. And I'll explain everything when we get there."

Magnolia just bit her lip and nodded, and I could tell she was still pretty shook-up.

I glanced at my brother. "But first we have to get *back* inside our house."

Bogey nodded toward our driveway. "Not a problem, kid. But we'd better hurry. Because I see our Dad driving up the street. And last I heard, he was bringing pizza home for dinner."

"And pizza comes in a very big box," I added. "A really wide, flat box."

Which meant he would walk in without even being able to see his feet. That made it the perfect time for us to sneak back inside.

So we took off running again. Right after I put Magnolia back in the saddle, so to speak. Bogey managed to keep our clue jar rolling while Mitzi ran beside us. In a matter of minutes, there we were — sneaking back into our house at the feet of our very tired Dad. Of course, he held the door open a little bit longer than usual. Since he was carrying his computer case and holding that big box in front of him. I had to say, it took some doing for him to get it all through the door. But it gave us plenty of time to sneak inside. Our Dad didn't even know we'd come in with him. And he sure didn't see me give the little clue jar a final push through the kitchen door. It helped, too, that our Mom wasn't in the kitchen right at that moment.

Especially since we'd just brought a new kitten home with us.

Then as our Dad headed for the kitchen, I slid the little jar into the family room. I hid it safely back in the corner by the couch.

Bogey touched Mitzi on the shoulder. "Take your pal up to the sunroom, Short-stuff. Find the Princess. She'll know what to do."

Mitzi saluted him, and the two calico kittens were off and running.

And that's when Bogey and I finally had a chance to investigate our latest clue. I turned the lid to unscrew it, and then I dropped it to the floor.

Right away, the scent of the clue hit me even before I had a chance to look at it. And my mouth began to water when I finally got a good glance inside that jar. I could hardly believe my eyes.

"Are those what I think they are?" I kind of murmured.

Bogey's brows shot up. "I'd say so, kid. Sure smells like it."

I crinkled my own brows. "Why would somebody put those in a jar for us to find?"

"Beats me, kid. But whoever did this knew what they were doing."

I glanced up at my brother. "Why do you say that?"

"Because these are some of the finest cat treats I've ever smelled."

And if anyone would know, it was Bogey.

I took a good whiff myself and I had to agree. These cat treats were top-of-the-line. No doubt about it. Now the question was, what were they doing inside that little jar? And why were they in Mrs. Bumble's backyard?

Funny, but it seemed like the more clues we found, the more questions we had.

And this case was just getting more complicated by the minute!

Holy Catnip!

CHAPTER 15

Holy Mackerel!

There we were, just enjoying the scent of those high-end cat treats. Someone had put ten of them in the jar, and I have to say, I have never smelled anything so delicious in my whole life. But if I thought they *smelled* good, well, let me tell you, that was nothing compared to how they *tasted*! Of course, Bogey and I had no choice but to sample a few of the treats. For the sake of solving the case, naturally. As cat detectives, it was always important for us to do a thorough investigation.

Okay, maybe we didn't *really* have to sample some treats, but gee, a guy's gotta have a few perks on the job. Doesn't he?

Anyway, those treats were so scrumptious I could hardly stand it.

And I couldn't help but smile. "Mmmm . . . Bogey. What is that flavor? I don't think I've ever tasted anything like it."

Bogey's eyes took on a dreamy, faraway look. "It's been a long time, kid, since I've had something like this. It's probably goose liver and caviar. And you can bet these treats cost a pretty penny."

"I guess this is supposed to be our next clue," I murmured. "Because it's in the same kind of jar as the others. Though why someone would leave cat treats as a clue, I have no idea." I put the lid back on the jar and pushed it behind the couch.

For a moment or two, Bogey just stared at that jar, like he

was in a daze. I could tell he really wanted another one of those extra delicious treats. But I'm sure he knew better than to eat our whole clue. So he just took a deep breath . . . and then another . . . before he finally looked away from the jar.

Then he blinked a couple of times. "Okay, kid, back to business. Whoever put those treats near that bee house knew it was a bad spot. Especially for a cat."

I was already nodding. "Because any cat would swat at those bees. And when you swat at a few of them, it makes the whole bunch mad. That's when the swarm attacked. We sure found that out."

"Yup, kid. But that little kitten didn't know any better. And she was too scared to move by the time the bees started to circle. We got there just in the nick of time. Otherwise, she would've been a goner."

I'm sure my eyes went pretty wide right about then. "But who would want to hurt a little kitten?"

Bogey shook his head. "Only a real rotten-to-the-core kind of person would set up a trap like that. And as traps go, that was a bad one."

That's when I gulped. "And when you think about it, that trap was probably set for . . ." Suddenly, my tongue seemed to be tied up in knots, and I couldn't get the rest of my words out.

So Bogey took care of that for me. "For us, kid. Someone set that trap for us."

My heart started to pound just thinking about it. "I wonder if they'll try to do something else like that. Or leave us any *more* clues."

Bogey furrowed his brow. "I don't know, kid. Might depend on *why* the person is doing all this. They may not know we survived the last round. Then again, maybe they do. Though one thing's for sure, I don't like this little game they're playing."

That made two of us. "So maybe we should stop playing it."

Bogey sighed. "Nice idea, kid. But it seems our crook just upped the ante. And it's getting ugly. You know what would've happened to that kitten if we had stayed home."

Well, I had a pretty good idea. Especially after being so close to that loud, buzzing swarm.

"Maybe Magnolia saw something," I suggested. "Maybe we should talk to her."

"Good idea, kid," Bogey said with a nod. "Let's run up and see what she knows. Because this last clue has got me stumped."

I looked at the little jar cross-eyed. "Funny, but even with all the clues we've already gotten, we don't have a *clue* where to go *next*."

Bogey nodded. "Don't I know it, kid. Don't I know it."

Then without another word, we trotted from the family room and through the kitchen, where our human family was eating dinner. And I hesitated for a moment when I heard Gracie explain something to our Mom and Dad. I could hardly believe how excited she sounded. Let me tell you, it sure made me happy to know that she was happy. Especially after the bad day she'd had.

"It's going to be the best party ever," she gushed. "A no-cell-phone party."

Our Mom smiled at her. "A no-cell-phone party. What a wonderful idea! Sounds like you figured out a way to solve your problem."

Gracie smiled back. "Well, it was the funniest thing. Lexie hopped up on my desk while I was doing some research. She walked across the keyboard and accidentally hit some of the keys. And the next thing I knew, this party idea popped up on the screen."

"That was fortunate," our Dad chimed in.

Gracie giggled. "If I didn't know better, I'd say little Lexie typed that in on purpose."

Our Mom and Dad laughed. But Bogey just arched an eyebrow in my direction and grinned.

Because we both knew the truth.

"I'm going to make cupcakes in the morning," Gracie went on. "And when everyone gets here, we're going to play a game to get people talking. It's called an 'icebreaker game.' But I don't know why they call it that. There isn't any ice involved with it at all."

Our Mom wiped her mouth with her napkin. "An icebreaker game just means that you're 'breaking the ice.' It's an expression for getting a group warmed up and talking to each other."

"Oh, that makes sense," Gracie said and took a bite of her pizza.

Now I grinned at my brother. It turned out I wasn't the only one who didn't know what some expressions meant.

"Anyway," Gracie went on, "I already sent out emails to everyone and they're all coming. Then I sent them a second email and asked them to tell me two interesting things about themselves. Something the others probably don't know about them."

"Will you use this in your icebreaker?" our Mom asked.

Gracie smiled. "Uh-huh. I'm going to put all the stuff together in a list. But I'm going to leave the names off, so nobody will know who is connected to which items. And when the party starts, everyone has to go from person to person and guess which items on the list belong to each other."

"Sounds like a lot of fun, Gracie," our Dad added. "You've always hosted great parties. Your friends are lucky kids."

Boy, he could sure say that again!

I was so proud of Gracie. Here she'd had problems with using her cell phone too much. And she didn't like that her friends didn't talk much anymore. But she figured out a way to stay off her cell phone *and* get her friends talking again. She was so smart and so sweet. Us cats were lucky to have her as our human sister.

I gave her a quick rub around the legs before Bogey and I left the kitchen. Then we raced right for the stairs and took the steps two at a time.

"We'll have to run security for Gracie's party, kid," Bogey said on the way up. "Maybe Lil and Trixie would lend us a paw. It wouldn't hurt to have some extra paws on board."

"What about Mitzi and Magnolia?" I suggested. "Maybe they could help, too."

"Nice idea, kid. Maybe when they're a little older. But you know how kids are around kittens. They'll be gushing all over that pair and forget to play Gracie's game."

I nodded just as we reached the upstairs landing. "That's probably true. And Gracie will have her hands full already. It won't be easy to get all her friends to give up their cell phones for a while."

"You got that right, kid. Could be dicey," Bogey added as we ran down the hallway.

We turned into the sunroom, and right away, we spotted all the other cats in the house. Mitzi, Trixie, Magnolia, Lil, the Princess, and Miss Mokie. Of course, we paid the proper respect to Miss Mokie the very second we entered the room. Then we joined the rest of the group.

Or maybe I should say, "the party." Because that's exactly what it looked like the moment we walked in. Even Miss Mokie seemed to be enjoying herself.

She sat up straight on her purple velvet couch. "My, what a delightful group we have gathered here this evening." Then she leaned forward, stretched out her legs, and started to purr. Something I hadn't heard her do in a long time.

Lil and the Princess were both smiling, and Trixie grinned, too, as she towered over everybody. Including me. I couldn't believe how much better she looked already, even though it hadn't been long since we'd rescued her. It even seemed like she'd put on a little weight, but it also seemed like a weight had been lifted off her shoulders. It was so good to see her doing so well.

When I thought about it, I could hardly believe that we'd been through two rescues in just a few days. First Trixie and then Magnolia. And it was the only thing anyone wanted to talk about tonight. Sure, at the time it had been really scary, but now it all seemed kind of fun and exciting. Especially now that everyone was safe and sound.

And as near as I could tell, Mitzi and Magnolia weren't fazed by it at all. They were playing and laughing and just having fun. I was amazed by how much they looked alike, and at the same time, how different they were. They were both tiny and probably about the same age. And they were both calico cats with the exact same colors in their fur. But that was as far as it went.

Because the weird thing was, those colors weren't in the *same* places on both girls. Magnolia's face was mostly white while Mitzi had an orange nose and a black mustache. Mitzi also had orange across her shoulders, and black and orange swirls on her back. But Magnolia was covered with big splotches of orange and black that mostly went down her back.

It was like someone had taken a big paintbrush, dipped it in paint, and then dropped it on those kittens just any old place.

Funny, but when I thought about it, Trixie had the same colors, too. Colors that looked like they had been painted on.

I was amazed at how well the three girls had made themselves at home, even though I knew our house was only a pit stop for them. Since Trixie and Mitzi were both foster cats, I figured Magnolia must be, too. Just as soon as our Mom and Dad realized we had another calico living with us, that is. I only hoped all three girls would end up together in the same forever home. Because they sure made a happy bunch.

Though at that moment, Mitzi appeared to be the star of the show. She was busy showing off her new cat karate moves. She kept on jumping high into the air and spinning in tight circles. Then she did some fast kicks with her tiny feet — all before she landed again.

She paused for a moment and turned to her friend. "Now you can take cat karate lessons with me, Magnolia! And you can take lessons from Buckley with me, too. He's teaching me to be a cat detective. Wouldn't it be fun if you were a cat detective, too?"

Magnolia nodded really fast. "That *would* be fun! Lots of fun!"

I waved to get Mitzi's attention. "You did a really good job out there today. You followed orders just like you were supposed to. And you helped us save your friend."

"And get our latest clue," Bogey added with a grin.

Tears suddenly formed in Mitzi's eyes and she reached over to hug the other kitten. "I was so scared out there, Magnolia! I was afraid something really bad was going to happen to you. I didn't think I'd ever see you again."

"I was even more scared," Magnolia answered back in a sweet Southern accent.

The two girls hugged for a moment and I looked over to see Trixie fighting back tears. The Princess dabbed at her eyes with her paw and the Wise One gave them a queenly nod.

Then Mitzi broke away and pointed to me. "Buckley is the one who gave me my name, Magnolia."

The other kitten smiled. "It's such a pretty name. I never thought it was right that I got a name but the other cats didn't."

Mitzi pranced over to me. "Magnolia got her name when a lady found her under a Magnolia tree. And that lady brought her over to Mrs. Bumble's house to be one of the foster cats."

"The lady who dropped me off told Mrs. Bumble my name," Magnolia said as she joined Mitzi. "Later, I met my friend here when I was sitting in the screened-in porch. She was outside and couldn't get in. So I sneaked some food to her through a hole in the screen."

"So she wouldn't go hungry," Trixie murmured with a smile.

"That's right," Magnolia said. "Because Mitzi wasn't officially one of Mrs. Bumble's foster cats."

Mitzi shook her little head. "Mrs. Bumble didn't have any more room when she found me. So she brought me over here."

"But now we're together again," Magnolia said. "And I can't even thank y'all enough for saving me. Those bees were mean and they had me surrounded. I don't know what I would have done if you two hadn't rode in to the rescue."

I didn't even want to think about what might have happened.

But I did want to find out if she knew anything that might help us with our case. "Believe me, Magnolia, we're really happy we found you just in the nick of time. But how did you end up there in the first place?" I asked her. "Right by that jar?"

She sat back and looked up at me. "Well, I wanted to go outside and play. So I snuck out this morning when Mrs. Bumble left. And I had plenty of fun for a while. I played and played in the flowers and the grass. But then I got tired and fell asleep. I guess I slept for a long time."

Bogey raised an eyebrow. "I'll bet you were pretty hungry when you woke up."

She nodded her little head. "Uh-huh. I sure was. Really hungry. So I tried to figure out a way to get back inside the house to get some food. But all the doors and windows were shut up tight. Mrs. Bumble doesn't like to keep anything open because of the bees."

"Probably so they won't come into her house," I suggested.

"She's really careful about that," Magnolia went on.

"So were you in the backyard?" Bogey asked.

"Nope, I was in the front. But I wandered down the driveway to the garage. To see if Mrs. Bumble's car was there. But it wasn't. So then I decided to go through that hole in the fence and into the backyard. That's when I smelled those treats in that jar. They smelled so good that I could *even* smell them with the lid on. And I was so hungry . . ."

Bogey nodded, and I knew if anyone understood what it was like to be tempted by cat treats, well, it was him. "So you were willing to take a chance," he said. "And go near all those bees. Just to have some treats."

"*Uh-huuuh.*" She shuddered. "But I didn't know it was going to be so dangerous."

I shook my head. "It's not your fault. Nobody should've put cat treats out there in the first place. While you were outside today, did you see anyone near the house?"

She crinkled her tiny forehead. "Well . . . something woke me up when I was sleeping. I'm not sure, but I think somebody went by me. I sort of remember a big shadow going past."

Mitzi joined us. "Did you get a good look at that shadow, Magnolia?"

She shook her head. "Nope. I sure didn't. I'm so sorry I can't be more help."

I smiled at her. "It's okay. I'm just glad you're safe. And I'm glad you didn't get hurt."

"Me, too," the Princess said as she stood between the kittens and put an arm around them both. "And since you two want to be cat detectives, I'd be happy to give you a little lesson on diamonds tonight. Would you like that? We can start right after our human family has gone to sleep. I know a lot about gems."

Mitzi started to bounce around. "That sounds so cool! What do you say, Magnolia?"

Magnolia smiled. "Why, yes, ma'am," she drawled. "That would be swell!" And then she started to bounce around, too.

The Princess beamed at them both. "We'll have our lesson in the dining room. There's a little jar down there with some diamonds in it. It'll be perfect for teaching you all about them."

"Can't we do it now?" Mitzi sort of whined.

I shook my head. "Remember what we practiced? About being patient?"

Mitzi turned to Magnolia. "I've just got to show you the trick that Buckley taught me last night. It's about learning how to be patient. There's some treats behind a plant in the dining room. We can go down there and try it out. Right now."

And before I could say another word, they were off.

The Princess glanced at me with her big, green eyes. "Should we go help them, Buckley?"

She stared into my eyes and batted her lashes, and right away my insides went kind of mushy. Before I knew it, I found myself nodding my head yes. I have to say, I sure didn't understand it. I could manage to be big and brave and do things like save a kitten from a bunch of bees. A whole, huge swarm of bees. Yet when the Princess stared at me with her big, beautiful eyes, well, I couldn't even think straight. And I sure couldn't say no.

So the next thing I knew, the Princess and I were following those two girls down the stairs and to the front room. We used the same, exact trick that we'd used the night before to teach the little kittens about patience. Soon, Mitzi was getting so good at waiting that she even started to help Magnolia. Finally, they could both wait an entire minute before going after a treat.

We practiced clear until Gracie went to bed. That's when I asked Mitzi to hide Magnolia on a dining room chair under the table. And we kept her hidden while our Mom and Dad locked up the house for the night.

Along the way, our Mom reached down and picked me up. "Buckley, I could sure use a hug after today."

That made two of us. So naturally, I gave her a nice, big hug.

"I can't believe anyone would think that Gracie or I would rob a jewelry store, Buckley," she murmured. "Anyone who knows us knows we'd never do something so horrible."

Well, she sure had that right. I gave her a goodnight kiss on the nose and meowed to her. It was the first time I'd seen her laugh all day.

"You always know the right thing to say," she said as she

put me down again.

Then she gave me a rub around the ears before she turned
out the rest of the lights and headed for bed.

And that's when the Princess decided it was a good time to
teach Mitzi and Magnolia about diamonds.

So I helped her move that little clue jar out from behind the
potted plant. I used my big paws to unscrew the lid, and then I
tipped the jar on its side. So the diamonds all tumbled out. I
have to say, those diamonds were really sparkly. Even in the
little bit of light that came in from the porch light.

"My goodness, these are nice ones," the Princess said with
a smile. "I'll bet they even have serial numbers on the side."

Mitzi raised her paw to ask a question. "Diamonds have
numbers on them?"

The Princess nodded. "Some diamonds do. Especially
diamonds that are really valuable. But the numbers are so tiny
that even cats can't see them without a microscope."

Magnolia crinkled her brow. "If they're so small, then how
do they get the numbers on there?"

"Jewelers use a very special machine with a tiny laser
cutter," the Princess told her. "It's all done by computer."

Bogey joined us and let out a low whistle. "Those are some
pretty spiffy stones, all right."

The Princess moved them around with her small paw,
making them twinkle and sparkle even more.

That's when Bogey murmured to me. "Time for us to run
our rounds, kid. Let's leave the Princess and her students to
their gems."

So I said a quick good-bye before my brother and I took off.
We ran to the kitchen door in the back first and checked every
window along the way. By the time we returned to the front of
the house, the Princess was just finishing up her talk. Mitzi
and Magnolia were both batting the diamonds from one side to
the next. Giving them a really good going over. As near as I
could tell, the Princess had given them lots of good
information.

Not a one of them even glanced up as we trotted past and
headed for the front door. After we finished there, we planned
to check out the windows, too. Then we would race up the
stairs and run our surveillance on the second floor. Just like

we did every night.

Only tonight, we didn't get that far. Because I barely started to sniff the edges of the front door when I heard something.

Outside.

Right away, I froze in my tracks and every hair on my entire body stood at attention. Bogey must have heard it, too, because he stood perfectly still.

"Somebody's out there," I said just above a whisper as chills ran all over my body.

"Get the girls upstairs," Bogey murmured back.

I nodded and tiptoed into the dining room.

I must have looked pretty rattled because the Princess' eyes went wide when she saw me. And all I had to do was motion toward the stairs, and she knew just what I meant.

She put a paw to her lips to let the kittens know they should be quiet. Then she quickly scooted them out of the room and straight up the stairs. On tiptoes. How she managed to keep them quiet the whole way up, I'll never know. But for some reason, they sensed the danger and obeyed her. Just like we'd trained them to do.

In the meantime, I moved closer to the window in the dining room. I could hear someone moving around outside. And I could hear a little sliding noise. The same kind of sliding noise that one of those clue jars had made when I moved it across our front porch.

Was someone out there, leaving us another clue?

Whoever it was, they had no business being on our front porch at this time of night.

That's when it dawned on me. If I peeked out carefully between the blinds, I might just catch them in the act.

The thought of it sent my heart racing.

Because there was one thing we knew about the person who'd been leaving us clues — they were pretty nasty. Very nasty, you might say. And I wasn't exactly crazy about the idea of having nothing but a window between me and such an awful person.

Still, a cat detective has a job to do. And scared or not, I had to do it.

So I put one of my big paws on the edge of the wide,

wooden blind. And I pulled it down, just a little bit. Enough so I could see the front porch outside.

And when I glanced out, I could hardly believe my eyes.

Holy Catnip!

CHAPTER 16

Holy Mackerel!

There I was, staring out onto the front porch of our house. My heart was pounding so hard and so loud I was afraid the whole neighborhood would hear it. Because I was pretty sure I was about to catch our culprit in the act. Meaning, I thought I was finally going to see the person who'd been leaving us clues.

But instead, I saw something completely different. Or maybe I should say, *someone.*

"It's Hector," I told my brother.

Bogey rolled his eyes. "Hector?"

"And it looks like he's got his brother with him."

Bogey sounded surprised. "Hector brought Henry this time? What are they doing out there?"

I pulled the blind down a little farther. "Eating cat treats from a little jar. One that looks exactly like all the other little jars somebody left us."

"Black shiny lid?" Bogey asked.

"That's the one," I told him. "They got it off."

Bogey joined me at the window. "They're eating our next clue."

I nodded. "Don't I know it."

My brother batted his paw against the window and got Hector's attention. "Put a lid on it, Hector. We need those for evidence."

But Hector just shook his head and passed another treat to his brother. "No way. These are the best cat treats I've ever had in my life. I couldn't quit eating them if I wanted to."

That sure sounded like something Hector would say. In case you didn't know, Hector is the Siamese who lives across the street and down a few doors.

A Siamese cat who is a really big blabbermouth.

And not only is Hector a blabbermouth, but he's very, very nosy. If you've got a secret that you don't want anyone else to know about, well, don't tell Hector. Because he loves to find out any juicy gossip about anyone. And whenever Hector gets any juicy gossip on anyone, he quickly passes that on to *everyone*.

"Evidence for what?" Hector finally decided to ask when he came up for air. "Are you on a case, Buckley and Bogey? You can tell me. I won't tell anyone."

Now I rolled my eyes. "Fat chance, Hector. What are you doing here anyway?"

"We got locked out," he said between mouthfuls.

"Again?" came Bogey's reply.

Hector shook his head. "It wasn't my fault this time. Henry sneaked out when our Dad took out the trash. And if Henry gets out, that means I have to go, too. After all, Henry is deaf and he can't exactly hear if a car is coming. And he can't hear our Mom call his name. So I had to follow him. To make sure he got home okay."

Just then, Hector raised his paws and did sign language to Henry. Henry grinned and did sign language back. Henry was a good-sized cat with long white fur and blue eyes. He may have been deaf, but he was as good a guy as you could ever find. And since Henry had been adopted into the family, he'd turned Hector into a better cat.

I waved at Henry and caught his attention. He grinned and waved back. Then we did a little "signing" and he told me how delicious those treats were. He even said it was really thoughtful of us to leave them out on the porch for them.

Right about then, I sure didn't have the heart to tell him that we weren't the ones who'd left those treats. Though I did know exactly how delicious they were. Probably just as good as the ones we'd had earlier.

I could tell Bogey was dying for one of those treats, too.

"Did you leave any, Hector?" he asked through the window.

Hector shook his head. "There weren't very many. Maybe ten. But we left you the message inside."

Chills raced across my fur once again. Did he say message?

"Can you read it to us?" Bogey asked.

"Sure," Hector said as he pulled the paper out and unfolded it. "It says, 'St. Gertrude Cat Treat Factory. Gourmet cat treats. Best cat treats money can buy.'"

Well, let me tell you, I've lived my whole life in St. Gertrude and I've never even heard of any cat treat factory. I turned to my brother who had the strangest look on his face. If I had to describe it, I'd say he seemed sort of shocked and happy and a little annoyed. All at the same time.

Hector ate the last treat and wiped his mouth with his paw. "Say, Buckley and Bogey, can you get us back inside our house?"

Bogey rolled his eyes again. "Don't we always, Hector?"

Of course, I already knew the answer to that question. Because, yes, we always did help Hector get back into his house. Every single time he got himself locked out. Which was a lot.

So Bogey loped on into the office, got on the computer, and typed out a message. Then he used that message to call Hector's Mom and Dad. The message came through in a computer voice, saying, "Please let Hector and Henry back inside your house."

A few seconds later, I watched as the front door of Hector's house opened up. Hector's Dad was calling his name.

"Gotta run!" Hector said. "Thanks for the treats. Thanks for getting us back inside."

With that, he signed to his brother. Henry waved good-bye before the two of them took off. They raced across the street and ran into their house.

"Thanks for nothing," I said as I glanced at that empty treat jar.

Then I joined my brother in the office. "Did you know St. Gertrude had a cat treat factory?"

Bogey had already called up their webpage on the computer. "Looks like they're new, kid. Brand new. And you'll never believe who owns the company."

"Who?"

"Mr. Pennypacker."

That's when my breath got stuck right in my throat. When Bogey said I wouldn't believe it, well, he wasn't kidding. Because I was shocked.

In fact, I was so shocked that I stayed frozen to the spot for a minute or two. Right until I heard someone pounding on our front door. Pounding really, really hard.

"Is Hector back?" I asked my brother.

Bogey was already up and headed for the door. "Couldn't be. Hector can't pound that hard. It's gotta be a human out there."

That certainly made sense to me. Especially when the doorbell rang. And rang again. Whoever was out there sure wanted us to open the door.

Before Bogey and I could go and look out the front window, a light went on in our Mom and Dad's room. And the next thing I knew, they were coming down the stairs in their bathrobes.

"Who could that be?" our Mom kind of mumbled as she half-tripped on the last stair.

Our Dad caught her just in the nick of time. "Must be some kind of an emergency," he murmured. "For someone to be so frantic at our front door."

He took a couple of long strides and reached the door in record time. Then he peeked through the peephole and turned on the front hallway light.

"What in the world . . .?" he muttered before he opened the door.

That's when Garnet Gabinski jumped inside our house and practically flung herself into our Mom's arms. Garnet was wearing pajamas and a bathrobe, too. And she was crying so loud that the sound of her sobs practically filled our whole house.

"Oh, Abby," she wailed. "I feel horrible! Absolutely horrible! There I was, just lying in bed. And I couldn't sleep a wink! I felt so awful about the way I treated you and your daughter today. I never should have said the things I said. I don't know why I acted like that! This burglary has got me so upset that I'm not even myself. I just had to run over here and apologize. I couldn't wait another minute. I never meant to hurt you and Gracie."

"There, there," our Mom said as she patted Garnet on the back.

"Can you ever forgive me?" Garnet sobbed. "I'm so, so sorry!"

"Of course," Our Mom said.

"I said all that without even thinking," Garnet went on.

And on. Sobbing and wailing and making strange gurgling noises.

Our Mom glanced at our Dad and he just shrugged. Then he raised his eyebrows and looked at Garnet like she had just landed in a spaceship from outer space.

"Why don't you sit down and rest," our Mom went on. "I'll get you a drink of water and some tissues." She led Garnet into the dining room and held out a chair for her.

Garnet practically collapsed into the chair, still wailing. Then she put her head on the table and cried.

Our Dad cringed and turned on the light in the dining room. "I'll go get the water," he said to our Mom. "You stay here with Garnet."

So our Mom took the seat beside her and patted Garnet's hand. And Garnet kept on crying until our Dad came back with some tissues and a glass of water. She wiped her eyes and blew her nose with a loud *pbbllltt*!

Then after a few minutes, she finally calmed down a bit. She sniffled and blew her nose a few more times and stared right in front of her. And kept on staring. To the very spot where the Princess had been teaching the two kittens about diamonds.

"Wait a minute . . . what are those?" Garnet gasped and pointed to the diamonds that were still on the hardwood floor. They sparkled in the light.

Our Mom squinted and glanced in the direction of the stones. "I have no idea. Whatever they are, they're shiny. Must be something off one of Gracie's costumes. And I don't know what that little jar is doing there."

Garnet suddenly bolted upright and placed her hands firmly on our Mom's antique dining room table. "I know

exactly what they are. They're diamonds! Stolen diamonds!
And I have a pretty good idea where they came from — my
store. You and your daughter really did break in and steal my
stuff!"

"No, we did not," our Mom said calmly. "I'm sure those
aren't real. Probably just something the cats found and were
playing with."

"Those are real, all right! And I'll bet they're mine!" By
now, Garnet was shouting. "I'm calling the police! And I'm
calling them immediately! I can't believe you did this to me,
Abby. And to think, I was feeling so horrible, after I thought
I'd falsely accused you of robbing my store. When it turns out,
you really *did* rob my store!"

And with that, Garnet pulled her cell phone from the
pocket of her bathrobe and dialed nine-one-one.

Our Dad rolled his eyes. "My wife and daughter didn't
steal your stuff, Garnet. Let me prove it to you." He strolled
over to pick up the diamonds.

Whereby Garnet shrieked and pointed at him. "Don't you
touch a thing! Not till the police get here. I don't want you to
hide those stones or switch them out for something else."

Our Dad glared at her. "May I remind you that you are in
our home? And you barged in on us? In the middle of the
night. For all you know, those gems belong to us. They're
probably just something Gracie had laying around in her
jewelry box."

"We'll let the police pick them up, and I'll prove they're
mine," Garnet went on. "They'll all have serial numbers on
them. And I'll have records of them back at my store."

Our Mom shook her head and held her hands open wide.
"There must be a rational explanation for this. If we stole your
diamonds, would we really just leave them lying around on the
floor like that?"

"Maybe," Garnet sniffled. "After all, you probably never
imagined that I'd be coming over tonight. And there was so
much jewelry that was stolen, I'll bet you didn't even miss that
handful of diamonds over there. You probably just dropped
them and didn't even realize it."

Right at that moment, Bogey motioned for me to join him
on the stairs. "Best we keep a low profile right now, kid," he

meowed quietly.

"But don't you think we should do something?" I whispered to my brother.

Bogey shook his head but kept his eyes glued to Garnet. "Not much we can do right now, kid. It'll just make things worse if we jump in. It's best if we wait it out and come up with a game plan. Once we figure out what's really going on here."

Seconds later, Officer Phoebe arrived with another officer, a young man named Officer Peyton. They had barely walked in the door when Garnet started hollering and carrying on even worse than she had before. And let me tell you, Officer Phoebe had to work pretty hard to get Garnet to calm down enough to explain the situation. In the meantime, the other officer carefully picked up the stones with tweezers and dropped them into little plastic bags. He also took a few photographs of the place where they'd been found.

"I'll have these checked out," Officer Phoebe said grimly. "If the stones have serial numbers, we'll find them. Then we can compare them to your records, Garnet. Have you already filed your insurance claim?"

Garnet crossed her arms. "Yes, I did it this afternoon. Once the police were finished at my store. But if these diamonds have been found, I can take them off my claim. I never thought I'd ever see any of my jewelry ever again!"

Officer Phoebe turned to our Mom and Dad. "Any idea how those stones got there?"

Our Dad shrugged and our Mom shook her head.

"I haven't got a clue," our Mom said.

"Could Gracie have been playing with them . . .?" Officer Phoebe started to suggest, but quickly let her words die out.

"On the floor?" Our Mom said with a laugh. "I don't think so. Gracie was busy all afternoon on her computer, getting a party set up. I don't think she even set foot inside this room tonight. And we had dinner in the kitchen."

Now Garnet stomped her foot. "Arrest them! All of them!"

That's when Officer Phoebe turned to Officer Peyton. "Would you please escort Garnet off the Abernathy's property? And take her statement outside?"

The other officer nodded and took Garnet's arm. That's

when Garnet started sobbing and sobbing again.

Once she was gone, Officer Phoebe sighed and sat down with our Mom and Dad.

Our Mom rubbed her forehead. "I'm so sorry you had to come out in the middle of the night like this, Phoebe. I honestly don't know what's going on. Or how those diamonds got there. If they even are diamonds."

"Did anything strange happen today?" Officer Phoebe asked our Mom. "Anything out of the ordinary?" She pulled her little notepad from her pocket.

Our Mom sighed. "The whole day was filled with strange things. First, we had a gigantic crowd at the store today. I sold more antiques in one day than I've sold in weeks. So we definitely had our hands full."

Officer Phoebe jotted down a few notes. "Anything else?"

Our Mom was already nodding. "Well, you were there when Garnet came in and accused Gracie and me of robbing her store. She was just so out of control that she wasn't even making any sense. One minute she thought we had robbed her and the next minute she apologized. The whole thing upset poor Gracie so much that I had no choice but to bring her home early. I had to leave Millicent and Merryweather there by themselves. Not that they couldn't take care of things."

"They do a good job," Officer Phoebe said with a smile. "So then what happened?"

"A large package got delivered here by mistake," our Mom went on. "It should have gone to the store, but the driver said it was rerouted."

I glanced at my brother and he raised an eyebrow. After all, we knew the real story behind all that.

Officer Phoebe kept on writing. "Do you remember, Abby, did you lock the door after the driver had gone?"

Our Mom looked in the direction of the front door. "I don't know. I'm not sure."

"So anyone could have gotten in," Officer Phoebe suggested.

Our Mom's mouth fell open wide. "I suppose so."

Our Dad glanced at the floor where the diamonds had been. "And someone could have planted those stones right there."

Our Mom gasped at the idea. "But who would want to do something like that?"

Officer Phoebe shook her had. "I don't know, Abby. Though I do know that neither you nor Gracie could break into a jewelry store. Even so, I still have to investigate this and see what's going on. First I'll have to find out if those stones really are from Garnet's Jewelry Store. And if they are, then I'll have to figure out how they got into your house. I'm sure you know that I may have to question Gracie."

"As long as we're with her," our Dad said. "And quite frankly, I'd rather not tell Gracie just yet. Not until we find out if those stones are real. Because I don't want to upset her before we even know if there's a problem or not. As I understand it, all the drama today really shook her up."

Officer Phoebe nodded. "Absolutely. I couldn't agree more. We'll check out the stones first and go from there. I'll be in touch soon." Then she said good-bye and left for the night.

Once everyone had gone, our Dad put his arm around our Mom. "Don't worry, honey," he told her. "You and Gracie haven't done anything wrong, and it will all be okay. I'm sure Phoebe will get this straightened out soon."

Our Mom let out a big sigh, and I could tell she was really upset.

"I sure hope so, Mike," she murmured. "I sure hope so."

He gave her a kiss and walked her up the stairs. I knew how much our Dad wanted to protect our family.

Just like Bogey and I wanted to protect our family, too.

So we raced right back to the office the second they'd gone back to bed. And we got right to work on the case.

"Someone has raised the stakes, kid." Bogey grabbed the bag of cat treats that he kept hidden behind some books. "I don't like this. Not one bit." He pulled the bag open and passed out a round of treats.

"Somebody raised the stakes? Were they building a fence or something?" I munched on my treat and thought about what he'd said.

Bogey shook his head and practically inhaled a treat himself. "Just an expression, kid. Meaning, the situation just got a lot more risky. And dangerous. For us and our family."

He passed me a couple more treats and took some for himself.

I shivered. "You can say that again."

"We are being played, kid," he went on. "Whoever sent those diamonds is probably the same person who robbed Garnet's store."

I glanced at the ceiling for a moment as I ate my treat. "Wait a minute . . . didn't we get those diamonds before Garnet's store was robbed?"

"Yup, kid. So either those diamonds don't belong to Garnet, or Garnet was actually robbed twice. And didn't even know it. Could be someone stole those loose stones before they did the *big* robbery. Maybe they were doing a trial run before the real thing."

I gasped. "Wow, we're dealing with a really smart crook."

"You got that right, kid," Bogey said with a nod. "And now they might be trying to set up our family. To take the fall."

My mouth dropped open wide, because I sure didn't like the sound of that. "Take the fall?"

Bogey passed us each some more treats. "Go to jail, kid."

Right about then, I think my heart skipped a beat. Maybe even two. "That would be horrible! I don't want our Mom and Gracie to go to jail! What do we do now?"

Bogey shook his head. "I don't think we have much choice, kid. Like it or not, we've gotta go to that cat treat factory."

"We do?" I swallowed another treat.

"Yup, kid. We need to follow the clues. Because there's something pretty suspicious about that Mr. Pennypacker. And I'd like to know what he's got to do with all this."

I thought of the swarm of bees that almost got us today and my paws started to shake. "We might be walking into another bad setup. An even bigger trap," I sort of murmured.

"Don't I know it, kid. Don't I know it," Bogey said before he passed us each another round of treats. Then he stashed the bag of treats back into their hiding place. "It's a chance we'll have to take. To keep our family safe."

Deep down inside, I knew Bogey was right. We had to stop the person who was doing all this. Before they tried to hurt our family even more. Or tried to hurt some innocent cats like they'd done today. Still, I didn't exactly *like* the idea of going smack dab into another scary situation. A possible setup.

But when it came to protecting my family, there was nothing I wouldn't do. Even if it was scary.

Holy Catnip!

CHAPTER 17

Holy Mackerel!

That night, I was so nervous I could barely even sleep after Bogey and I ran our last surveillance round. I just kept on wondering what was going to happen when we went to the cat treat factory the next day. Thanks to our encounter with the bees, I wondered if we might be walking into a very big trap. Plus, I also wondered why we'd never heard of the St. Gertrude Cat Treat Factory before. And with all that *wondering*, it sure made it hard for a guy like me to get some shut-eye.

But I must have fallen asleep at some point. Because I woke up when the sun started to peek in through the windows. Much to my surprise, Bogey was already out of his bed and nowhere in sight.

A few minutes later, Gracie was up, too. She made a beeline for the kitchen and got right to work making her cupcakes. I watched her from my bed as she gathered all the ingredients and mixed everything in a bowl with some beaters. Then she poured the batter into cupcake pans that were lined with cupcake papers. After that, she popped the pans into the oven.

Then Gracie set the timer and smiled. I knew she had hosted lots of parties before. And there was something about getting ready for a party that always made her extra happy.

Though I didn't think she would have been so happy if

she'd heard the commotion Garnet had caused the night before. Right in our very own dining room. Thankfully, Gracie must have been so worn-out yesterday that she slept through the whole thing.

She glanced my way and her eyes went wide. "Buckley, you look pretty tired! Maybe you should just stay in bed for a while and get some sleep."

If only I could.

Our Mom and Dad didn't exactly look rested, either, when they finally made it down to the kitchen.

Gracie shook her head at them. "Am I the only one who got a good night's sleep last night?"

Our Mom wrapped her arms around Gracie and gave her a nice hug. "I smell cupcakes baking. You're getting really good at this."

"Thanks, Mom," Gracie said. "It's so much fun to make cupcakes. I love baking."

Our Mom yawned. "Do you need any help getting ready for your party?"

"Nope, Mom, I've got it covered," she said with excitement in her voice. "After I make my cupcakes, I'm going to decorate the living room a little bit. And I've got my game all ready to go. Plus, I've got a basket where everyone is supposed to leave their cell phones when they come in."

I had to say, I really hoped Gracie's party turned out to be terrific. And I sure hoped Officer Phoebe didn't have the answers about those diamonds until after the party was over. But most of all, I hoped Bogey and I *did* have some answers before the day was through. Answers that would help us put a stop to the person who had been leaving all these clues for us. Not to mention, causing big problems for our family and putting innocent kittens in danger.

I got up and stretched as our Mom filled our dishes with cat kibble. Then I grabbed a quick bite while she started to cook breakfast for the humans in the family. Once my belly was nice and full, I headed to the office. In search of my brother.

Along the way, I ran across the Princess. "Oh, Buckley," she moaned. "I heard what happened last night. And it's all my fault. I never should have left those diamonds out there. I should have put them away before we ran upstairs. I was just sure I'd have time to come back down and get them. Before any people were around." Her eyes were misty and she kept wringing her paws.

I shook my head. "It's not your fault, Princess. Someone set us up by putting those diamonds on our front porch in the first place. Now Bogey and I just need to figure out who's behind all this. To keep our family safe."

"Thank you, Buckley. You're so brave," she murmured as she stared at me with her big, green eyes. And she kept on staring. Finally, she gave me a quick hug and raced for the stairs.

Well, it was a good thing the Princess took off when she did, or I would have been in big trouble. Especially since the room had already started to spin, and I had to take a whole bunch of deep breaths so I didn't flop over. When I finally recovered a little, I blinked a few times and made a beeline for our home office. Bogey was just hopping down from our Mom's desk when I got there. For some reason, I had the idea that he might be upset after all that had happened the night before. Or I thought he might be tired. Or something.

Instead, he just greeted me with a big grin. "You ready to roll, kid? I've got the whole thing set up."

I'm sure my chin practically hit the hardwood floor. "You do?"

More than ever, I wished I could be like my big brother. Even when bad things happened, he was never too upset to do his job. He could always think about the case and stay focused, no matter what was going on around us.

He gave me a nod and glanced up at the front door. "Yup, kid. The doorbell will be our cue. When it rings, get ready to zoom outside. We'll hide on the porch until our ride gets here."

I blinked a few times. "Huh?"

He grinned again. "I ordered flowers. For Gracie," he explained.

Well, to tell you the truth, Bogey's explanation left a lot more *unexplained* than it left *explained*.

I tilted my ears in his direction. "So the flower delivery person is going to give us a ride to the cat treat factory?"

Bogey motioned to the front door. "Nope, kid. I've got something else arranged."

I crinkled my brow. "You do? How . . .? When . . .?"

"Just finished, kid. Did it all online and paid for it from my bank account."

"The one our Mom and Dad don't know about?" I asked him, though I already knew the answer.

Bogey grinned. "That's the one, kid. From the money I made doing cat food commercials. Long ago."

I glanced up the stairs. "Is Mitzi coming, too?"

Bogey shook his head. "She and her pal have cat karate lessons this morning. Then Lil, Trixie, and the kittens are going to run surveillance. Before Gracie's party. They'll hand the reins over to us when we get back. And then we'll handle security during the party."

Holy Catnip! Bogey sure had done a lot already this morning. And to think, the only thing I'd done so far was to get up and eat breakfast. Maybe I needed to do a better job as a cat detective. After all, how could I teach CDITs if I didn't step up to the plate myself? And take on a little more responsibility?

But I didn't have a single second to dwell on it. Because the doorbell rang, and that's when Bogey and I stood at attention. Ready to jump into action. Especially when we saw our Mom head to the door with her coffee cup in hand.

She peeked through the peephole and shook her head. "Well, once again, we have a surprise visitor at our front door. At least this one looks like a happy surprise." She pulled the door open, and we saw a blonde lady standing there with a vase full of pretty pink flowers.

"Delivery for Gracie Abernathy," the lady said.

Gracie joined them at the door. "For me? Nobody's ever sent me flowers before."

"Who are they from?" our Mom asked.

Gracie pulled off the little card that was attached to the flowers and read it out loud. "It says, 'From your friends. Looking forward to the party.'"

And that's when Bogey gave me the signal to run.

So we did. We slid smoothly past everyone's legs and took a sharp left turn. Then we hid on the front porch behind some chairs with big cushions.

We heard Gracie gush from inside the house. "Awww . . . that was really sweet of my friends to send me flowers."

"It certainly was," our Mom agreed.

"Somebody sure likes you a lot," the delivery lady said to Gracie. "Because this was a rush order. Whoever ordered these even paid extra to have them delivered right away. And I do mean, 'right away!'"

"That's so nice," Gracie said. "I'll be sure to put them out for my party."

And with that, the delivery lady said a quick good-bye and ran down the steps. She got in her car and took off.

I tilted my head at my brother. "Umm . . . so far so good. Now how do we get to the cat treat factory?"

"Drive-N-Dash, kid," Bogey said with a grin. "I ordered and paid for it over the Internet. They've got instructions on where to take us and when to pick us up."

"Huh?" I turned and watched the little blue car that was practically crawling up our street. "Drive-N-Dash?"

"Yup, kid. It's like a taxi. Only drivers use their own cars to take people around. That's how they make their money."

I felt my eyes go wide. "And I guess they drive cats around, too?"

Bogey shrugged. "Their website didn't say otherwise."

"So we don't know . . ." I started to say.

But Bogey interrupted me with, "Let's shake a leg, kid."

And I knew just what he meant. So we raced to the curb together. Then we sat up nice and tall as the car pulled up.

A young man got out and came to the passenger side of the car. He had long, silky brown hair and lots of earrings in his ears. He was wearing a shirt that looked like a whole bunch of paint bottles had exploded on it.

At first he glanced at our front door and then he looked down at us. "I have a pickup order for Buckley and Bogey."

Bogey grabbed the hem of the driver's long shorts and tugged.

The young man smiled. "What is it, little cat dude? Do you know who Buckley and Bogey are?"

We both responded by meowing at him. A bunch. Then Bogey reached up to the door handle on the front passenger side. I did the same, only on the back door.

The young man's eyes went wide.

Really, really wide.

"Dudes . . ." he sort of choked. "Are you . . . are you . . .?"

Bogey meowed again and reached up to give the young man a paw bump.

The driver gasped in amazement. "Did you just fist bump me, little cat dude? Seriously? Okay, okay . . . I'm cool with that. So I'm guessing you're Buckley and Bogey. And you ordered a Drive-N-Dash. Wow! I never had any cats order a Drive-N-Dash before. But hey, sure . . . I'll take you. I don't discriminate against Feline-Americans. Let me get the door for you. My name is Dave and I'll be your driver."

He opened both the front and back doors on the passenger side of his car.

"Which one of you cats is Bogey?" Dave asked.

Bogey gave him a nod and jumped in the front seat.

"Cool!" Dave said with a big smile. "So I guess the big dude is Buckley."

I purred up to him and then jumped into the backseat.

"Nice to meet you both," he told us.

Well, I had to say, it was nice to meet him, too. He buckled us in with seat belts before he shut the doors and got back in the driver's seat. Then he drove very carefully and talked to us the whole way to the cat treat factory. He even pointed out some historic landmarks and told us about how he was going to school to be an auto mechanic. All in all, I thought it was pretty interesting. Not to mention, it was a really nice service for us cats. Plus, it only took twenty minutes to get there. Then Dave opened our doors, unbuckled our seat belts, and let us out.

"Have a good time tasting all those cat treats, little dudes," he told us as we all stood in the parking lot. "I'll pick you up in an hour. Nice doing business with you."

Bogey and I each gave him paw bumps, and his eyes went even wider than before. "Dudes!" was the last thing he said before he got in his car and drove away.

After that, we joined a group of people who were carrying their cats into the front room of the cat treat factory. Once everyone was inside, the whole group stood in a half-circle, like they were waiting for something. Bogey and I hid behind the legs of a large man who was holding a couple of gray kittens.

"Bogey," I whispered. "What's going on?"

"Don't sweat it, kid. I signed us up for a tour of the factory. So we could get inside the main areas. With no questions asked."

Well, I could always count on Bogey to come up with a good plan. Though I sure wished I could come up with some good plans myself a little more often. But the truth was, Bogey was still the pro and I was still the rookie. No matter how much I learned about being a cat detective.

I glanced up as a lady came through some swinging metal doors and stood in front of our group. She had long, shiny silver hair and wore a shiny silver top. She welcomed our whole group and started to tell us all about the cat treat factory. She also pointed out big barrels full of cat treats. And bags and bags of cat treats on the shelves.

After that, she held one of the swinging doors wide open. Then the whole group went in to the giant room where they mixed and baked the treats.

And let me tell you, I could hardly believe my eyes. I glanced around and I was absolutely amazed by all the different kinds of treats that were being made. There were some on pans that had just come out of the oven and were ready to be put into bags. Then there were others that were still in the oven. But whether those treats were already cooked or just being cooked, their scent filled the air.

I've never smelled anything so wonderful before in my life. Not even when our Mom and Dad cooked a turkey on Thanksgiving Day. Because the whole big room was just filled with a huge cloud of delicious scents. It made my heart start to pound and my mouth start to water. Right before my stomach started to growl. It even kind of gave me the shivers. I smelled turkey and fish, and caviar and liver. All fresh. All being made that very day. The different smells were all mixed up together, making one big, heavenly scent. For a moment or two, I felt like I was floating on a sea of cat treats. Treats as far as the eye could see. I was surrounded by so many treats that I could never ever eat them all.

It even made me forget that we were on a case.

And that I was supposed to be investigating.

But I came right back down to earth when I spotted a little jar with a shiny black lid. Hidden right behind one of the huge mixing bowls. The beaters in that bowl were whirring around and around and around as they stirred cat treat batter. Almost like the beaters Gracie had used to mix her cupcakes. Only much, much bigger. Probably about forty times bigger. And faster.

And scarier.

Yet if we wanted to get to that clue, I knew we had to go right past that bowl with those big, gigantic spinning beaters. Just the thought of it made me start to shake in my paws.

I gulped and turned to my brother. To see if he had spotted the clue, too.

And that's when I saw something so shocking that I could hardly believe it. If I thought I'd been scared before, well, it was nothing compared to how I felt right at that moment. Because Bogey's eyes had taken on kind of a glazed look. And he seemed to have trouble breathing. In fact, he was kind of panting and gasping.

He finally managed to sputter, "*Sooooo* many cat treats, kid. So many, many, many treats . . . everywhere . . . all around us. Can't think straight, kid . . . eyes hazing over. Brain fogging up. Just *soooo* many treats . . ."

Then I saw his eyes start to roll and he began to wobble.

I'd never seen Bogey like this before.

Was he going to be okay?

Holy Catnip!

CHAPTER 18

Holy Mackerel!

There we were, at the St. Gertrude Cat Treat Factory, and we were practically surrounded by cat treats! And let me tell you, I was having a tough time concentrating with all those treats around. But Bogey was having an even harder time than I was.

He just kept babbling on and repeating things like, "*Soooo* many cat treats, kid." He wobbled when he walked and he drooled when he talked. And when he did talk, he didn't exactly make a lot of sense.

All the while, I was busy staring at the clue that I figured we were supposed to find. I could see the little jar with the shiny black lid on the other side of the room. It was just behind a gigantic mixing bowl that was turning around and around. With big, scary beaters whirling inside that bowl.

And if all that wasn't bad enough, well, things got even worse when the lady who ran the tour started to pass out samples. Because Bogey seemed to get even more muddled with every treat we tasted.

I waved one of my big paws before his eyes. "Umm . . . Bogey, do you think we should check out that clue?"

But it was like he didn't even see me. "Clue, kid? There's a clue? All I can see are cat treats." And then he went back to repeating, "Cat treats. *Soooo* many cat treats. Everywhere.

Can't think. Can't focus." He acted like he was in a trance.

And before long, I realized that Bogey was pretty much out of commission. I guess the sight and smell of all those cat treats was just more than he could take. Obviously he wasn't in any kind of condition to investigate our case. Let alone make full sentences.

That meant it was up to me to take the lead and make the decisions for us. For once, I had to be the one in charge. There was just no way around it.

I gulped at the thought. Especially since I was starting to worry that my brother might be in trouble. I knew I needed to get that clue and get us out of there. And fast.

"Lean on me," I told him. "And I'll stand you up next to a wall. Then I want you to stay put for a minute."

"Sure thing, kid," he managed to mumble.

He put his weight against me and I half-carried him to a corner. When we were just a few inches away, I leaned him against the wall. It was enough to keep him standing on his feet.

"I'll be right back," I told him. "I'm going in. After the clue."

"Be careful," was all he could manage to mutter. "Looks dangerous."

"Aye, aye," I told him.

Then for some reason, I stood up straight and saluted him. Perfectly. I was amazed that my big paw went exactly where I wanted it to go.

Bogey gave me a nod and then raised a paw to his own forehead. He did a sliding salute and quickly put his paw back on the ground again. "Back at'cha, kid. Now hurry up and save the day, would ya? Daylight's burning."

So I turned in the direction of that big mixing bowl. The lady giving the tour was now showing the group how the whole setup worked. And wouldn't you know it, she decided to turn those beaters on extra fast, just to demonstrate. The gigantic stainless steel bowl started to shudder, like it was alive.

Oooohs and aaaahs rose up from the tour group.

But I just wanted to tell the lady to turn those beaters off!

Only I couldn't exactly do that.

Instead, I took a deep breath and tiptoed around the outer

edge of the group. Then I inched closer and closer to that giant mixing bowl. The closer I got, the louder it got. And the louder it got, the more scared I got. To tell you the truth, I was pretty sure it was going to break free from its stand and come right after me. Any second now.

Holy Catnip!

More than anything, I wanted to turn around and run. But I knew I couldn't. So I kept on inching forward, closer and closer to that little jar. By now my heart was pounding almost as loud as that big bowl. And with Bogey fading fast, I knew I'd better hurry up. That's when I decided to do something I'd heard our Mom talk about — I took a big, giant leap of faith. I closed my eyes for a second, gathered up all the courage I could find, and then I jumped in behind that big bowl.

And right beside that little jar.

Without waiting a single second, I batted the jar with my big paws and kept it moving. I batted it all around the backs of the whole tour group while everyone watched the lady demonstrate how those beaters worked.

I kept on moving that jar until I reached Bogey. He was still wobbling back and forth, and mumbling about cat treats with a glazed look in his eyes. So I opened the lid of the jar and looked inside myself. And I could hardly believe what I found.

A little note.

Written to Bogey and me.

It said, "I know your weaknesses. Shut down the BBCDA or else . . ."

Shut down the BBCDA? Were they crazy?

That's when my heart started to pound even more. Whoever was doing all this *really* was out to stop us. They didn't want us to investigate any more cases. To top it off, they were right about one thing — they sure knew Bogey's weakness. Cat treats! And they had proven it by putting Bogey out of commission with more cat treats than he could handle.

But more importantly, they knew *our* biggest weakness of all. They knew they could get to us by putting our family in peril. And in this case, the diamonds that were planted on our front porch sure got the job done, all right.

So at that very moment, I knew we had to get out of there.

And I knew I had to get my brother to safety.

I put my arm around him. "Bogey, let's go!"

He blinked a couple of times. "What about the clue, kid?"

"I'll tell you all about it when we get home."

"Was it bad?"

"Uh-huh . . ." I murmured. "Now lean on me and I'll get you outside."

But I'd barely spoken the words when I realized I had no idea *how* I'd get Bogey out of the building. Even so, I kept on going anyway, and I helped him move toward the swinging doors that led to the front room. Once I got there, I found the doors were completely shut. So I stood up on my back legs and put my front feet on one of the doors. Trying to figure out a way to open it.

And I have to say, I was pretty happy that I did. Because there are times when it pays to be an extra big cat. One who weighs a whole bunch. And it turned out this was one of those times, since the door swung right open when I put all my weight on it. Then all I had to do was drop my front paws to the ground and keep the door open.

Well, okay, maybe that wasn't *all* I had to do. Because I also had to get Bogey to go through the door as well. Yet with him being so hazy, I knew it was going to take a lot to get his attention. And get him to "amscray, skedaddle, or vamoose," as he would have said.

So I took a deep breath, crinkled my brows, and commanded him to, "Follow the sound of my voice! And come with me, Bogey. Right now!"

I couldn't believe how bossy I sounded. But I guess a guy has got to be a little bossy sometimes. Because it was enough to get Bogey moving.

"Right behind you, kid," he mumbled as he wobbled on through to the front room.

Thankfully, getting through the outer door turned out to be pretty easy. We just waited until some people opened it, and then I half-pulled, half-dragged my brother outside.

Bogey started to come around the minute we hit the fresh air. Then he shook his head and blinked a few times. As though he finally knew where he was.

Dave was already waiting for us in the parking lot. He'd

gotten there early and he helped us to his car when he saw us. I had to say, I was really starting to like this Dave guy. A lot. Especially when he picked up Bogey and put him in his seat.

"Whoa . . . little dudes," he said. "Bogey doesn't look so good. You must'a had too many cat treats."

Bogey took some deep breaths and kept on looking around. He even sat up as Dave drove the car through the parking lot. I can't even begin to say how relieved I was to see my brother doing better. But then I glanced out the side window as we turned onto the street. And I got nervous all over again.

For standing behind the factory's huge picture window was a man.

A man who was staring at our car as we drove away.

A man holding a bowler hat.

It was Mr. Pennypacker. And he had a very big frown on his face.

Holy Catnip!

CHAPTER 19

Holy Mackerel!

I nearly fell off my seat when I saw Mr. Pennypacker staring at us as Dave drove us out of the parking lot. Thankfully, Dave had buckled us in with seat belts. Otherwise, I probably would've gone right over the edge when I spotted Mr. Pennypacker.

Funny, but I hadn't seen him on our tour. So where had he been? And did he have anything to do with the clue that had been left for us?

More than anything, I wanted to talk to Bogey about it. But I wasn't sure if he was in any kind of shape to discuss our case at the moment. Plus, I didn't want to interrupt Dave who kept on pointing out different sights as he drove us home. That would have been just plain rude. Especially since he was so nice to Bogey and me.

When we got home, Dave let us out in front of our house, just as some of Gracie's friends were showing up for the party. They gave us some pretty funny looks when we jumped out of Dave's blue car.

But the timing sure made it easy for Bogey and me to get back into our house. Because we just slipped right in with some of the kids who were walking inside. Then I guided my brother to the office, so I could make sure he was okay.

Bogey shook his head. "I don't know what came over me

back there, kid. That place really knocked me out."

I nodded. "That's for sure. It was pretty weird to see you like that."

He rubbed a paw over his head. "Thanks for getting me out of there, kid. Don't know what I would have done without you. Mind filling me in on the details of what happened back there?"

And just as I was about to open my mouth, Lil came running toward us. "Thank goodness you two are back! Because we're going to need all paws on deck for this one."

Bogey raised an eyebrow. "Do tell, Lil. What's got your dander up?"

Lil shook her head. "Gracie's having a tough time. Because the kids are refusing to go along with her idea and give up their cell phones for the party. Some of them are even being pretty mean to her."

Somebody being mean to Gracie? That sure made my ears stand at attention!

And Bogey's too. "Count us in, right, kid?" he said with a nod to me.

"Right!" I practically hollered.

Then the three of us raced to the living room to find Trixie standing guard over a basket. Attached to the basket was a sign that read, "Be present at my party and not on your phone. So put your phone here and leave it alone. You'll get it back later, before you go home."

The only problem was, there were only three cell phones in that basket. And there were a whole bunch of kids at the party.

That meant most of the kids still had their phones. In fact, three or four of them were on their phones right now. I suddenly understood why Gracie had planned for them to put those phones away for a while. Otherwise, they would've been off in their own little world, you might say. And not even thinking about the party.

A girl named Marissa had one hand on her hip and her phone in her other hand. "Why should I give up my phone for your stupid party, Gracie? It's my business when I'm on my phone. Not yours."

I could tell Gracie was near tears. She had put on her pretty red dress and it looked like she'd even decorated the room. She'd gone to a lot of work for her friends, and some of them sure didn't appreciate it.

"I'm just asking you to give up your phone for a few hours," Gracie explained. "Not forever."

"What if I get a message from Violet? What if I miss it?" Marissa demanded.

"I'm sure Violet will understand if you're busy," Gracie told her.

"I wish I hadn't come here at all!" Marissa practically snarled.

And that was about enough of that for me. I sure didn't like anyone talking to Gracie that way. I nodded to Bogey and I knew he understood exactly what I was thinking. So while he scooted the cell phone basket over, I reached up and pushed the cell phone right out of Marissa's hand. It dropped straight into the basket with a loud *Plop!* Then we scooted over to a boy who was on his phone, and we did the same thing. After that, Trixie joined in to help with a taller girl. Since, well, Trixie was a taller girl herself.

And we kept on going, filling that basket up one cell phone at a time. As we went along, the kids sort of gasped and choked and made all kinds of funny noises. Some even laughed and smiled.

"Did your cats just . . .?" One girl started to ask.

"I can't believe it," another girl said. "But I think your cats are gathering up the phones."

Well, he sure had that right! Once we had all the cell phones, I went back to Gracie and rubbed around her legs. Just to let her know I had her back. So to speak.

She smiled down at me. "In case you didn't know it, I have some very smart cats."

"I'll say," a wide-eyed boy agreed.

"Now that we're all here," Gracie went on, "I came up with a little game for us to play. Remember when I asked you to email me with some interesting things about yourself? Well, this is what I did with it."

And with that, Gracie passed out a copy of the game she had made up the night before. Plus, she passed out pencils to everyone.

A boy named Tommy looked at all the lines printed on the

paper. "This is two pages long! I don't want to read all this."

Gracie shook her head. "It's only one page. Front and back. This will be fun, believe me."

"I don't believe you at all," Marissa whined as she flopped into a chair. "First you take my cell phone away. And now you expect me to read something? What kind of a party is this?"

And that's when us cats jumped into action again. I leaped up onto the chair right next to Marissa and I pointed one of my huge paws right at that sheet of paper. Then I stared at her. I even squinted my eyes so I'd look kind of mean myself.

The other cats did the same thing to some of the other kids.

Trixie sat right next to Tommy. "Okay, okay," he finally agreed. "I'll play this game."

Somehow, Gracie managed to put a big smile on her face. Though to tell you the truth, I'm not sure how. Because I had a pretty good idea that she didn't exactly feel like smiling at the moment. But I knew she was a good hostess, and she was working hard to make sure all the kids were going to have fun.

Only, they didn't know it yet.

"All right, everyone," she said. "Here's how we play. I've got the things you sent me all typed down here. There are forty of them altogether. But I jumbled them up so they're not in any kind of order. Now you have to figure out what items belong to each person. Then fill in the blank beside each item with the correct person's name. And you have to do that by going around the room and asking each person one question at a time."

"Huh?" Marissa said.

I gave her another squinty-eyed look.

"Well," Gracie went on. "For instance, the first statement says, 'Find someone who has been to Australia.' Then fill in the blank with that person's name."

Tommy shook his head. "But everybody already knows the answer to that one. It's . . . it's . . ." He knitted his brows together and glanced around the room. "Wait . . . I can't remember who . . ."

"That's right," Gracie said, never letting her smile dip. "Now you have to find that out. But you can only ask each person one question at a time. So if you ask Sophie question number ten, and that's not her item, then you have to move on and ask someone else. And you can't cheat off anyone else's paper. The first person who gets all the right answers wins. And I baked a very special cupcake for the winner. So let's get started. Ready, set, go!"

So they did. Everyone got to their feet and turned to the person next to them. I heard kids asking things like, "Do you fit question number eight? Did you win a dance contest?"

Gracie's friend Sophie turned to a girl named Laura. "Are you number fourteen? Do you know how to sew clothes?"

Laura quietly nodded yes.

Sophie's eyes went wide. "I didn't know that! That's really awesome!"

"I made the dress I have on," Laura told her.

Sophie's mouth dropped open wide. "That's amazing! Could you please show me how to sew sometime?"

"I'd be happy to," Laura answered with a big smile. "Now, let me guess, are you number twelve? Do you own a St. Bernard dog?"

But Sophie shook her head. "Sorry. It's not me. Guess we'd better move on to the next person."

And they did just that.

All the while, I watched as some kids wrote names on their papers and some didn't ask the right people the right question. Yet all the kids kept moving along, asking questions as they went.

Marissa even got in on the fun. She turned to another girl and asked, "Are you number sixteen? Did you once win a spelling bee?"

In the meantime, Tommy turned to Gracie. "Do you have some of your things on this paper, too?"

Gracie nodded. "Yes, I do."

Tommy moved closer to her. "Well . . . I see you have cats. Are you number twenty? Do you make Christmas cat collars every year? And sell them at the St. Gertrude Craft Fair?"

Gracie smiled and nodded. "That's me. My Mom and Dad let me set up a booth of my own."

Tommy's eyes went wide. "Really? So you sell your stuff and you make your own money?"

"Yes, I do," she told him. "It's fun to make my own money. I spend some and I save some. And I buy Christmas presents for my Mom and Dad all by myself."

"I didn't even know that," Tommy told her. "And we've known each other for years."

"It's so true," Gracie agreed. "We've all been friends since we were little. But there's lots of stuff we don't know about each other."

And so it went. The kids kept on moving from person to person. Everyone asked questions and then stood there and talked. And laughed.

A bunch.

Before long, the living room got pretty loud with kids talking. It was clear that everyone was having a great time.

Us cats just stood there together and kept an eye on things. Usually Bogey would have pulled out a bag of cat treats at a time like this. But today, he just left the closest treat bag stashed behind a couch.

Bogey turned to Lil. "Did the kittens stay upstairs? Like they were supposed to?"

Lil gave Bogey a nod. "They're taking a nap up in the sunroom. They're pretty worn out after practicing their cat karate all day. Plus, I took them on their very first surveillance run. But now the Princess is keeping an eye on them. And Miss Mokie, too. Her eyes sparkle so brightly every time she wakes up and sees them."

Somehow, just knowing that made me smile. And I kept on smiling as I looked over to see Gracie laughing and talking with everyone else. It took almost a whole hour before a girl named Brianna completed both sides of her game sheet. After that, Gracie announced her as the winner.

But not before she had checked all her answers, that is.

And Gracie even read all the answers out loud, for the kids who hadn't completed their game yet. Plus she awarded Brianna the special cupcake that she'd made. One with jelly in the center and the word "Winner" on top in red icing.

Then Gracie served the rest of her cupcakes, too. Along with some pink punch that she'd made.

"That was so much fun, Gracie," a girl named Jennifer announced so the whole group could hear. "You did a great job making that game."

"You really did," Marissa even chimed in. "I'm so sorry I

was such a pain. You really got us talking to each other."

"Without our cell phones," Tommy added. "We all see each other at school. But I didn't even know all this stuff about each one of you. It was fun just to . . ."

"Talk?" Gracie said, finishing his sentence for him.

"Yeah," he told her. "It was fun to talk. We should all talk more often. Face to face. Without our cell phones."

"That's right, Gracie," a boy named Bryson chimed in. "There's so much I didn't know about everyone else. You're the best, Gracie!"

And with those words, Bryson started to clap for Gracie. Then a few more kids started to clap, too. Before long, all the kids were clapping for her.

Once again, Gracie had tears in her eyes. But this time, they were *happy* tears. Several of the kids gave her hugs, and then everyone just started talking and talking and laughing. Mostly about the things that Gracie had put in her game. Plus, everyone ate lots of cupcakes, and as near as I could tell, it was the best party that Gracie had ever hosted.

When the party was over, everyone thanked her and picked up their cell phones on the way out. Our Mom stood by Gracie as she said good-bye to her guests.

When the last one had gone, our Mom turned to Gracie. "I am so very proud of you, honey. You had a problem and you found a solution for it. But you went above and beyond all that. I'll bet you and your friends will be having great conversations from now on, all because of your party."

"Thanks, Mom," Gracie said as she gave our Mom a hug. "I haven't decided what to do about my cell phone yet. I'm not sure I need it. Not unless there's an emergency."

Our Mom wrapped her arms around Gracie and kissed the top of her head. She smiled and I could see she had happy tears in her eyes, too.

And let me tell you, anytime there were hugs and kisses going on, well, I wanted to be right in the middle of it all! So I reached up Gracie's side and meowed until she picked me up. Then I gave her a kiss on the nose.

Right before I glanced out the window.

And saw Officer Phoebe coming up the front walk. She had a big frown on her face, and all of a sudden, I felt like frowning, too.

A few seconds later, she knocked on the door, and our Mom let her inside.

Officer Phoebe said a quick hello to all of us before she turned to our Mom. "Could I please talk to you alone for a minute, Abby?"

I had to say, Officer Phoebe sounded upset.

Very upset.

In fact, I'd only ever heard her voice sound like that when something bad had happened.

Our Mom's voice sounded pretty serious, too. "Sure, let's just step into my office."

Gracie bit her lip and put me down. "I'll go clean up from the party."

"Sounds good, honey," our Mom told her.

Thankfully, Bogey suddenly appeared, and together we followed our Mom and Officer Phoebe into the office. We jumped right up on the desk so we wouldn't miss a thing. Our Mom shut the French doors, probably so Gracie couldn't hear what they were saying.

Then she turned to Officer Phoebe. "What's going on?"

Officer Phoebe sighed and stared at her shoes. "We checked the diamonds under a microscope and we found serial numbers. And I'm afraid I've got some bad news."

Our Mom put her hand to her chest. "No. It can't be. It's not possible."

"I don't understand it, either," Officer Phoebe said quietly. "But I'm afraid those diamonds belong to Garnet."

"Phoebe, none of this makes sense," our Mom gasped. "I don't know how those diamonds got there. I didn't take them and Gracie certainly didn't. She's just a girl. A good girl! Not a thief. She wouldn't even know how to steal diamonds."

Officer Phoebe shook her head. "I don't believe it myself, Abby. But any way you look at it, I'm afraid I've got to bring both you and Gracie in for questioning. Down to the station."

And that's when I think my heart skipped a beat or two. Maybe even three. I could hardly believe that Gracie and our Mom were going down to the police station. Bogey and I both knew they didn't take those diamonds! Somebody had put them on our front porch. The very person who was playing some kind of a rotten game with us.

Now, more than ever, I knew that Bogey and I had to solve this case. It had taken a lot for me to step up to the plate today. And now I knew I had to do it again. I needed to be the best cat detective that I could possibly be.

Just like our Mom had told Gracie that she had gone above and beyond, well, now I had to do that, too!

For the sake of my family.

Holy Catnip!

CHAPTER 20

Holy Mackerel!

Let me tell you, I've had to do some pretty scary things since I became a cat detective. Things I sure didn't want to do. Yet they were things I knew I *had* to do. To solve a case or to help a cat in need. But of all the scary things I've ever had to do, the thing I had to do today was the absolute scariest.

And the hardest.

Because I thought my heart was going to break into a million tiny pieces when I had to step back and watch our Mom and Gracie head to the police station. I couldn't help but wonder if they would ever come home again. What if they were put in jail and had to stay there?

To make things even worse, I didn't think Gracie really understood what was going on. Our Mom and Officer Phoebe sort of explained it to her. But they left out a lot of details.

"Glad to see they candy-coated it," Bogey meowed, just under his breath. "Makes it easier on Gracie."

"Candy-coated?" I repeated. "They're going to give Gracie some candy?"

Bogey shook his head. "Just an expression, kid. It means they're not making it sound as bad as it really is."

Well, if you asked me, it *all* sounded pretty bad. In fact, I thought it sounded downright awful. One of the worst things that could ever happen.

I remembered the note that I'd found in the clue jar at the cat treat factory. The person who wrote it said they knew what our weaknesses were. And well, they weren't kidding. First they'd put an innocent kitten in danger, even though I was pretty sure the whole trap in Mrs. Bumble's backyard was meant for Bogey and me. Then they'd put Bogey out of commission at the cat treat factory. And now they were setting our family up to be accused of a crime. A bad crime. One that might land Gracie and our Mom in jail.

Yet according to the note in that jar, all Bogey and I had to do was close down the BBCDA. But was it too late? Now that our Mom and Gracie were headed for the police station?

Thankfully, Officer Phoebe had let our Mom call our Dad before they left. And she even said our Mom could follow her down to the police station in her own car.

Of course, I didn't let them go without putting up a big fight. I made a beeline to the door to the garage just as our Mom and Gracie were about to leave. Then I stood on my hind legs and put my front paws on the door. I stretched up just as tall as I could go, and I did my best to block them. And I let out such a yowl that even Bogey jumped.

"Buckley doesn't want us to go," Gracie said softly.

Our Mom sighed. "That makes two of us. But like it or not, we have to get this sorted out." Then she reached down, slid her hands around my ribcage, and gently pulled me away from the door.

But I wasn't about to give up so easily. Not at all. So instead of backing off, I made a big, flying leap straight into Gracie's arms. She caught me, and I immediately wrapped my arms around her neck. I buried my nose in her hair while she circled me with her arms and held me tight. I could hardly believe it — she hadn't even had a chance to change out of her pretty red dress yet.

"I love you, Buckley," she whispered into my fur.

And that's when I hung on extra tight. If she was going to the police station, well, then I was going with her. And if she went to jail, then I was going to jail with her. Because nobody was going to pull me away from her.

"Can we take Buckley and Bogey?" Gracie asked our Mom. "They go lots of places with us."

"I know, honey," our Mom answered gently. "But this time they have to stay here."

How could that be? Bogey and I needed to be there, too. To make sure they were okay.

"I have to put you down now, Buckley," Gracie told me. She leaned over and tried to pry my arms from her neck.

"*Nooooo!*" I yowled again as an ice-cold chill raced through my entire body.

"Let her go, kid," Bogey meowed. "We'll work on the case from here. No more chasing clues. Time for us to take the bull by the horn and put two and two together."

"Bulls? And math?" I meowed back. "What's that got to do with Gracie and our Mom going to the police station?"

"Just expressions, kid," he told me. "Meaning, let's solve this case. The crook has left us plenty of clues."

And with that, I allowed Gracie to put me on the floor next to my brother. Then she and our Mom went out the door while Bogey and I just stood there. Staring. My stomach did so many somersaults I wasn't sure I'd ever be able to eat again. More than anything, I really wanted to yowl some more.

Bogey set his mouth in a firm line and squinted at the door. "No time for wallowing, kid. We'll have the office to ourselves. So let's go roll up our sleeves and put the pieces of this case together."

"We have sleeves . . .?" I started to ask.

"Nope, kid," he said as he turned around. "It means 'dig in and get to work.'"

"Um . . . okay," I sort of sniffled, right before I took a deep breath and followed him to the office.

And I do mean followed! Because Bogey ran so fast that I'm pretty sure he went airborne. I couldn't keep up with him at all as I raced behind him. By the time I jumped up on our Mom's antique desk, he was already at the computer.

He glanced at the screen and reached for a hidden bag of cat treats with one arm. As near as I could tell, he sort of did it automatically. Without thinking at all. But then he hesitated for a moment and stared at the bag. Right before he shrugged and pulled the bag open.

"Tough times call for tough measures," he said as he passed me a couple of cat treats. "Now let's go over this case, kid. Maybe you should start by telling me about the last clue. The one at the cat treat factory."

I sat up nice and tall. "The only thing in that jar was a note. But it wasn't just *any* old note. Oh, *no*. It was addressed to us and it said, 'I know your weaknesses. Shut down the BBCDA or else . . .' Or else!" I repeated.

Bogey shook his head. "Or else, huh? Sounds like quite a threat. And whoever wrote it knows our weaknesses, all right."

I was already nodding. "And they really figured out how to get to us when they set up Gracie and our Mom. Making it look like they robbed the jewelry store. That's when they hit us right here." I put my paw to my chest to emphasize the words. Right over my heart. Which, by the way, actually felt like it hurt at the moment.

"You got it, kid," Bogey agreed. "We're dealing with a real nasty piece of work."

I practically gulped down my cat treats. "And I'll bet they just keep on getting nastier. Do you think we should close down the BBCDA?"

Bogey arched a brow. "We've solved a lot of crimes, kid. And we've helped a lot of cats. Not to mention, we've helped plenty of people, too. Do you really want to give that up? And spend your days batting around cat toys? Just waiting for your next meal? Sounds pretty dull, if you ask me."

Well, when he put it that way . . . I guess there really was only one answer.

"No, I sure don't," I told him.

Bogey grinned. "Me either, kid. Not on your life. Especially if we only shut down the agency just because some rotten crook tries to force us to."

I glanced out the window. "But won't they just do meaner and meaner things? To us and everyone around us?"

Bogey downed another treat. "Not if we start running the show, kid. And quit jumping every time they drop a clue on our doorstep. Because think about it — they've had us running all over town, right?"

I nodded. "Uh-huh."

Bogey passed us each a couple more treats. "They've got us chasing our tails and we've been going nowhere fast."

"Really fast," I said and practically gulped down a treat.

"All because somebody left us a bunch of clues, kid. Too many clues. Clues that never added up to much of anything."

I nodded. "And clues usually lead us *somewhere*."

Bogey squinted his eyes and glared at the computer screen. "As near as I can tell, it all boils down to one thing."

"It does? What?" I leaned forward, dying to hear what Bogey was going to say next.

"A giant distraction, kid. Somebody wanted to distract us and they've done a fine job of it."

Bogey's words almost knocked me right over, and I wondered why I hadn't seen it sooner. "They sure have."

"And we took the bait, kid," Bogey said, shaking his head slowly. "We've been reeled in since the crook put that first jar on our front porch. They knew we couldn't resist investigating a bunch of suspicious jars. Jars with clues that led to more clues and even more clues. Whoever did this must know us and know that we're cat detectives. And they knew we'd drop everything to investigate."

I felt my eyes go wide. "But how would they know? We always thought humans had no idea that the BBCDA was run by a couple of cats."

Bogey munched on a treat. "I hear ya, kid. As a general rule, humans have no idea how smart cats are. But somebody must've figured it out. Then they sent us on a wild goose chase."

Right at that moment, I had a pretty good idea there weren't any actual geese involved. I figured this was probably another one of Bogey's expressions.

He downed another treat and went on. "It's gotta be somebody who's close to us, kid. Somebody who's been watching us."

Shivers suddenly ran up my spine. "That's easy. Mr. Pennypacker was watching us when we drove away from the cat treat factory today. And we've seen him staring at us a few other times. Plus, he does *own* the cat treat factory. He could have put that clue with the note there."

"Could be, kid. But we've hardly ever run across him before. Not until this week. So the odds of him knowing the truth about us are pretty slim."

I munched thoughtfully on a treat. "What about Mrs.

Bumble? She lives only a few doors down from us. And she brought Mitzi over. Plus, we found a clue right in her backyard. Maybe she's been watching us and figured things out."

Bogey put a paw to his chin. "Maybe, kid. But we're just guessing here. Let's look at this from a different angle. *Why* would anyone want to distract us? And why would they want to see the BBCDA shut down?"

The answer to that question popped right into my head. "Because they wanted to commit a crime and they didn't want us to investigate it."

Bogey grinned at me. "And they knew we'd solve the crime. Especially since we've solved crimes that the police couldn't solve. So that brings us to another question. What is the crime that someone doesn't want us to investigate?"

"Well, there was the robbery at Garnet's Jewelry Store," I suggested.

Bogey stashed the bag of cat treats back in its hiding place. "It's a possibility, kid. The crime is unsolved, and somebody's trying to pin it on our Mom and Gracie. Do you remember what we saw when we were in the jewelry store? When Mitzi knocked over Garnet's bills?"

"Um . . . well . . . bills?" I crinkled my forehead.

"But what kind of bills, kid?"

"Oh . . . um . . . there was one for her insurance company. She uses the same insurance company as our Mom does for her store."

Bogey grinned. "Yup, kid, and if Garnet's store was robbed, what would happen?"

"Her insurance would pay for all the stuff that was stolen," I said with a nod.

"You got it, kid." Bogey flexed a paw and examined his nails. "Now let me ask you another question. What *didn't* you see while we were in her store?"

I glanced at the ceiling and tried to remember. "Well . . . there was lots and lots of jewelry. Everywhere. But there weren't any customers. Except for Mr. Pennypacker."

"So maybe business wasn't exactly booming," Bogey went on. "And remember the night she knocked on the door? She told Officer Phoebe that she'd already filed a claim with her insurance."

"She sure didn't waste any time," I added. "She should be getting lots of money pretty soon.   From the insurance company."

Bogey was already nodding. "You got it, kid."

I tilted my head. "And there's one other thing. The night that she was here . . . the night when she spotted those diamonds . . . Why didn't she make a big commotion and tell Officer Phoebe to search the rest of our house? Just like she did at our Mom's store?"

And that's when Bogey's mouth dropped open. "Kid, I believe you just cracked the case."

For some reason, I felt all tingly. "I did?"

Bogey gave me a paw bump. "Way to go, kid! Garnet already knew that our Mom and Gracie didn't steal those diamonds.   Otherwise, she would've raised a ruckus and insisted that Officer Phoebe search the whole house. For the rest of the missing jewelry."

I stared at my brother. "But she didn't."

Bogey grinned. "That's right, kid. Because she knew those diamonds were the only stones here."

By now I felt like bouncing around like Mitzi always did. "Probably because she planted them on our porch. For us to find."

"That would be my guess, kid," he said and turned back to the computer. "It's time we took a closer look at Garnet."

And without another word, he typed her name into the computer and ran a quick background check on her. That's when he found a video of Garnet talking about the sale at her jewelry store. Right away, Bogey clicked on the little arrow to make it play, and we watched the video together.

When it was almost over, Trixie appeared in the hallway and poked her head into the office. "Excuse me, was that a video you were watching?"

I nodded to her. "Uh-huh. We're investigating a case."

"That's interesting," Trixie added. "Because I recognized that voice."

Bogey sat at attention. "Well, Trix, that's even *more* interesting. Mind telling us where you've heard it before?"

Trixie made a graceful leap up onto the desk, reminding

me of a beautiful, flying horse. "Not at all," she said. "That's the voice of the woman who owns the house where I was being held captive."

Holy Catnip!

CHAPTER 21

Holy Mackerel!

Did I just hear what I thought I'd heard? Did Trixie really say what I thought she'd said?

Bogey's ears immediately pointed in her direction. "Trix, are you sure about this?"

Trixie shuddered. "Believe me, I could not be more sure. You don't forget the voice of the person who only shows up every once in a while to feed you. I spent hours and hours, and days and days, listening for that voice. Hoping and praying that I would hear it. Because that meant she might bring me some food and water. Or maybe she would let me go free, so someone else could take me in. I would've rather been out on the streets than locked in that room."

I reached over and gave her a hug. "That must have been terrible, Trixie. I'm so glad you're here now. I don't know what kind of a person would want to starve a poor, helpless cat."

"A real, rotten-to-the-core kind of person," Bogey practically growled. "And after hearing your story, Trix, I think Garnet's name just climbed to the top of our suspect list. Especially since her late-night visit to our house sent our Mom and Gracie off to the police station. I'll bet she's also the one who sent us on this wild goose chase, kid."

I put my paw to my chin. "It sure does add up. Because,

when you think about it, one thing led to another. The only reason we went to Garnet's store in the first place was because we found that clue on our doorstep. If we hadn't gone there to investigate, we never would've been caught in her store."

Bogey frowned. "All this time, we thought we got caught because Mitzi jumped the gun. And landed on Pennypacker's hat."

My heart started to pound as I put more of the pieces together. "But Garnet probably left that clue of the diamonds on our doorstep because she *knew* we'd make a beeline to her store to investigate. Maybe she was just waiting there for us to sneak in. And maybe she knew we were there the whole time."

Bogey shook his head back and forth, very, very slowly. "Could be, kid. Then she put on quite a show, acting like she'd caught us red-handed. So she could call our Mom and Gracie to come get us."

I nodded. "Everybody knows our Mom and Gracie would come running for us. Just like they always do."

Bogey rubbed his forehead. "You can bet it was a real stroke of luck for Garnet when Gracie bumped into that display. And sent that jewelry crashing to the ground. Because Garnet probably planned to blame them for a crime they had nothing to do with. Her crime. Gracie's little accident made it all that much easier. I can't believe we fell for it, kid."

All the while, Trixie just watched and listened, taking it all in. The sadness in her eyes told me the whole case was really hitting home with her. So I figured now might be a good time for a round of treats. I grabbed the bag from its hiding place and passed a couple of treats to Trixie and Bogey. Then I took a couple for myself.

Trixie thanked me and smiled. As she ate her treats, I couldn't help but notice how different she looked now. She had been skin and bones when we rescued her. She could barely even walk then. Yet here she was, putting on some weight and teaching cat karate to kittens. Not to mention, enjoying life in a house where she was safe and cared for. Even so, she acted like the cat treats in front of her were the most precious thing in the world. I probably would've felt the same way if I had been in her paws. And if I had been through the same things that she'd been through.

I had to say, I was so happy we'd rescued her. Even more now than I had been before. Sure, we'd gone through a lot to save her from that creepy house. A house that we now knew belonged to Garnet. And that night had been extra scary, since there'd been thunder and lightning and wind and rain. Lots and lots of rain. Yet it was all worth it just to have Trixie out of that horrible place.

And that's when it hit me.

Really hit me.

How much I enjoyed being a cat detective. No, it wasn't all cat treats and Drive-N-Dash rides. But it still felt good to help out another cat or person who needed us. And I realized that, more than anything, I didn't want to close down the BBCDA. Especially not when one rotten crook was trying to force us to.

Instead, I wanted to put that crook behind bars, where she belonged. So she couldn't harm any more cats. Or people.

"It would have been easy for Garnet to put clues on our porch," I told my brother. "Since she lives so close by. She could have dropped those jars off and left, without anyone even seeing her."

Bogey nodded. "You got it, kid. Nobody would've given her a second look. They probably thought she was just out for a stroll."

Trixie's big ears perked up. "I think Garnet's capable of doing all kinds of horrible things. And if you're investigating her, I'd really like to help. Any way I can."

"Me, too," Lil said as she suddenly appeared in the doorway and stepped into the office. "When someone harms my friends or family, I take it very personally. So if you'd like some extra paws on the case, I'd be happy to join in. Just say the word."

Bogey glanced at me and I nodded in agreement. Without one bit of hesitation. If Trixie and Lil wanted to help out, then I was all for it. After all, the more cat detectives we had on this case the better. Especially since our Mom and Gracie still hadn't come home from the police station.

"We'd be glad to have you gals join the party," Bogey said. "Because the stakes couldn't be higher."

Lil jumped up onto the desk. "Mind catching us up to

speed? It sounds like quite a case."

"It's a real doozie, all right," I agreed.

Then Bogey and I filled them in on all the details. Starting with the first jar on the porch and ending with the jar I found at the cat treat factory. And then our Mom and Gracie going down to the police station.

"Whew . . ." Lil said, shaking her head. "I guess I've been too busy teaching cat karate and catching up with Trixie to pay attention to anything else. So tell me, any ideas on how Garnet figured out that you're behind the BBCDA?"

I passed out another round of cat treats. "Maybe she overheard us talking when we were running surveillance at our Mom's store."

Bogey arched an eyebrow. "Could be. We chat in human language sometimes. But only when we're sure nobody is listening. Even so, it's possible she caught us off guard and put two and two together."

"It makes sense," Lil said before munching on another treat. "Since she sounds like a pretty sneaky character. She's probably the type who eavesdrops."

Trixie's mouth formed a grim line. "Then she used me as bait to confirm it. She probably figured you'd hear about my captivity and come to the rescue. I'll bet she even left that laptop in my room to see if I would contact you somehow. Of course, I did, through Lil."

Lil's eyes practically gave off sparks. "And she probably watched us the whole time we rescued Trixie."

"How creepy," I murmured. Just the *thought* of Garnet watching us during that awful thunderstorm gave me the shivers.

"You got that right, kid," Bogey said under his breath.

"So that's why nobody came running right away when we set off the alarm," I added.

"I think you nailed it, kid," Bogey went on. "In the meantime, she'd already set up her little game. We even had that first clue jar inside our house before we took off to rescue Trixie."

Trixie picked up a treat and held it in her paw. "And from that moment on, Garnet kept you good and distracted. So you wouldn't interfere when she robbed her own store."

I nodded. "Uh-huh. Officer Phoebe even made the comment that the robbers had gotten all the jewels out *really* fast. Between the time when the alarm went off and then the police got there."

Lil glanced my way. "Which makes sense. Since Garnet would've taken all the jewels out earlier. Then she set the stage to make it look like someone had broken in. Right before she set off the alarm."

"So where is all the loot?" Bogey asked.

Trixie gave us a sly smile. "Probably in the big safe she's got in her house. On the third floor."

Bogey turned an ear toward Trixie. "You've seen the safe, Trix?"

"Yes, I have," Trixie told us. "Garnet took me in there right after she brought me to her house. She put me down inside the safe and let me walk around while she got something out. I even watched her punch in the code for the keypad lock. This was all before she shut me away in that upstairs bedroom."

Bogey squinted his eyes. "Then it sounds like we'd better have a look-see inside that safe. What do you want to bet it's full of jewelry? The stuff that was in Garnet's store?"

"I'll bet it is, too," I said as I stashed the cat treat bag back in its hiding place. "When should we go and look?"

"Tonight," Bogey said without even batting an eye. "Before Garnet has a chance to move any jewelry out. And sell it. Or stash it someplace else."

"But what if she's home?" I sort of choked. "We could get caught." The very idea of going back to that big, creepy mansion made my fur stand on end. Going there once had been plenty for me.

Trixie shook her head. "She and her husband always go out for dinner and a movie this night of the week. So this is the best night for us to go in. And I even know the code for the burglar alarm. I saw her punch the numbers into the keypad at her back door when she first brought me in. She's got a double-redundant system."

Lil nodded. "That means you have to punch in the code twice. If you only punch it in once, it just becomes a silent alarm. It's something they use to trick burglars."

"Exactly," Trixie said. "A burglar might think they've

turned off the alarm, but the police still get notified. It's very sneaky."

It seemed like everything about Garnet was *very sneaky.*

"Great information, Trix," Bogey said as he glanced at the clock on the computer. "Could save us a lot of headaches. So why don't we figure out a game plan and get this show on the road."

Lil smiled. "Don't forget, those two kittens are getting pretty good at cat karate. I think we should take them with us. They could come in handy."

"Huh . . . what?" I gulped. "Do you really think Mitzi and Magnolia are ready to go out on a case?"

Lil smiled at me and nodded. "You should see those two girls, Buckley. They're naturals. And they're very advanced already. Some of the best students I've ever seen."

"Yes, they are," Trixie added. "They've got feet of fury."

Feet of fury?

I had to say, I didn't exactly like the sound of that. And I didn't like the idea of them going with us tonight. After all, it had only been yesterday when I watched Mitzi *pretend* like she knew cat karate. Okay, maybe it had actually been a few days ago. But any way you looked at it, it hadn't been very long at all. And the thought of those two little kittens going into that big, scary house . . . well, let's just say that a lot of bad things could happen to a couple of little kittens in a place like that. Especially since it was the same place where Trixie had been held prisoner. And she was fifteen times the size of one of those kittens. Plus, Trixie was a seasoned cat detective. Not just a CDIT.

But whether I liked the idea or not, the four of us cat detectives still got down to business and came up with a plan. A plan that included Mitzi and Magnolia. Though I did have to admit, it was a really *good* plan. Provided everything went just like it was *supposed* to go.

Then afterward, everyone elected me to go tell the two kittens.

So I made a beeline for the sunroom. I found Mitzi and Magnolia there, practicing their cat karate while the Princess and Miss Mokie watched. And when I told the kittens about our plan, they started to bounce around with excitement.

"Oh, Buckley, that's the best news ever!" Mitzi gushed. "Mags and I are going to be *real* cat detectives!"

"This is going to be fun," Magnolia said before she did a somersault.

The Wise One looked down from her purple velvet couch and nodded. She was clearly pleased with the two kittens.

But the Princess sat on the floor nearby, and for once, her beautiful green eyes were clouded over with worry. "They're awfully young for this," she murmured. "Please promise me you'll watch over them, Buckley."

"He will, he will!" Mitzi and Magnolia both said at once.

"Don't worry, Princess Alexandra," Mitzi chirped. "We'll be fine!"

Then both girls went back to practicing their cat karate moves. Mitzi went spinning into the air with a roundhouse kick and Magnolia did kind of a paw-spring and came up kicking.

I had to say, I was really amazed by what I saw. I even felt like clapping for them. Because they were already pretty good when it came to cat karate.

But that didn't mean I wasn't nervous about taking them with us. Sure, Mitzi had tagged along a couple of times. And she was doing so much better than when I'd first met her. Even so, we were going into a very creepy house that was owned by a very nasty person. One who wouldn't hesitate to harm a kitten, or us big cats, for that matter.

I put my paw in the air to get the young kittens to settle down. Just like I'd done when I had started to train Mitzi. And right away, they both sat at attention. Very, very quietly. Then they stared up at me and waited for my command.

I stood just as tall and straight as I could. "Umm . . . okay, you two, it's very important that you can take orders tonight. Do I have your word that you'll follow instructions?"

They both nodded their little heads. "Yes, Buckley."

"Good," I said. "We'll be leaving in five minutes. We're all going to meet at the back door."

"Okay, Buckley," they chimed in together. Their tiny faces were practically bursting with excitement.

"There's one more thing," I started to say. "I'm very . . . I'm very . . ." Then for some reason, I suddenly had a hard time getting the words out. Because my throat felt funny and my mouth just wouldn't work right and I got all choked up. What was going on?

"Are you all right, Buckley?" the Princess asked in her sweet voice.

I shook my head and coughed a couple of times. "Everything is fine," I finally squeaked out. "I just wanted to say that . . . well . . . I'm really proud of you two kittens. I can tell you've both worked extra hard to learn cat karate. And you're both doing such a great job."

Mitzi looked at Magnolia, and the two kittens absolutely beamed at each other.

While I just kept on choking up. "Now be sure to stick with me when we go on this case. So you can come home safely. Because I don't know what I'd do if . . ."

And those were all the words I could manage to get out at that moment.

Little Mitzi raced right over to give me a hug. "Buckley, you're the *best*! In the whole wide world! If it wasn't for you, I wouldn't even be going on a case. Now I'm going to be a real cat detective! It's a dream come true!"

Then Magnolia joined her and gave me a hug, too. "I'm so happy, Buckley. I can't believe Mitzi and I are going to be cat detectives! Together!"

I hugged them back and for some reason, now my voice wasn't the only thing that wasn't working. Because my eyes started to feel strange, too, and they got a little misty and kind of blurry. Especially when I looked over at the Princess and she absolutely sparkled up at me with her big, green eyes. Of course, looking into those beautiful eyes didn't exactly help things. Because I suddenly started to feel dizzy on top of everything else.

Thankfully, the Princess spoke up. "I'd better get you girls ready to go. Come with me." Then she herded the young ones out.

Right after she'd gone, I couldn't help but sigh. I really didn't want those two little kittens to go with us tonight. Even if Lil and Trixie and Bogey thought they were ready.

Because, the truth was, *I* wasn't *ready* for them to be ready. How could they grow up so fast? How could they be ready to go into a dangerous situation when they were still so tiny? All of a sudden, the whole world seemed pretty topsy-turvy to me. It was spinning like a cat toy that someone had batted across the room.

"I can see that you are troubled, young Detective," the Wise One said from her position above me on the couch. "Clearly something is weighing heavily on your mind. Do you wish to tell me what has distressed you so?"

I was about to say no, since, after all, I had to join the others and get ready to go. But apparently my mouth had other ideas. And it seemed to run away without me. And I do mean run! Because my words just flew right out. Almost as fast as Bogey flying down the stairs.

"Everything feels like it's spinning out of control," I told her. "From Gracie having problems with her cell phone to a lady we barely even know trying to hurt our family. Then there's the way Bogey was out of commission at the cat treat factory. And our Mom and Gracie had to go to the police station. And now these little kittens are going with us on a case, and I don't want them to go. I don't like the way everything seems to be in a big, giant mess. But no matter what I do, it seems like I can't get things to go back to normal."

She nodded to me. "Ah, yes, young one. You have been through some trying times. As you grow older, you shall learn there are some things you can control and other things you cannot."

I frowned. "I sure don't like it when things are like this. And I really hope that everyone will be okay."

That's when Miss Mokie's eyes sparkled with kindness. "It appears that you are rather worried about those around you. And that you cannot control what's happening to them."

I glanced at the floor for a moment. "Uh-huh, I am, Miss Mokie. I didn't like seeing Bogey in such bad shape at the cat treat factory. He couldn't even think straight when he was surrounded by all those cat treats. Then I didn't like it when Gracie first got her cell phone. She acted almost like Bogey did today. She couldn't think straight, either. And she couldn't put that phone down to go to sleep or even walk across the room. That's how she ran right into a jewelry display. For a while, it seemed like her cell phone was more important than .

. . well, everything else. Her cats and her family included."

The Wise One frowned and shook her head. "I fear that is a rather common affliction among humans these days. They can't part from such devices for even a moment or two. They truly miss out on the joys of life, simply because they spend too much time staring at a small device in their hands. And that, I fear, is a very different kind of being out of control."

I crinkled my brow. "It is?"

"Ah, yes, young one," she said, closing her eyes for a moment. "For there are things in life that are meant for use in moderation."

I tilted my head and looked up at her. "Moderation?"

She sat up straighter. "It means, 'not to excess,' young Detective. For it is important to have balance in life."

"Oh, okay," I told her. "I think I have pretty good balance. I can walk across the stair railing without falling off."

Miss Mokie gave me a small smile. "Perhaps I might explain it this way. Imagine a seesaw. If it has too much weight on one end, that end will go to the ground and the other side will tilt up. But if you have the *same* amount of weight on either end, the board will be level. When the board is level, you might say it is balanced."

I glanced at the ceiling for a moment. "Hmmm . . . okay. But what does a seesaw have to do with cell phones?"

She lifted a front paw, flexed her claws, and examined them. "If a human were to use their cell phone too much and not spend much time with their friends or family, you might say they're giving more weight to the cell phone."

That's when the light finally dawned on me. "Then the seesaw would tip to one end. And it would be out of balance."

She put her paw back on her purple velvet couch. "You are correct, young Detective. And it's important to have balance in your life. You should spend some time working and some time with your family. There should be some time spent eating and other time spent sleeping. But if you spend too much time on one thing, you will be out of balance."

I nodded. "Then one end of the seesaw will be down."

"Precisely. You have learned much today, young one. And now I must leave you with these parting words. As the years go by, you may find there are things in your life that are out of control. Things that need to be changed. Sometimes those things are harmful things. And if you have the power to change those things, then you should do all that you can to change them."

"Like Gracie did with her cell phone," I said. "She realized that it got her into trouble. So she did everything she could to change that and quit using it so much. She even got some of her friends to do that, too."

Miss Mokie's eyes lit up. "An excellent example. Gracie is a very good-hearted and sincere young girl. Her efforts are to be commended."

Thinking of Gracie made me smile. And that's when it dawned on me. Maybe Gracie hadn't been the only one whose seesaw had been tilting to one end. After all, Bogey and I had been so busy with the BBCDA that we hadn't been spending as much time as we usually did with our family. Especially Gracie.

So right then and there, I vowed to pay more attention to her. In fact, I decided I would start right this very minute. And then I remembered that she was still down at the police station.

"Thank you, Miss Mokie," I murmured. "I think I understand."

Miss Mokie lifted her paw and held it in the air above me. "You have done well, Grasshopper. But now you must take your leave, for I must rest. Know that your efforts in training these young kittens have not gone unnoticed. And know that I, too, am rather proud of you, young Detective."

With that, my mouth fell open just as Miss Mokie's eyes fell shut. To know that Miss Mokie was proud of me . . . well, there weren't many things in the world that could make me feel any better than that. Especially since the Wise One didn't exactly say things like that very often. So when she did, it was a pretty big deal.

I smiled and tiptoed out of the room, so Miss Mokie could get her sleep.

Her words stayed with me as I left her and headed down the stairs to join the others. Because I knew there was something else in my life that really needed to be changed. Something that I *could* change.

I needed to stop Garnet from harming my family and friends.

And the only way I could do that was to prove that she had robbed her own jewelry store.

So with the help of Bogey, Lil, Trixie, and the kittens, I intended to do just that.

Even if it was scary.

Holy Catnip!

CHAPTER 22

Holy Mackerel!

Everyone was already at the back door by the time I got there. Trixie and Lil were busy talking and pointing up at the doorknob. And the Princess was fussing over Mitzi and Magnolia.

Bogey pulled me aside the second he spotted me. "Everything okay, kid?"

"Not just yet," I told him. "But I'm hoping it will be. Really soon."

Bogey raised an eyebrow. "Not sure I follow you, kid. But as long as you've got your head in the game, you can fill in the blanks later."

I glanced over at the two kittens and did a double take. In fact, I had to blink a couple of times just to make sure my eyes weren't playing tricks on me.

I leaned toward my brother. "Bogey . . . are Mitzi and Magnolia . . . are they wearing . . . sunglasses?"

Bogey grinned. "Yup, kid. It would appear so."

I almost gasped. "Do we need sunglasses, too?"

"Only if you want them," my brother replied as he stretched his back legs.

I crinkled my brow. "I don't know . . . I guess I never thought about it before."

Though I had to say, the girls did look pretty fierce with

their glasses on. And it was sort of strange that I couldn't see their eyes. It made them look like they had no expressions at all. For the life of me, I couldn't tell what they were thinking. But one thing *was* for sure — they didn't look one bit scared.

"We'll figure it out later, kid," Bogey told me. "After we get back." Then he waved his front paw to get everyone's attention. "Okay, folks. Let's get this show on the road. Got the camera, Lil?"

"Got it." She pointed a paw to our dad's little camera that she had attached to her collar. "We only need a couple of pictures to prove that Garnet's missing jewelry is in her safe."

"And then we'll be out of there and headed home," Bogey said as he turned to me. "Okay, kid. You're up. Ready to help Trix get us out of here?"

"Aye, aye," I told my brother.

Then I tried to salute him. But I missed and just touched the top of my head. If nothing else, at least Trixie, Lil, and Bogey had all glanced at the back door right at that moment.

Though the kittens both bowed and said, "*Oooss.*"

I sighed and went to join Trixie for phase one of our plan. The part where I was supposed to help her push a chair up close to the door. Trixie put her huge paws against her side of the chair and had no problem moving it right into place. Almost like the bottom of the leg had grease on it.

As for me, well . . . that was a whole different story. And one I sure didn't want to talk about later. Because when I put *my* big paws on *my* side of the chair, the back leg seemed to be stuck. It wouldn't budge one inch. No matter how hard I pushed.

So I decided to give it a running start. I backed up, ran straight for that chair, and smacked into it with a loud *whomp!* The chair went flying and bashed right into the door. Unfortunately, the whole thing also sent me flying. And I ended up doing a somersault and crashing into the wall. Then I just stayed there for a second or two, all sprawled out while the room kept on going in circles.

Not exactly the kind of move a guy wants to make in front of a whole bunch of cat detectives. And not a great way to start out on a very important case.

Above me, Bogey's face came into focus. "Well, kid, I gotta

hand it to you. You really know how to give it your all. But maybe we should save the rough stuff for Garnet's house."

Rough stuff? I sure hoped there wasn't going to be any rough stuff. *Especially* not at Garnet's house.

I blinked a couple of times and rolled over. Just in time to see Bogey climb up onto the chair and wrap his arms around the doorknob. He squeezed it tightly and managed to turn the knob. Then he leaned back and pulled that knob with him, until the door opened an inch or two. Finally, he jumped off the chair, and Trixie and I scooted it out of the way.

This time the chair moved just like it was supposed to.

Then Lil used one of her paws to tug the door open wide enough for all of us to run through.

Bogey turned to the Princess. "You know what to do if our family gets home early, right?"

She nodded her little head. "Uh-huh. I'm supposed to make a big fuss about this door being open."

"You got it," Bogey said with a grin.

With that, we waved good-bye to the Princess, and we were off. We took the same route to Garnet's house as we'd taken the last time. To speed things up, Magnolia rode on Trixie's back and Mitzi road on mine. Though I had to say, it seemed like it was easier going this time. And before I knew it, we were all in position in the backyard. Thankfully, the whole house was dark and it looked like nobody was home.

Trixie directed us all to a mat by the back door. "This is where Garnet keeps a key hidden. I saw her put it here from the window of the room where she held me captive."

For a moment, Trixie glanced up at that very window. And I could have sworn I saw that big cat shudder. Then again, it probably wasn't easy for her to visit the place that had basically been her prison.

I put my paw on her shoulder. "You're not by yourself anymore, Trixie. You've got all of us now."

"And we're not going to let anything bad happen to you, Trix." Bogey hooked his claws into one end of the mat and pulled it up. "We'll just get in and get out. Nice and easy like."

Trixie swallowed hard. "Thanks, boys. And everyone. I can't even tell you how much I appreciate it."

I grabbed the key with one of my claws and Bogey let the

mat fall back into place.

"Don't sweat it, Trix," Bogey said while he stared up at the door. "We've all been in a pickle a time or two ourselves. Now, let's get to work. Time to get that door unlocked and opened up."

Trixie nodded toward the door. "Once we're inside, we've got exactly thirty seconds to turn off the alarm before it starts to blare out with full force."

Thirty seconds? That wasn't much time. But first we had to *get* inside. So I quickly passed the key to Lil and made a beeline for a plastic porch chair. Trixie followed me, and together, we had the chair in place next to the door in a hurry. Then we both helped to lift the kittens up to the seat. Lil stood beside us and handed the key up to Mitzi. She put the key in her mouth and stretched up to the doorknob. With Magnolia's help, Mitzi used her tiny paws to guide the key right into the slot on the lock. Once it was firmly in place, the kittens jumped back to the porch while Lil leaped up onto the chair. She was all set to use her strong arms to turn that key and open the door. Just like we had planned.

But then a funny thing happened.

She had barely leaned into the door when it suddenly opened up all on its own. The hinges even creaked a little as the door moved a couple of inches.

Right at that moment, my heart started to pound really hard inside my chest. Bogey, Trixie, Lil, and I all turned to stare at each other. The kittens just stood at attention, without one bit of expression on their faces.

Let me tell you, finding an unlocked door sure wasn't part of our plan. Especially one that just pushed right open. Like it wasn't even latched properly. If you asked me, I thought the whole setup looked pretty suspicious.

Trixie shook her head. "I can't imagine that Garnet would leave a door unlocked. It's not like her."

"Could this be a trap?" Lil suggested quietly.

Bogey tilted his head. "Could be. If we go in, we could be in trouble. But if we don't go in, *our Mom and Gracie* could be in trouble."

I gulped. Because I really didn't like either one of those options. Even so, I knew we had to prove that our Mom and

Gracie were innocent. And the only way we could do that was to prove that Garnet was guilty.

I couldn't believe the words that came out of my mouth next. I blurted them out without even thinking. "I think we should go in. There are six of us, so we're not going in alone. And I sure don't want Gracie or our Mom to go to jail."

Bogey put his paw on my shoulder. "I'm proud of you, kid. You've got enough guts for all of us."

But the truth was, I didn't really have any "guts" at all. And I sure didn't have enough for the whole group. Because I was already shaking in my paws, just thinking about Garnet laying a trap for us.

"Count me in," Lil said.

"Me, too," Trixie added.

And I knew it probably took more bravery for her to go in than anyone else. After all, she had already escaped from this place once. Now here she was, going back in so she could help our Mom and Gracie.

"Maybe we should leave the kittens out here," I suggested.

Mitzi's mouth fell wide open. "No way! You're not leaving us behind!"

"We're here to be cat detectives," Magnolia jumped in. "We're not staying outside."

Bogey pushed the door open a little wider. "Well, any way you look at it, we've only got ten seconds left to punch in that alarm code. So we'd better run in and turn it off before it starts making a racket."

"The code is 5-5-5-5," Trixie said quickly. "And the keypad is right by the door."

Bogey motioned to me. "Let's go, kid. I need you to give me a boost."

And the next thing I knew, I was leaning against the wall and holding Bogey up as he stood on my shoulders. I tried to hold us steady while he used his narrow paws to punch in the code.

But let me tell you, it wasn't easy being a feline ladder. Because Bogey weighed a lot more than I thought he did, and it was really hard to balance. For a second or two, I felt us start to lean to the right. I did my best to straighten us out, and then we started to lean to the left.

It was a good thing Bogey and I were cat detectives. Because we sure wouldn't make it as a circus act.

It felt like an hour went by while I stood there and waited for Bogey to finish pushing the buttons of that alarm. All the while, I just stared at the floor, wishing he would hurry up.

At long last, he jumped down. Then I stepped outside and motioned for the other cats to come in. They didn't waste a single second before they tiptoed inside. Like it or not, we were now officially inside Garnet's creepy mansion. And the sooner we got the job done, the sooner we could get out of there.

Naturally, we let Trixie take the lead since she knew her way around. The rest of us followed, and we barely made a sound as we walked up a set of stairs and into a big hallway. From there, we made our way to a huge curved staircase, deep inside the mansion. The rooms all around us were dark, and the whole place was really, really quiet.

Too quiet, if you asked me.

Without a word, we started up the stairs, going in a single-file line. Trixie stayed in the lead, followed by Bogey and then Lil. I came next, with Mitzi and Magnolia behind me. And while I was worried about us all, I was especially worried about having those two tiny kittens with us. Every inch of my being just wanted to get them back outside and let them wait out there until we were all finished. But I knew that would never happen. Because it was too late. We were too far inside that mansion already.

So I just kept on moving behind the rest of the bunch. And before long, we started to pick up the pace a little bit. That was, until Trixie accidentally stepped on a loose board in the stairs. I nearly jumped to the ceiling when I heard the loud *creak!* Then we all froze in our tracks and listened for any movement upstairs. To see if anyone had heard us.

When we didn't hear a thing, we kept on going. Of course, the rest of us were really careful to walk around that creaky board. I wasn't sure about the others, but every hair on my body felt like it was standing on end. I could barely even breathe. I just wanted to get to that safe, open it, and take our pictures.

And then amscray!

It seemed like it took us forever before we reached the second-story landing. From where we stood, we could see the room where Trixie had been held. I shuddered, just looking at it.

But we didn't take any time to dilly-dally. Instead, we just kept on going up those stairs. Up and up and up. Inside that very silent mansion.

Finally, we got to the third floor, where the safe was supposed to be. That's when Trixie made some motions with her paw and gave us some silent directions. She pointed down another hallway and then tilted her head to the right. Which meant the safe was clear back on the far side of the house.

By now, we'd had enough of taking it slow. So we picked up the pace and trotted down a hallway. Together, we all turned a corner, ready to head for the safe.

That was, until we saw a sight that made me feel like someone had just dunked me in water. And I don't mean warm water, either, like our Mom used when she gave us a bath. No, I felt like I'd been dropped smack dab into freezing cold water that was filled with ice cubes.

I'm sure the rest of the cats were just as horrified, too, since we all came to a screeching halt. For there, right in front of us, were two big dogs. Dobermans, I think they were called. And they must have been lying in wait for us at the top of the stairs.

But no matter what kind of dogs they were, they suddenly sprang to life and snarled at us. Drool dripped from their teeth and their eyes practically glowed an eerie yellow. Clearly it was only a matter of seconds before they attacked.

And we would be goners!

Holy Catnip!

CHAPTER 23

Holy Mackerel!

There we were, on the top floor of Garnet's mansion, practically standing face-to-face with two nasty guard dogs. Dogs with very sharp teeth, I might add.

And before we could turn around and run, Lil hollered, "Mitzi! Magnolia! Full claws! Pounce!"

After that, everything happened in a flash. I caught glimpses of tiny, needle-sharp claws as the two little calicos went flying through the air. And I do mean flying! Of course, they were also sort of spinning and flipping at the same time. The next thing I knew, there was fur and dust and dander coming up in kind of a cloud around the two dogs. There was yelping and hollering and the whir of tiny feet as the attack went on.

Much as I wanted to jump in and help those two girls, everything was moving so fast before my eyes that I wasn't sure who was who. In fact, I even thought the girls switched sides a couple of times. And to be honest, it looked like they had the situation under control.

Feet of fury was right!

The whole scuffle ended in about a minute. Then I could finally make out the two dogs who were now covered in scratches and big bare spots where their fur had once been. Their noses were scratched and their ears were scratched, but their eyes were wide and their mouths were hanging open in shock and terror. They looked like they weren't sure whether they should run or just stay put. But one thing *was* for sure, those two dogs looked more scared than *I* have ever been in my whole life.

Mitzi and Magnolia, on the other hand, landed on their feet in front of me. As near as I could tell, they didn't have a scratch on them. And they didn't have a single strand of fur out of place. They hadn't even lost their sunglasses in the whole scuffle.

Both girls just bowed and said, "*Oooss.*"

Then without so much as a "woof," those two dogs just amscrayed on out of there.

I watched them go and my chin practically hit the floor. One minute I thought we were goners, and the next minute I could hardly believe what I'd just seen.

While Lil and Trixie congratulated the girls, I glanced over at my brother. His eyes were wide and his eyebrows had practically shot up to the top of his forehead. To be honest, I don't think I've ever seen him look so shocked before. He blinked a couple of times and then he shook his head slowly.

"Bogey," I muttered under my breath. "Do you think we might've overdone it with the kittens' training?"

"Could be, kid," he choked. "Could be. But they saved us from those dogs. And right now we've gotta think about the bottom line here."

"There was a line somewhere?" I gasped. "I didn't see any lines anywhere."

"Just an expression, kid," Bogey told me.

Trixie shook her head. "I was not expecting those dogs. They're new. I know Garnet didn't have any dogs before."

Bogey frowned. "Not a good sign. So let's shake a leg, folks. Time to get this safe open and snap a few photos. And then get out of here."

With those words, we all trotted right up to the safe, which was about the size of a closet. Then I leaned up against the door, and Bogey jumped up onto my shoulders again. Using all my strength, I boosted him up so he could reach the keypad.

But unlocking the safe turned out to be a lot trickier than punching in the alarm code at the back door. Sure, Trixie had given us the code to the safe. And I was pretty surprised when she told us the numbers were 1-2-3-4. Because that sure didn't seem like a very sneaky code for someone who was as sneaky as Garnet. But even with the code, the safe's keypad was a lot more difficult to work with. Mostly because it was so small, and even Bogey's lean paws were too big to hit those numbers. So he had to extend one of his claws and use it to punch in the numbers very carefully. One at a time.

Thankfully, he got the job done pretty fast. Then he was ready for the next part of the plan. And he didn't waste a single second before he got right to it. He leaped off my shoulders and grabbed onto one of the spokes of the safe handle. Then he hung on tightly and used his weight to make the spoke turn downward. Which unlocked the safe.

We heard a loud *whoosh* sound and the door of the safe popped open just a crack. And that's when Lil and Trixie went to work. They used their paws and claws to tug that heavy safe door open. A half an inch at a time. It wasn't easy to do, but they kept at it until there was enough of a gap for Lil to reach her arm through. Then, little by little, Lil pushed her shoulder in and then her head. At long last, she got her whole body through the gap, pushing the door open wider as she went. Trixie jumped in next and leaned up against the door, until she and Lil had pushed it fully open.

A light automatically went on inside the safe. And that's when I gasped. In fact, we all kind of gasped. Even Bogey. Because, just like we had suspected, the whole thing was filled with jewelry. Shelves and shelves of jewelry. The exact same stuff that had been in Garnet's store.

And let me tell you, it sure did sparkle!

Of course, we all stepped inside to take a better look. Lil let out a low whistle and I just kept on looking around in a daze.

"Now, that's what I call evidence," Bogey said with a grin. "But no time to be dazzled, ladies and gent. Let's get to work."

So we did just that. Mitzi and Magnolia used their tiny claws to remove Lil's collar, so we could use the camera she'd been carrying. Then Bogey leaned down while Lil and the kittens managed to move the camera onto the top of his head. I held the camera in place as Bogey sat up slowly, bringing it up with him, like he'd now become a camera stand. Then

Trixie got into position and started taking pictures right away. Every time she snapped a photo, Bogey very carefully turned in a different direction, and I held the camera steady. So Trixie took pictures from all around the safe. I even leaned the camera back once or twice, to make sure she got photos of the upper shelves full of jewelry, too.

And as she worked, I noticed Trixie did the same thing that Bogey had done — she extended one huge claw to push the button on the camera. And it worked really well. Especially since her paws were even bigger than mine.

Finally, Bogey said, "I think we've got it. Let's wrap this up."

Then he leaned down again and the girls took the whole setup — collar and camera attached — and moved it back to Lil's neck. While Trixie held it in place, the kittens went to work fastening the collar. That's when I stepped over to a tall, narrow chest that was near the door of the safe.

One that looked kind of familiar.

Probably because I'd seen that very chest in our Mom's store. And when I used a couple of claws to pull open a drawer, I saw some jewelry from our Mom's display case.

Jewelry that I was sure she hadn't sold to Garnet or anyone else.

Holy Catnip! Not only was Garnet trying to blame Gracie and our Mom for her own crime, but *she'd* even stolen stuff from our Mom!

"Bogey, take a look at this," I murmured.

Just as a dark form moved right in front of the safe. I glanced up to see a face surrounded by fluffy, bright red hair.

Garnet.

And her two dogs were right behind her, blocking our way out.

She looked down at us and started to laugh. Though let me tell you, it wasn't a happy kind of laugh like most people laughed. Instead it reminded me of the noisy crow that always landed in our yard and cawed at us through the window. The sound made the fur on my back stand on end. Without even thinking, I jumped in front of the kittens and put my big paws out to protect them.

"*Ah-hah-hah-hah-hah!*" Garnet cackled on. "My, my, my,

but who do we have here? The famous cat detectives, Buckley and Bogart. Along with their cronies. Amazing, isn't it? For a couple of cats who think they're so smart, you certainly did a good job of falling right into my trap. Hope you've all had a nice life, little felines. Because it's about to be curtains for you."

Funny, but up until that moment, I had thought the whole situation was pretty scary. And now here she was, talking about decorating.

I glanced at my brother. "She's giving us curtains? What does she want us to do with them? Decorate our Mom and Dad's house?"

Bogey shook his head but kept his eyes trained on Garnet. "Nope, kid. Not that kind of 'curtains.' It's just an expression. It means she wants to put an end to us all."

"Oh . . ." I kind of muttered.

Well, I had to say, I didn't exactly like *that* kind of curtains. And just thinking about it made me start to shake in my paws.

"Any last words?" Garnet jeered. "After all, I know you can talk in human language. I caught you one day when you didn't know I was around. I was at Abigail's store, looking at her jewelry and trying to figure out what I wanted to steal. That's when I saw you in the window, and I sneaked up behind you. Then I listened in. And believe me, I got an earful. So now I suggest you start talking to me in human language. For I wish to be amused by you before I finish you off."

Bogey responded by meowing. Not to her, but to us cats instead. "Whatever you do, everyone, don't speak in human language. Just keep meowing. And Lil, lean over to Trixie, would ya? So she can use her claw to hit that little red button on the side of the camera? The one that starts recording a video?"

And that's when I stretched out my front paw and meowed, too. To distract Garnet from what Trixie was doing. After all, Garnet had been doing things to distract us for days. And like Bogey had once said, two can play at that game.

Garnet's eyebrows knitted into a deep *V*. "Cat got your tongue?" she said before she started to laugh again. "Well, that's enough of that. I *demand* that you speak to me. In human language."

"Keep your cool, everyone," Bogey commanded. "In fact, let's give her a good show. Act like you're bored."

So we did. I yawned and stretched. Then Mitzi and Magnolia both flopped over on their sides and closed their eyes. All the while, Bogey just stared at Garnet.

And it seemed to make Garnet madder by the moment. "Oh sure," she went on. "Just pretend like you don't know what I'm talking about. But I *do* know what I'm talking about. I know all about you. I also know you were the only ones who could have stopped me in my little scheme."

Bogey responded again by meowing to us. "Keep it up, folks. You're doing great."

"You don't think I'm very smart, do you?" Garnet went on. "Well, I'll have you know, I am *very* smart. I set up everything. I knew you couldn't resist those clues I left for you on your front porch. And I knew you couldn't resist rescuing a cat that I had locked up. Especially when I didn't feed her or give her water. That's why I left that laptop in her room. Because I knew she'd contact you. And I was right."

About then, I was starting to feel pretty mad myself. Especially when I thought about the way she'd treated Trixie.

"Take it easy, everyone," Bogey meowed. "She's just trying to bait us."

And she was doing a pretty good job of it.

"I knew you couldn't resist bringing the little jar with the diamonds into your house," she sneered. "Then I knew I could frame Gracie and Abigail for stealing the jewelry from my store. It was so easy to sneak my jewelry home and make it look like my store had been robbed. I knew I could get away with it. I only had to tie up one loose end, and that was to get rid of all of you. And I knew just how to do it. I knew you couldn't resist coming over here to investigate. After all, that's what you do, isn't it? Investigate? I even made it easy for you. I left the back door open and I made sure Trixie knew all the codes. I made them so easy that I knew even she could remember them."

"Wow," I meowed to my brother. "She sure does *know* lots of stuff."

Bogey held up a paw and glanced at his claws. "Yup, kid, she sure does. But there's one thing she doesn't know."

"Oh? What's that?" I asked him.

Bogey grinned. "She doesn't know that I didn't turn off the alarm."

My jaw practically dropped to the felt-covered floor of the safe. "You mean . . . you mean . . ."

Bogey grinned. "Yup, kid, I only punched the numbers in once."

I gasped. "And since you didn't punch the numbers in twice, you set off the silent alarm."

"You got it, kid," he said. "The police should be on their way."

Then right on cue, we heard sirens in the background. And they were getting louder and louder by the second.

Garnet's eyes went wide. She was so mad that smoke practically came out of the top of her head.

She stared right at Bogey. "You didn't . . ."

And he just kept on grinning.

Then Lil issued a command in cat language. "Mitzi! Magnolia! Full claws! Pounce!"

And the next thing I knew, the two kittens went airborne. Garnet screamed and hit a button on the side of the safe door. Without warning, a big, dark object fell from the ceiling of the safe. It knocked the kittens to the ground and covered all my friends.

But I reacted with lightning speed and jumped right up next to the tall jewelry chest. The one that held the jewelry from our Mom's store. Thankfully, the falling object only skimmed the side of me, but it didn't cover me. And that's when I finally got a good look at the thing.

What I saw made my heart skip a beat. Maybe even two or three. For the object that was covering my friends and pinning them to the floor was a net. A big, dark net. One that would take a long time to escape from.

Worst of all, Garnet had started to push the door of the safe shut. That meant she planned to lock us all inside. And the walls of that safe were so thick that nobody would ever hear us hollering for help. So even when the police showed up, they would have no idea we were in there.

Right away, I knew exactly what I had to do. I pushed off the side of that jewelry box with all my strength and went airborne myself. I practically flew past the door of the safe, just as Garnet was pushing it shut. I'd barely gotten out when I heard that door close behind me with a loud *thud*! It even caught a few of the hairs on my huge tail and yanked them right out. But I sure didn't let that stop me. After all, Garnet had just locked my friends in her safe. And it was up to me to save them.

Yet the instant my feet touched the ground outside the safe, I came face-to-face with one of the dogs. That's when I did something so brave and so daring that I even shocked myself. Because instead of shrinking back, I charged at him with everything I had. I tried to make it look like I was a big tiger and not just some housecat. I guess I really took that big dog by surprise, and maybe even scared him a little.

Because he backed right out of my way.

But only for a moment.

And as I raced off, both of the dogs were already nipping at my huge tail.

I heard Garnet scream, "Get him!"

Then I dug my claws in deep for traction and zoomed out of there just as fast as I could go. I fought to keep my legs in control as I skidded around the corner and ran down the hallway. I reached the staircase and flew down the stairs, taking them three at a time. All the while, those dogs were right on my heels. One of the dogs even passed me before I reached the second-floor landing. Then he turned around so he could catch me when I tried to run down to the first floor.

With one dog behind me and one in front, I did the only thing I could do. I took a quick zigzag into the hallway and made a beeline for the very room where Trixie had been held prisoner. It was just enough to fool the dogs and buy me a little bit of time. I'm pretty sure I was going about a million miles an hour when I flew into that room and skidded around the corner. Then with all my might, I reached up and slammed the door shut. And I quickly scooted a chair in front of it. I even leaned the chair at an angle, so nobody could open it from the other side.

I knew it wouldn't hold for long, but I figured I might have enough time to escape through the window. And go get help. So I ran right to the window where we'd rescued Trixie, and I tried with all my might to pull it open. But no matter what I did, I couldn't make it budge. Then I headed for the laptop computer sitting on a desk. Probably the same one that Trixie had used to contact Lil days ago. Now I only hoped that I could get a message out, just like she had, asking for help. Then I might have a chance to save the other cats.

So while the dogs banged on the door outside, I got that laptop up and running. But now I had one more problem — how would I type out a message? With my huge paws, I'd never been able to type on a computer keyboard. Bogey had always handled that, since his paws were so much slimmer than mine. Plus he could make his paws go where he wanted them to go. When he wanted them to go there.

Yet I could never tell for sure what my paws were going to do. In fact, it always seemed like they had a mind of their own.

But now, like it or not, I was going to have to type on that keyboard. Big paws and all.

Because there was one thing I knew beyond a doubt — it was up to me to save Bogey and Lil and Trixie and the kittens. Otherwise, like Garnet had said, it would be curtains for them all.

Holy Catnip!

CHAPTER 24

Holy Mackerel!

There I was, shut up inside the very room where Trixie had once been held captive. But I wasn't locked in like Trixie had been. Instead, I just barely had the door blocked off. And I sure hoped it would hold long enough for me to get a message out. A message to someone who could save us. But who?

I knew Officer Phoebe would already be on the way. Though I couldn't reach her anyway since I didn't know her cell phone number.

But there was one cell phone number that I *did* know.

Gracie's.

So I did my best to type out a message to her. Yet no matter how hard I tried, my big paws were all over the place, and the message I wrote didn't make any sense. So I deleted all that and started again. Then I remembered what Bogey had done when he punched in the code for the safe keypad. And I remembered how Trixie had managed to hit the button on the camera. They had both used just one claw instead of their entire paw!

And I decided to try the same thing. I extended my strongest claw and hit the first letter on the keyboard. It made a big difference, but I still had trouble getting my paws to go where I wanted them to go.

The next word I tried to type came out as, "Hdlp." But I

deleted that in a hurry and kept on trying. I fought with everything I had to hit the right keys. And believe me, it wasn't easy.

I finally managed to type out, "Hlp. 911. Garnet's house. Cats locked in safe. Hury."

It wasn't perfect, but it would have to do. I sent the message without waiting a single second. After all, I knew Gracie was a very smart girl and she'd figure it out.

Funny, but all of a sudden, I almost went limp with relief. Talk about a big weight being lifted off a guy's shoulders. I knew Gracie would be here before long. And she'd be smart enough to bring our Mom. Not to mention, I was pretty sure she'd alert Officer Phoebe, too. So all I had to do was wait for her to get that message and we would be rescued.

That, and I had to survive the nasty dogs who were barking out in the hallway. By now they were making quite a racket as they kept on trying to get inside the room. And every time they jumped up against the door, the chair holding that door budged just a little bit more.

I only hoped Gracie would get here soon.

But then I remembered something — after her bad experience, Gracie had said she wasn't going to use her cell phone anymore.

Did that mean she wouldn't have it with her? That she wouldn't even keep it in case of an emergency? Because, let me tell you, if ever there was an emergency, this was it! My heart started to pound at the thought of Gracie not getting my message. With everything I had, I hoped and prayed she would look at her phone.

Outside, I heard tires skid to a stop and then the sirens died down. I figured that meant the police were here. Especially when I heard some really loud pounding, followed by a doorbell ringing and ringing.

And that's when it dawned on me — if I could get past those two snarling dogs outside the door, maybe I could get to Officer Phoebe. But that meant I'd have to outrun those dogs who wanted nothing more than to sink their teeth into me.

Just the thought of it made me start to shake all over. And for a moment or two, I couldn't decide whether to wait or make a run for it. Past the dogs and down the stairs.

But then I realized I didn't really have a choice. If Gracie didn't get the message, the police would never know that the other cats were locked in the safe. Because Garnet would probably convince them that she'd set off the alarm by accident. And the police would leave.

So the only way I could save everyone was to get to Officer Phoebe! Then I had to convince her somehow to come up the stairs. To the safe. Where she could rescue the other cats.

But how could I get past those two dogs?

I glanced around the room and spotted a tall bookcase right next to the door. At the top of the bookcase was a huge, heavy glass vase. Probably an antique one, like our Mom sells in her store.

And that's when I put two and two together, as Bogey would say, and I quickly came up with a plan. A plan that I sure hoped would work. But was I brave enough to go through with it?

Then I remembered something Lil had once told me, days ago when we were trying to get out of the house to go rescue Trixie. She'd told me that everyone had things they were afraid of. But sometimes we had to muster up courage we didn't even know we had. And it helped if we remembered *why* we were about to do something that was scary.

So I did just that. I thought of how badly I wanted to save Bogey and Lil and Trixie and the kittens. And how sad I would be if I never saw them again. Then I took a deep breath and gathered up all the courage I could find. Without wasting another minute, I leaped onto the floor and ran straight up that bookcase. Kind of like climbing a ladder. Once I got to the top, I scooted that big vase around until I had it in the perfect position.

Then I shoved that vase with all my might. And let me tell you, I hit a perfect bull's-eye! Because the vase landed right on the chair that I had leaned up against the door. And it hit that chair *hard*. The vase shattered into a million little pieces and made such a loud *boom* that I'm pretty sure everyone all over the mansion must have heard it.

But best of all, it knocked the chair to the ground and the door flew wide open. Probably because the dogs had been leaning on it from the other side. They came stumbling in and practically slid across the floor. And that's when I made a gigantic flying leap from the top of the bookcase and out into the hallway. I sailed right over the heads of those dogs and took off running the second my paws touched the ground. I raced straight for the stairs just as fast as I could go.

Because I knew I had to beat those dogs down the stairs and to the front door. Right about then, I sure wished I could fly like Bogey. Though just thinking about Bogey and the others locked up in that safe made my stomach turn a million somersaults. And it made me run even faster.

Thankfully, I had a pretty good head start on those dogs as I skidded around the corner and straight down the steps. Still, it wasn't long before I heard them barking and making a beeline for me again. I was halfway down that big, long staircase when they caught up to me. I could even smell their hot, stinky breath on my back.

Yet somehow, I just knew I had to outrun them. If those dogs caught me, I wouldn't be around to save my friends. So like it or not, I was their only hope. I had to get to the front door without the dogs catching me.

I heard the closest dog open his strong jaw, and just before he was about to chomp into me, I leaped up onto the staircase railing. Then I just kept on running all the way down that banister. Talk about having good balance!

My move was enough to really confuse those dogs. Especially since they tried to jump up and join me. Thankfully, it bought me a few more seconds time. And once I got near the first floor, I leaped off the banister, took a right and raced for all I was worth through the front room. Then into the hallway. Those dogs really started to gain on me just as the front door came into sight.

So that's when I picked up the pace even faster. Especially when I saw Officer Phoebe at the front door. Talking to Garnet. And the next thing I knew, a girl in a red dress came right into view.

It was Gracie. She must have gotten my message!

By now the dogs were barking louder, and all the people turned to stare at us as we came thundering down the hallway. Garnet and Gracie and Officer Phoebe all gasped with wide eyes. And if nothing else, at least I knew they'd seen me.

Though from where they stood, I probably looked like nothing but a black streak.

One of the dogs opened his mouth to take a bite out of me. Just as I made one final, big push, and I leaped high into the air.

And I went flying, flying, flying . . . right into Gracie's arms.

My Mom suddenly stepped in front of Gracie. "Stay! Don't even think about it!" she screamed at those two dogs. And I do mean screamed. She put her hand out, like a crossing guard.

I could hardly believe it, but both those dogs stopped dead in their tracks. Then again, I could see why. Especially when I saw how our Mom glared at them. Even those fierce, scary dogs knew better than to mess with someone who looked as mad as our Mom did right now.

"What are you doing here?" Garnet half-shrieked to Gracie and our Mom. "I can understand why the police are here. But you two are another matter. You have no business coming to my home. And I already explained to the police how I accidentally set off the alarm."

Gracie moved right in front of Garnet. "Would you like to explain to me why you have my cat at your house?"

She shrugged. "How should I know? Clearly he was trespassing."

I wrapped my arms around Gracie.

"Do you have a safe?" Gracie demanded of Garnet. "And do you have the rest of my cats locked up in your safe?"

"What a ridiculous idea," Garnet cackled. "You've been a thorn in my side since the day I met you. Now you're even more of a bother than ever before."

Gracie took a step closer to Garnet. "I got a strange emergency message on my phone. And it said my cats are locked up in your safe. I would like to take a look, please."

"Stay out of my house," Garnet told her.

"I'm going in there," Gracie yelled in a way that I've never heard her yell before. "Whether you like it or not." And she stepped right past Garnet and into her mansion.

Our Mom and Officer Phoebe followed.

"You can't come in here," Garnet screamed. "Not without a search warrant."

"I believe this falls under the rule of 'Probable Cause,'"

Officer Phoebe informed her. "Cats being locked in a safe is a very dangerous situation. They might be running out of air."

"You'll never find my safe," Garnet sneered.

And that's when I let out a very loud yowl! I jumped out of Gracie's arms and trotted down the hallway. I glanced back for a moment and looked straight into Gracie's eyes. To get her to follow me.

"C'mon!" she hollered. "Buckley is leading the way!"

Which is exactly what I did. I stepped right beside those nasty dogs and gave them a good, solid glare as I went. Then I picked up my speed when Gracie started to run behind me. Our Mom followed, and Officer Phoebe came, too, making Garnet walk in front of her.

I took the whole bunch up one staircase and then the other. And finally, I turned the corner into the room with the safe. Everyone else followed. Except for the dogs, of course.

"Big deal," Garnet said. "I've got a safe. Who cares?"

"Open it! Right now!" Gracie commanded.

"I don't remember the combination," Garnet seethed.

But I did.

Though I had a pretty good idea that Garnet was lying. Either way, I jumped into Gracie's arms and then put my big paw next to the keypad.

More than ever before, it was up to me to save the other cats. And it all depended on me being able to make my big paw go where I wanted it to go. Because this time, I had no choice.

So I extended one claw and took a deep breath. Then I concentrated really, really hard and pushed the first button. Number one. I took another breath and fought to hit the number two button. And on I went, working and fighting so hard to make my claw hit the right buttons. Number three. And finally, number four.

With that, Gracie turned the handle the door *whooshed* open. Lil, Bogey, and Trixie were standing up against the door on the other side, and they quickly pushed it open all the way.

Gracie cried out in shock when she saw the other cats. While I jumped to the floor, she reached down to take them all into her arms.

Just as Garnet tried to back out of the room.

But Officer Phoebe was a step ahead, and she caught her right away.

"You stole my cats . . ." Gracie's voice came out in an angry whisper. "We found the back door of our house open . . . How could you take them? How could you try to hurt them like this?" To tell you the truth, I don't think I've ever seen Gracie so mad before in my life.

Our Mom clenched her jaw and her eyes blazed with anger. "And it looks like that's not all Garnet took." She pointed to the jewelry box that came from her store.

"I'll say," Officer Phoebe added. "And if I'm not mistaken, that's the jewelry you claimed was stolen, Garnet. So it appears that you robbed your own store. And got the insurance money on top of it all."

"I would have succeeded, too," Garnet sneered. "If it weren't for those meddling cats. Don't you know who they are? They are cat detectives. They run their own agency."

"Uh-huh," Officer Phoebe said as she put handcuffs on Garnet. "Tell it to the judge. I'm sure he'll find it interesting."

Right about then, Bogey decided to play back the video that Lil and Trixie had taken with our Dad's camera. Officer Phoebe and our Mom listened closely. Then they looked from us cats to Garnet and back at us again.

"You don't think it's possible . . .?" Officer Phoebe sort of murmured.

Our Mom picked up Bogey and held him tight. "Who knows?" she half-laughed. "I'm just glad they're all safe. Plus you've got all the proof you need that Gracie and I didn't rob Garnet's store. In fact, you've got proof that it was the other way around."

After that, more police officers arrived and Garnet was taken away.

It seemed like hours passed before Gracie and our Mom got us all back home. Safe and sound. Though they did seem a little confused about Magnolia.

Of course, she just climbed up into our Mom's arms, started to purr, and then went to sleep.

"I don't remember this little one," our Mom said softly. "When did we take her in?"

Gracie crinkled her brow. "Maybe she came with the other

little calico kitten." She pointed to Mitzi, who was busy trying to climb up and join her friend. "She must be another one of the foster kitties."

Our Mom picked up Mitzi, too, and then beamed at Gracie. "By the way, honey, I am so proud of you for what you did back there. You knew enough to follow Buckley. Otherwise, we might not have rescued all the cats in time. You're really growing into a remarkable young woman."

Bogey and I rubbed up against Gracie's legs.

"Thanks, Mom," Gracie said as she kneeled down and put her arms around us. "I'm just trying really hard to do my best."

"That's all any of us can do," our Mom told her with a smile. "Now, let's get these kitties some dinner. If ever there was a night for tuna fish, I think this is it."

Holy Catnip!

CHAPTER 25

Holy Tuna Fish!

That night, our Mom fed us tuna fish, all right. She and our Dad and Gracie brought plates up to the sunroom so all the cats in our house could enjoy it. Then our human family went downstairs to eat their own dinner.

"This tuna is absolutely divine," Miss Mokie proclaimed. "Quite fresh. Excellent vintage."

And after that, well, it turned into quite a party. Bogey passed around some turkey-flavored cat treats that went really well with our dinner. And the Princess made sure everyone got a turn at the water dish. Then we all started talking about how we had fooled Garnet and made sure she went to jail. I heard about how the cats had gotten out from under the net while they were locked in the safe. And they heard about how I had escaped from those dogs and managed to bring Gracie and Officer Phoebe to the rescue.

"Outstanding," Miss Mokie said with a smile. "Absolutely outstanding work done by all of you. It's a shame that humans have no idea how supreme cats are in their intelligence. Though I suspect Garnet may have figured that out. Still, she was no match for this group."

"She sure wasn't," I agreed. "And, umm . . . I've got something I'd like to say . . ." I paused and glanced from one cat to the next. "After today, I think Mitzi and Magnolia can officially be called 'cat detectives.'" Then I turned to face the kittens directly. "You two did such a great job today. You saved us all from two scary dogs, you did some amazing cat karate, and you followed orders just like you were supposed to. I would be happy to have both of you on any case."

Right away, those two kittens came up and gave me a hug. I was so proud of them that I felt like I was going to burst.

Now Bogey sat up nice and tall. "Mind if I say a few words, too? Because the real hero of the day was my fellow cat detective here, Buckley. You've got guts, kid, and you sure know how to think on your paws. You saved us all, and I'm proud to run the BBCDA with you."

And with that, the other cats cheered and gave me a "paws up." Even Miss Mokie gave me a glowing smile.

Funny, but right at that moment, I really didn't know what to say. Who would've dreamed that a former shelter cat like me would one day be called a hero?

The Princess sidled up to me. "You deserve this, Buckley. You went through a lot with this case, and you got everyone safely back home."

And when I thought about it, I knew that's what mattered the most.

Later, Gracie came up and joined us. She gave each one of us a hug and a kiss, and she told us how much she loved us. Then she played with the kittens and watched them do their cat karate moves. I had to say, she looked pretty surprised when they did their kicks and jumps and things.

"Wow," she kind of murmured. "I've never seen cats do anything like that before. It's almost like you kittens have been taking lessons or something . . ."

That's when I decided it was a good time to climb into her arms and tuck my head in under her chin. I was so glad she didn't go to jail. Especially since she didn't do anything wrong. And as much as I loved being a cat detective, I knew I always had to make sure I had enough time for her, too.

"I learned something important today," she whispered into my fur. "My cell phone is really great for emergencies. But I'd rather talk to my friends in person. Sophie is going to host the next party."

If you asked me, I thought that sounded like a really nice

idea.

"There is one thing I don't understand, though," Gracie went on. "I'm not sure who sent that message to me. The one that said you cats were locked in Garnet's safe."

She pulled back and looked right into my eyes. But I didn't say a word. Instead I just purred and gave her a big kiss on the nose.

She giggled and hugged me again. "I don't know what I'd do if anything ever happened to you, Buckley. You and all the cats."

The feeling was mutual. I didn't know what I would do if something bad ever happened to her, either. Then again, just like the Wise One had told me, if anything bad ever happened to Gracie, I would do everything I could to change that. And to save her. Just like I'd done today.

I wrapped my arms around her neck and suddenly my eyes felt really heavy. Now that I knew we were all safe, and with so much happiness all around me, I let my eyes fall shut. Then I slowly drifted off to dreamland.

The next morning, I woke up in my cat bed in the family room. Everyone else was already up, and it sounded like something big was going on out in the front hallway. So I yawned and stretched and went out to see for myself. Mrs. Bumble was there, talking to our Mom.

"Big day," Bogey said with a grin. "You'll never believe it, kid. The calicos are all being adopted."

I crinkled my brow. "You mean . . .?"

"Yup, kid. Someone is taking all three. Together. They're going to have a new home."

"Trixie, Mitzi, and Magnolia? They're going to leave us?" I kind of gasped.

Okay, I know I should have been excited and happy for them. But I'd gotten used to having them around. In fact, I really *liked* having them as part of our family. Sure, I had been pretty annoyed with Mitzi when she first came to us. But she'd come a long way in just a little bit of time. Especially for such a tiny kitten.

And who was going to watch out for that tiny kitten now?

Right about then, my heart started to pound. "I don't think they should go, Bogey. This sounds like a really bad idea to me. I think we should try to stop this. Maybe we should hide them."

Bogey shook his head. "No can do, kid. It's a big day for them. They're going to have a real home of their own. A forever home. The day a cat gets adopted is the happiest day of their lives."

Well, I had to agree with him on that.

Still . . .

By now I was starting to panic. "But the new people won't know anything about them. They won't know that Trixie got rescued. And she needs to eat lots so she can put on weight. And they won't know that Magnolia almost got stung by bees. And they won't know . . ." All of a sudden, I started to choke up. "They won't know Mitzi's name."

Bogey put his paw on my shoulder. "Don't sweat it, kid. I've got this covered."

Just as the doorbell rang.

Gracie was there to answer it with a big smile on her face. Much to my surprise, Merryweather, one of the ladies who worked at our Mom's store, walked in. Today she was wearing a pink dress with a big skirt and a pink scarf around her neck.

She greeted Gracie with a hug. "I'm so excited. I'm about to become a cat Mom. I've never had a cat family before. And you promise you'll babysit sometimes, right Gracie?"

Gracie's eyes danced with joy. "I would love to."

I glanced at my brother. "Merryweather is adopting them?"

Bogey grinned. "You got it, kid. We'll see them all the time. She'll probably even bring them down to the store."

Well, I had to say, that didn't sound so bad.

Merryweather glanced at her phone. "I got your message, Gracie."

Gracie tilted her head. "I didn't send you a message."

I turned to my brother. "Did you . . .?"

His grin got even bigger. "Wait for it, kid."

So I did.

"Okay," Merryweather said as she read something from her phone. "The big one is Trixie. She needs to put on some weight. And one of those little ones is Magnolia Belle."

Magnolia lifted her tiny head and let out a meow. A meow

with a Southern drawl, of course. So it sort of sounded like, "*Mee-yoow-wa.*"

"Finally," Merryweather went on. "We have Mitzi."

And with those words, Mitzi jumped into the air and did one of her roundhouse kicks.

Which made all the people say "*Oooh!*"

Our Mom laughed. "I didn't realize they all had names. And they're certainly very pretty names."

After that, everything turned into a big flurry of good-byes.

Trixie smiled at both Bogey and me. "I will never, ever forget what you did for me. Anytime you need an extra paw on a case, well, you can count on me. And us. The kittens and I are going to be starting our own agency. Calico Cats Consolidated, SWAT Team."

"Sounds like a plan, Trix," Bogey said.

"It would be nice to work with you again," I told her. "Plus, we've been so busy lately, maybe we could send some of our cases your way." I glanced at my brother. "So we can have more time to spend with our family."

"That would be terrific," she said. "It would be a great way to get our agency off the ground."

Bogey grinned. "Then count on it. We'll be in touch."

He gave her a paw bump and I gave her a hug. I was so happy to see her doing so well. And I knew Merryweather would take very good care of her.

Then Trixie went off with Lil for a moment, and Bogey and I said so long to Magnolia. And last of all, I found myself face-to-face with little Mitzi. That's when something strange started happening to my eyes.

"Be sure to keep practicing your cat karate," I told her. "And watch out for bad guys. And big nets."

"I will, Buckley," she said in her little voice. "I sure am going to miss you. I wish I didn't have to go."

Suddenly there seemed to be something wrong with my nose, too. "I'm going to miss you a bunch, too. But you have to go. The day you get adopted is the best day of your life."

She nodded her tiny head. "I'm really happy to have a home. And I think Merryweather is a very nice lady. But it's *not* the best day of my life."

I crinkled my brow. "Umm . . . sure it is."

She looked me right in the eyes and shook her head slowly. "No, Buckley. The best day of my life was the day I met you." Then she reached up and gave me a big hug.

I hugged her back and held onto her for a moment. And that's when wet stuff really started to roll down my cheeks. What in the world was wrong with me?

I let her go and wiped my face with my paw. Then I followed them all to the door. Merryweather carried the kittens while Trixie trotted along beside her. They all went to the curb and started to get into a blue car.

A blue car that looked familiar.

That's when I spotted Dave, our Drive-N-Dash driver. He looked up and gave us a wave. Bogey grinned and gave him a "paws up" while I just waved back. Then Dave helped Trixie into the front seat while Merryweather got into the back with the kittens. They took off just as another car pulled up.

Much to my amazement, it was Mr. Pennypacker.

"Excuse me, Mrs. Abernathy?" he called out as he hurried up the walk.

The next thing I knew, he was inside our front hallway.

"Please excuse the intrusion," he said as he removed his bowler hat. "But you weren't at your store this morning. And I have a special request that couldn't wait another minute. I've seen your stunning cats around town. Buckley and Bogey. And I was wondering if you would mind if they were models for my new ad campaign."

Our Mom's eyes went wide. "Ad campaign?"

"Models?" Gracie repeated.

"Yes, yes," he went on. "I just opened the St. Gertrude Cat Treat Factory about a month ago and I need to advertise. And I think Buckley and Bogey would be perfect for my ads. Though I'm afraid I can't pay much. The best I can do is to guarantee them a lifetime supply of cat treats. Delivered fresh a couple of times a week. Would that do?"

"Of course, Mr. Pennypacker," our Mom said. "I'm sure they'd be happy to model for a cat treat factory. Heaven knows the cat treat bags around here seem to disappear the second I get them home from the store. I'm always finding them in the strangest places."

I glanced at my brother. His eyes had taken on kind of a

faraway, glazed look, and he just flopped over onto his side.

Then Gracie picked me up and started to dance around the room with me. "Did you hear that, Buckley? You're going to be a model!"

The room whizzed by as she danced around and around. Funny, but I had forgotten that Gracie had once gone through her spinning phase. Though I had to say, I hadn't missed it one bit.

In the meantime, our Mom and Mr. Pennypacker made arrangements for us to get our pictures taken later that week. By the time Mr. Pennypacker had gone, Bogey had recovered a little, and Gracie had set me back on the hardwood floor. Though as near as I could tell, it still felt like the room was going around and around and around.

I waited till my eyes focused again, and then Bogey and I wobbled over to the front window. Together, we watched Mr. Pennypacker stroll down the walk.

"I like that guy," Bogey murmured as he pulled a bag of cat treats from behind the potted plant. "I think this might be the beginning of a beautiful friendship."

I nodded. "The cat treats from his factory sure were good."

"The best I've ever tasted." Bogey grinned and glanced at the bag. "Guess we won't be eating these regular old treats much longer." Then he passed us each a couple of treats.

"I guess not." I said before I put one of the treats in my mouth and munched away.

"Heck of a week, wasn't it, kid?"

I nodded. "You can sure say that again."

In fact, I almost said it myself. That was, until the Princess pranced right up to me.

Then she stared up at me with her big, green eyes. "Buckley, I just wanted to say . . ."

And suddenly the room started to spin all over again.

"You were so wonderful with those little kittens," she went on. "You made such a difference in their lives. I think you're just the best, Buckley." And with that, she reached up and gave me a kiss on the nose.

Well, it was all just more than I could take. Stars danced in front of my eyes, and now it was my turn to flop over onto *my* side.

The next thing I knew, Bogey was standing over me. "Dames, kid. They'll do it to you every time."

"Dames," I kind of mumbled.

He waved a cat treat in front of my nose. "Here you go, kid. This'll get you going again."

I took the treat and ate it slowly.

Bogey grinned. "As soon as you get your bearings, kid, we've gotta get back to work."

"Umm . . . okay. What's going on?" I asked him.

He arched an eyebrow in the direction of our Mom's office. "I checked the computer first thing this morning. Looks like we've got another case for the BBCDA."

I got to my feet and shook my head. "So soon?"

"Yup, kid. And this one's a doozie."

Somehow that didn't surprise me. I only hoped this new case didn't have nearly as many clues as the last one.

Holy Catnip!

THE END

About the Author

Cindy Vincent was born in Calgary, Alberta, Canada, and has lived all around the US and Canada. She is the creator of the Mysteries by Vincent murder mystery party games and the Daisy Diamond Detective Series games for girls. She is the award-winning author of the Buckley and Bogey Cat Detective Caper books, and the Tracy Truworth, Apprentice P.I., 1940s Homefront Mysteries. She lives with her husband and an assortment of fantastic felines — including the *real* Buckley and Bogey, who run surveillance on her house each and every night.